BITTER FEAST

PARADISE CRIME MYSTERIES BOOK 12

TOBY NEAL

Book Cover Design by ebooklaunch.com.

Print ISBN-13: 978-1-7337517-7-3

The father said to his slaves, "Quickly! Bring out the best robe and put it on him, and put a ring on his hand and sandals on his feet; and bring the fattened calf, kill it, and let us eat and celebrate; for this son of mine was dead and has come to life again; he was lost and has been found." And they began to feast.

Luke 15:22–24

CHAPTER ONE

Stevens

LIEUTENANT MICHAEL STEVENS HOOKED HIS thumbs in the pockets of his jeans and gazed down at his newest case. "Tell me what you see."

Detective Brandon Mahoe squatted in the narrow, chilly space of the walk-in refrigerator beside the corpse. Blood had spread in a pool beneath the victim, filling the round holes of a raised rubber floor mat. The smell, more of a metallic feeling in Stevens's nostrils, was almost lost in other competing odors: garlic, ripe fruit, mushrooms, scallions, and the produce lining the shelves.

"Male, six foot, trim build at a hundred and seventy-five pounds or so. Dark hair. Maybe thirties or younger. Cause of death appears to be stabbing." The young detective wasn't being sarcastic about the handle of a large butcher knife protruding from the man's back—Mahoe didn't do sarcastic. "Probably a kitchen staff employee, to judge by the chef's coat he's wearing."

Stevens dropped to his haunches beside Mahoe. He blew into a latex glove, inflating it to go on easy. He did the same to another, snapping it on. "Good start."

"Can we shut the refrigerator door?" A male voice, harsh with impatience, came from the doorway. "All this food. It will spoil."

Stevens slowly unfolded to his full, intimidating height. He turned and stared down at the stocky, belligerent figure confronting him. "And you are?"

"Chef Winston Noriega. This is my restaurant." The man, his chin outthrust, folded tattooed, muscular arms over a pristine white apron. "There are thousands of dollars of farm-fresh gourmet produce in this walk-in. I see no reason for it to go to waste just because François got himself killed in here."

"Back up out of this area." Stevens used his voice like a lash to cut across the arrogant chef's posturing. He advanced toward the man. "We'll close the door. But only so we can have privacy. I'm sure you wouldn't in good conscience serve food to your customers that has been part of a crime scene, even if we allowed it. Officer!" He gestured to one of the uniforms gathering the names of the kitchen staff. "Put up crime scene tape in this kitchen, clear this area, and put Chef Noriega in his office until I have time to interview him."

"Yes, sir." The officer gestured to his partner, who shooed the staff lookie-loos into an adjacent area and pulled out a roll of scene tape.

"You can't do this!" Noriega said. A muscle jerked in a jaw wide and square as a bulldog's. Stevens glanced over at the officer who'd approached and now stood behind the chef. First responders had told Stevens that the chef had discovered the body.

"What did you say the victim's name was?"

"That's François Métier, my sous-chef. Don't touch me." The chef shrugged away from the officer's hand and stomped toward his office. Stevens stared after the restaurateur thoughtfully, watching the officer accompany him to the door of his office. A woman, tall and elegant in black trousers, slipped in after the chef. Probably the wife—he'd heard she helped manage the famous restaurant.

Stevens pulled the door of the walk-in closed. Mahoe began photographing the scene. Flashes from the camera threw the tight setting into high relief repeatedly against Stevens's eyeballs: floor-to-ceiling shelves packed with every sort of foodstuff; the body on the floor, one hand down beside the body, the other curled near the man's face; the blood pool filling the rubber mat.

There was a gleam of something in the victim's hand lying alongside the body. Stevens bent low to investigate the object.

A familiar twinge in his side reminded him of a gunshot wound that had gone septic months ago. Healed now, that area still tickled him with his mortality whenever it had a chance. "Look, there's a ring in his hand. Photograph this."

Mahoe approached with the department's Canon and recorded the item in question; then Stevens lifted a diamond-encrusted band with a large center stone from the dead man's hand.

"Looks like an engagement ring." He slipped it into an evidence bag. "Did you call Dr. Gregory?"

"Yes, sir. The medical examiner's on his way."

"No need to call me 'sir.'" Stevens had been Mahoe's original commanding officer, but they were working as partners now.

"Yes, sir." Mahoe shook his head. "Sorry. Habit."

A tap came at the steel door. Mahoe, closer to the entrance, pushed the handle, and the unit opened with a pneumatic *whoosh*. Dr. Phil Gregory entered, carrying his kit and a body bag, cheeks pink with excitement. The portly medical examiner had been on a health kick lately, and his trademark aloha shirt, decorated with hula girls today, hung loosely from his shoulders. "A murder at Feast! This is my favorite restaurant!"

"You're looking good, Doc, so you can't have been eating here that often," Stevens said. "I've heard the food's good, but after talking to the chef, I'm not wild about coming here as a customer."

"Well, he's known for being a perfectionistic prick. That just makes for better dining, and this restaurant is all about the food." Dr. Gregory gloved up and slid booties on over his shoes as he approached the body, opening his doctor's bag to make his initial assessment.

Stevens nodded. "Gotta say, I wasn't impressed with the chef's response to all this. He seems more worried about losing his produce than his employee."

"That's consistent with what I've heard about Chef Noriega." Dr. Gregory squatted beside the body. "So how's Lei? Has she gone out on maternity leave yet?"

"She's hanging in there. Got a couple more days on active duty." Stevens's very pregnant wife had finally had to slow down and was often irritable. Being ungainly was tough for such a physical person. "Baby can't come soon enough for either of us."

The space felt crowded with three men and a body in the packed area, so Mahoe sidled past Dr. Gregory. "I'll go see what's happening outside. Gather our interviewees."

"Leave the camera. I'll need to get more shots when we roll the body," Stevens told his protégé. He turned back to Gregory. "So we got the call at oh eight hundred hours, when Métier's body was discovered by Chef Noriega, who came in early for some prep work." Stevens prodded the corpse with his foot. "I'm guessing this guy, identified by Chef Noriega as François Métier, his sous-chef, was offed last night sometime. He's in full rigor, plus the cold of the fridge, so probably after the night's rush. Must have been late in the shift or someone would have found him."

"Murder weapon appears pretty obvious." Dr. Gregory pointed at the knife protruding from the victim's back. "This stroke went in so deep that it broke the skin on the other side of his body. Went right through his kidney and probably nailed an artery. Bet it dropped him like a stone. Exsanguination will be cause of death, at a guess."

"No defensive wounds, either. There was a ring in one of his hands." Stevens withdrew the small plastic evidence bag and showed it to Dr. Gregory. "I'm guessing he knew and trusted his attacker."

"Maybe it was a woman," Dr. Gregory said. "He was going to pop the question in the fridge where they met, and she popped him instead."

Stevens's mouth twitched involuntarily at the gallows humor. "Very romantic. But doesn't the depth of the stab wound look challenging for a woman?"

"Easy with one of these chef's knives. This looks like one of those super-sharp ceramic blades. They go through meat like butter."

A flashback swamped Stevens's mind: his hand, fisted around a combat knife, driving up into a man's throat from below. Blood poured down his arm, only slightly warmer than the jungle air.

Not real. It never happened. He shook his head abruptly to clear it. "Early days yet for speculation."

"Of course, but this looks pretty straightforward." Dr. Gregory moved around the body, looking it over carefully, his glasses fogging slightly. "Dr. Tanaka's been called to another scene, so can you help me? Let's remove the knife and roll the body."

"Let me pull any prints first." Stevens used gel tape to gather impressions from the handle as Dr. Gregory bagged the man's hands. "Damn. Just looks like a few smears, but hopefully we can retrieve something back at the station. You do the honors, removing it." He took an evidence bag from his crime kit and snapped it open.

Dr. Gregory grasped the knife handle carefully, holding it with the tips of his fingers so as not to disturb any prints. He lifted it from the body with startling ease. "Whoever did this either knew exactly where to stab, or was damn lucky. It went right where it should go for maximum damage. Hit no bones along the way, which is harder than people realize."

Stevens held the bag open, and Dr. Gregory dropped the knife into it. While Stevens sealed and wrote on the bag, Dr. Gregory continued his examination.

Mahoe poked his head in. "I've got some interviews lined up, Lieutenant. Want I should start taking statements?"

"Sounds good. I'm helping Dr. G with the body. Need a little more time. Leave the chef for me to talk to, though."

"You got it." The young detective withdrew his head.

Stevens arranged the evidence collected so far in the open area of his briefcase-like crime kit as Dr. Gregory performed the body-temp indignity with a rectal thermometer. The ME spread the long, zip-up body bag wide in preparation for receiving its cargo. "The victim's way cold and in rigor, as you speculated, Lieutenant. Consistent with death last night. I'll know more after the full post. Let's roll and bag him."

Stevens took the man's feet and Dr. Gregory the shoulders, and they flipped the corpse onto its back.

Blood had pooled beneath the body where the tip of the knife had penetrated the abdomen, providing an exit wound for fluid to drain out. The vivid liquid, darkened with the hours, had spread to cover the white of the man's side-buttoned chef's coat and looked black in the fluorescent light. Blood still trapped in the body had gathered in bruise-like, purplish lividity in visible tissues. The smell of coppery fruit felt substantial in Stevens's nostrils.

"I'll deal with this back at the morgue." Dr. Gregory gestured to the blood-soaked clothing. The man's rigor held one arm up at his side, head turned and eyes closed, just as he'd fallen.

"Sounds good." Stevens picked up the Canon and photographed the front of the body.

François Métier had regular features and a square jaw decorated with a hipster swatch of beard. He'd been a handsome man before dusky lividity had stained his face. Stevens moved in close, photographing.

"Should be some interesting interviews ahead." Stevens set aside the camera and rifled through the man's pockets. He dropped a wallet and phone into evidence bags. "Don't see anything else of interest."

"I'll do a thorough check for trace back at my lab."

When they were both done recording and inspecting, Stevens lifted the man's heels, encased in rubber-soled work shoes, and Dr. Gregory grasped the rigid shoulders. They slid the body into the black bag.

"I brought the gurney. It's just outside," Gregory said.

"Well, I'm not throwing my back out—getting too old for that shit." Stevens opened the fridge's door. "Mahoe! Need help here."

"What's up, LT?" The detective stepped up into the narrow space.

"You've got the young back we need," Stevens said. With the three of them lifting, they soon had the black-bagged corpse on the gurney and strapped down.

"I'll let you know anything interesting I find." Dr. Gregory lifted a hand in farewell. The ME pushed his burden out through the kitchen, accompanied by one of the uniforms, as Stevens retrieved his crime kit.

"Mahoe, can you put crime scene tape across the walk-in? No one goes in or out until we have a chance to have Kevin go over every inch of it." Kevin Parker, MPD's pimply-faced University of Hawaii criminology intern, was proving a big asset at crime scenes, with an instinct for finding anything out of place and an eye for detail that had helped on several cases.

Stevens waited for Mahoe to seal the fridge with scene tape, using the time to organize his crime kit and label the evidence bags, but as he did so, a sense of dreamlike distance from his surroundings distracted him.

Stevens stripped off his gloves, flexed his hands, and rolled his neck as he looked around the clean, brightly lit kitchen. Months after a military contractor stint that had resulted in some serious injuries, Stevens still sometimes felt a sense of unreality about his perceptions, a barrier between himself and what was happening around him that his friend, psychologist Dr. Wilson, called "derealization."

"A symptom of your head injury," the psychologist had said when he'd called her not long ago to complain that the bizarre sensation was still happening. "Just weather it, along with the flashbacks. Be patient and try not to take it too seriously. Use a physical cue to ground yourself in the present moment's reality. Remind yourself that you're home, safe, and that your brain just isn't firing right."

Stevens had done a course of Eye Movement Desensitization and Reprocessing therapy, courtesy of Security Solutions, the company he'd contracted with, as part of his severance package. The EMDR had helped, but he still experienced these disorienting episodes. Looking down, he rubbed his steel watch against his wrist, eliciting a cool pinch of metal against skin as a physical cue. His wife also had a habit of rubbing something or squeezing her leg when she had symptoms—Lei still sometimes used the same sorts of techniques, though the source of her trauma was very different.

The jungle rose in his memories. Deep green light, almost black, was pierced by lance-like rays of sunlight filtering through the canopy. The smell of rot and growth was a rich synthesis in his nostrils. He moved forward through the damp mulch of the forest floor, pushing aside vines and undergrowth, the whoop and holler of monkeys in the distance, enemies at his back and hazards ahead. . .

Not real. Never happened. He wrenched himself back to the present. The men behind his kidnapping had been court-martialed. A thorough review of foreign contracted operations was underway at the federal level, Colonel Westbrook had assured him. Starchy and formal, the colonel, liaison between the army and his former private-contract company, had turned out to be a good guy.

A loud voice, vibrating through the nearby wall, broke his reverie.

"Hell if I'm going to sit on my ass a minute longer waiting for this cop!"

Chef Noriega was getting restless. Stevens heard a light feminine voice trying to calm the man. The two voices rose and fell in a familiar cadence that sounded like marital argument. He should have had the officer keep the wife out, but he'd been distracted.

"Let's go interview the man behind Feast," Stevens told Mahoe. "Got your recorder handy?"

"Sure, LT."

Stevens knocked once on the door marked OFFICE and turned the knob, pushing the door inward.

Chef Noriega had his hands around the throat of the dark-haired woman, pushing her up against a desk. She clawed at his wrists, her face congested. Bulging, panicked eyes begged for help from behind the chef's shoulder.

Lei

Lei had to grab on to the edge of the desk to heave herself out of the office chair. "Be right there, Captain," she said into the office phone, and hung up. Once standing, she leaned back, digging her fists into the small of her back, arching to stretch. The curve of her belly still brushed the edge of the desk. "We got a new case."

Pono, her longtime partner, looked up from his e-mail. "What the hell. You're supposed to be on light duty!"

"It is light duty. I hope. Another cold case. We've been summoned to hear about it."

"Yeah, and look how that last one turned out," Pono grumbled, referring to a cold one eight months before that was supposed to just be a time filler and had turned into one of the biggest cases they'd had in years.

"I don't know about the timing. I'm going on maternity in a few days." Lei waddled to the door of the cubicle, tugging down the dark blue maternity smock she wore over skinny black maternity jeans. She'd had Ellen, Stevens's mom, sew up a bunch of the same garment, a sort of uniform that, she hoped, minimized the obviousness of pregnancy.

Pregnant cops were awkward for everybody. The guys got all protective and mother-hen-like, the way Pono was acting, the women wanted her out of sight, and the perps didn't know how to act either. She was glad she wasn't the size her friend Marcella had been at approaching nine months—but still, a basketball-sized belly pressing on her bladder constantly was challenging, and even light duty as a cop wasn't a typical desk job.

Pono took her elbow in the hall, but she tweaked it away. "Quit fussing. I can walk on my own two feet. Just because I can't see them doesn't mean they aren't still there."

"Stubborn, you." Pono shook his head. "I can't wait for you to be done and out of here. I'm having a heart attack thinking you're going to drop it in our office or something."

"You must have really been a wreck when Tiare was pregnant," Lei panted, short of breath with her lungs so cramped. She tried to speed up, but felt the distinctive sensation of the baby moving. These internal feelings had gone from fishlike fluttering, to kicking that felt like tiny fists, to these late-term, long, slow rolls that inevitably ended up with feeling like she had to pee.

Which she now did.

"No one was more relieved than me when she declared she was done after we had a boy and a girl." Pono spun his Oakleys by a stem as he slowed his stride to match hers.

"Quick bathroom stop." Lei turned toward the women's room.

Pono rolled his eyes. "Of course. I'll see you in Omura's office." He continued on down the hall.

In the stall, Lei settled herself on the toilet and smoothed the sturdy navy cotton over her belly. It pushed back against her hand.

"You better be pointing downward. Not too long now, Baby," she whispered. "I can't wait to get this part over with and meet you." They'd decided not to find out the baby's gender, and she was glad of that choice, anticipating the surprise of what it would turn out to be. So far the pregnancy had been healthy and problem-free, but Lei knew she was still trying to guard herself from the grief of something going wrong—while knowing that there was no way to really do that.

If something went wrong with this baby, she'd never have the heart to try again.

She finished up and washed her hands. Her face was fuller in the mirror. Her hair was, too, and her breasts strained the fabric of a smock sewn two months ago. "Oh well. I'm out of here in two days, and I can wear nothing but sweats from here on out, right, Baby?" There was no comment from below but another jab to the kidneys. "Ow. Maybe you're planning to play soccer for University of Hawaii."

A few minutes later Lei pushed open Captain Omura's office door.

"Surprise! Happy baby shower!"

Everyone was yelling. A party squeaker went off, and a popper rained confetti down over Lei as she clapped both hands over her mouth in shock. It seemed like the entire department was crowded into Omura's little office, and they all laughed and clapped at her expression as Pono fired off another popper. More confetti spiraled down. It was going to be a pain to get out of her hair, but her partner's infectious grin brought an answering smile to Lei's face.

"Any excuse for cake," said Detective McGregor, a big, bluff, red-faced man she'd butted heads with on a few cases. Jessup Murioka, the department's teen tech whiz, came up to hug what he could reach of her and slip a sweet-smelling ginger lei over her head. Pono handed out pink-and-blue party hats and wrapped cigars. Standing guard in front of the huge cake on Omura's desk was Tiare, his wife, wearing bright purple scrubs. She'd clearly come straight from the hospital, and the only thing bigger than the cake was her smile.

Lei made her way through the hugs and shoulder smacks to Tiare's side. "You're the monster behind this idea."

"Of course. Couldn't just let my little sistah skulk off to that fortress house without a going-away party." Tiare enfolded Lei in her arms. She usually smelled of gardenias, and today was no exception. "Hope you finished that childbirth class. I know I agreed to be your labor coach, but I'm not going into it without you getting some instruction."

"We finished last week. Got the certificate at home to prove it. Thought Stevens was going to get sick during the videos, but he did the breathing and kept from fainting."

"The men get the easy part of the deal, not that they act like it." One arm around Lei's shoulder, Tiare addressed the milling officers and support staff. "I'll cut the cake as soon as you folks throw a few bucks in for the office gift." Tiare cut across the joking and horseplay. "We're getting the family one of those fancy strollers that does everything but change the baby."

She handed a gaily-wrapped box with a slit in the top to Pono. Lei's coworkers, teasing while doing so, dug bills out of their wallets and shoved them in.

Captain Omura, smiling and sophisticated as usual, came around her desk and patted Lei's shoulder. "How are you feeling?"

"Really huge, with bruised kidneys. Thanks for asking." Lei glanced around. "Where's my husband? And Dr. Gregory?" The colorful ME was one of her favorite people.

"They pulled a fresh homicide. Out at that chichi restaurant Feast."

"Oh, that should be interesting." Lei felt her heartbeat quicken with interest, and the baby kicked in response. "Do you think he needs any help at the scene?"

"Definitely not. Part of my present to you is sending you home after the party—a couple of days early. I checked with human resources, and you have some comp time coming to you along with the maternity leave."

"So there's no case for us? Your call was just to get us into the office?" Absurdly, Lei was disappointed. What was she going to do for the next month until the baby came? She hadn't let herself think too much about it, but now full-time motherhood was upon her.

"You've got a case all right." Omura patted her belly. "Right here, my little workaholic. Now, let's have some cake."

Kathy

Sergeant Kathy Fraser hesitated outside the open door of Captain Omura's office. She held a brightly wrapped gift, a box containing a new diaper bag that was more like a backpack. She'd spent considerable time puzzling over it online, looking for just the right item that seemed like something her ex-partner Stevens and his wife would use. Kathy had planned to just leave the baby gift for Stevens to find on his desk, but then the interdepartmental e-mail had gone out summoning everyone to Lei's shower.

Kathy smoothed her hair back and tugged on the edge of her buttoned-up uniform jacket, glancing around the noisy gathering.

Lei Texeira, Stevens's wife, was cutting into the cake on the desk amid much ribald joking—her rounded midsection, draped in a plain dark blue smock, got in the way of reaching the desk. Lei was smiling and pretty, a riot of curling brown hair flowing over her shoulders and her legs still slim in tight-fitting black jeans.

A coil of jealousy tightened Kathy's stomach.

Lei had everything—a home she owned, a loving husband, and a baby on the way—not to mention the best job in the world.

Kathy couldn't bring herself to enter the noisy party. Lei wouldn't want to see her anyway—she thought Kathy was after her husband, and nothing Kathy had said or done had dissuaded the other woman of it.

Kathy turned and walked rapidly back toward the stairs to her office on the next floor, an office she still shared with Stevens, though he'd gone back to full-time detective work after a brief, disastrous trip overseas. He now worked a full roster of cases while mentoring junior detectives, and she hardly saw him.

That was fine. There was an awkwardness between them that seemed permanent since his departure for that ill-advised venture. He'd returned from Central America damaged and distant, and the friendship they'd forged while working together in the new-hire training program was gone.

Kathy's shoes rang on the metal stairs as she rose to the third floor. It was just as well she and Stevens weren't friends any longer. She'd had a ridiculous crush on him, and thankfully that was over, too. She pushed the door open and went in, setting the baby gift in the center of Stevens's desk.

The cell phone in her pocket rang. She took it out, checking who it was before answering.

"Elena!" Kathy's friend Elena Noriega hardly ever called during the day, too busy with a three-year-old and helping manage her husband's famous restaurant. "What's up, girl?" It was good to hear from a friend when she was feeling so lonely and vulnerable.

"Oh, Kathy! You have to help!" Her elegant friend's Spanish-accented voice was distraught. "Please come to Feast—they're arresting Winston!"

"Oh my God. Who is? What for?" Kathy was already moving, grabbing her weapon and purse, heading for the door.

"Your ex-partner, Lieutenant Stevens, is arresting him!" Elena was sobbing now. "They're taking Winston away. You have to stop them!"

"Calm down, Elena." Kathy tripped down the stairs. "What's happened?"

"Someone stabbed François Métier, our sous-chef. And the lieutenant was investigating with his partner, and Winston, he . . ." Elena blew her nose, trying to gather her composure. "He was very upset. We have to close Feast, and we have thousands of dollars of food spoiling. François was murdered, and Winston—he got mad. He lost his temper and choked me."

"Oh my God." Kathy reached the exit and broke into a trot as she headed for the main doors of the police station in Kahului. She'd long suspected that demanding and brilliant Winston Noriega did more than just verbally bully his wife, though Elena had always denied it. "Are you all right?"

"Yes, yes . . . The…the lieutenant, he grabbed Winston and threw him against the wall. And when Winston came at me again, he punched him! And then he cuffed Winston and said he was charging him for the murder as well as assault. I don't want to press charges on Winston for that. He was just upset and stressed!"

Kathy frowned at this evidence of battered woman syndrome as she hurried across the parking lot. "Call your lawyer. I'll be there as soon as I can."

Kathy ended the call as she reached her vehicle, a white Nissan Rogue. She plugged in her Bluetooth and speed-dialed Stevens, setting her cop light on the dash and getting on the road for Lahaina at top speed.

Stevens didn't answer his cell. She doubted Mahoe would answer either—they probably had their hands full at the moment. She left a message on Stevens's voice mail.

"Hey, Stevens, please call me back. I don't know if you're aware, but Elena Noriega is one of my best friends and has called me for assistance. It would be great to know what was going on from your end so I could help support the investigation. See you shortly." She then called Dispatch, let them know where she was going and got details on the murder.

Surely Kathy could help in some way, even if it was just to comfort Elena—but apprehension tightened the muscles of her arms as she drove too fast along the steep, winding road. She wasn't sure how to handle it if her friend Elena was involved in murder.

CHAPTER TWO

Wayne

WAYNE TEXEIRA WALKED ALONG THE iron-rich red dirt path between rows of vegetables on his friend Teo's farm, carrying a couple of large canvas bags as he followed the farmer. Teo Benitez had twelve acres of former pineapple land on the west side of Maui, and he'd been putting every foot of it into growing organic produce to supply the farm-to-table movement that was sweeping the nation.

"Got some nice Japanese eggplant that are ripe," Teo said over his shoulder. "Good for stir-fry."

"Sure, show them to me." Wayne's long stride kept up easily with Teo's much shorter one. The enterprising Filipino was from a third-generation farming family on Maui, and he'd started out working on one of the upcountry flower farms. His aptitude with agriculture had led to leasing this parcel, backed by the owner of the flower farm. In a cross-cultural twist, Teo was studying Hawaiian agricultural practices and integrating them into his organic farming methods.

Wayne liked to come out once a week and walk the fields with

Teo, see what was coming into readiness, and plan his restaurant's menus with that in mind. His little place, Wayne's Hawaii Bistro in Haiku, was gaining a steadily increasing following as he sought to provide a varied, fresh menu that was Maui-grown.

"Ho, you get so many weeds." Wayne gestured to a field they were passing, green from watering but with the varied, uncultivated textures of local groundcovers.

"That field's resting—all those plants, they bind nitrogen in the soil. Those weeds never happened by accident—they're native Hawaiian plants. Takes a lot of effort and time to get this pineapple and sugar land back to where you can grow food crops with this used-up soil." Teo kicked a hard, clay-like clod out of the way as he gestured to a hillock of mulch that a worker was spreading out with a backhoe. "Got plenty of compost now though. I have a bunch of West side landscapers drop off their yard waste, and we grind it up."

"That's a mountain of compost." Wayne narrowed his eyes into the sun.

"That's what it takes to make the 'black gold' we need for growing." Teo's phone buzzed in his heavy-duty belt holster. He looked back at Wayne, squinting in the sunshine. "Gotta take this. One of my other restaurants."

"Sure, no problem." Wayne skirted his friend as the man took the call, squatting to inspect some bell peppers, plump and brightly colored. He plucked them and slipped them into the bag. Wayne felt content as he reached deep among the plants with their smell of mulch and growing.

His life was so different now than it had been all those dark years ago, when he'd done a twenty-year stretch for drug dealing. Wayne had his own business, he was helpful to those in recovery from addiction in the community, and he had the joy of living with his daughter, Lei, and her husband and son on a beautiful property —and soon he'd be a grandfather for the second time. Gratitude to God for redeeming his life filled Wayne—even as he felt a stab of familiar grief that his sister, Rosario, wasn't alive to enjoy these days with him.

Teo's voice rose in agitation, a spate of rapid speech as he strode up and down, waving an arm. His friend was usually so calm that Wayne frowned, glancing back, but he continued to pluck the bell peppers. He could stuff them with rice and spices and top them with Romano cheese for a nice baked vegetarian entrée.

Teo ended the call and returned to Wayne's side. "My friend Felipe told me that François Métier, the sous-chef at Feast, was murdered today. And Chef Noriega was arrested for it!"

"Whoa." Wayne stood slowly, an arthritic ache in his knees and lower back bothering him as he straightened. "They were your best customers."

"Yeah. François, he came to meet with me often over the produce. I planted with them in mind. Why would Noriega kill François?"

"Why do the police think that? They must have a reason." Wayne had become familiar with cops' procedural processes through years of living with Lei and Stevens.

"Felipe said Noriega was giving the cops attitude—you know how he is—and then he attacked his wife because he was pissed off about the murder. So they decided to slap the cuffs on him and take him in."

"Who were the investigators?" Wayne was pretty sure Lei wasn't doing any more cases so close to going out on maternity leave, but with his headstrong daughter, he could never be sure about anything related to her job.

"Felipe didn't get names, but they're all waiting in a room to be interviewed. He's pretty upset. He wasn't supposed to call me, but he wanted to let me know because he thinks Feast will be shut down for a while, and they were going to buy a whole lot of produce today." Teo took off his Maui Organic Gardens ball cap and ran a hand through his hair. "Said the main cop was a tall *haole* guy."

"Probably my son-in-law, Michael Stevens." Wayne set the bag down, knuckling his sore back in a stretch. "He's a good man and a good cop. He'll find the truth."

"I hope so." Teo frowned, gazing around at the sunlit field. "This is bad for me. I have all that lettuce they usually buy, and much more. I can't believe Noriega would kill Métier. Noriega's a hothead, but he'd never endanger his restaurant that way."

"People can surprise you. I'll take more produce," Wayne said. "All your peppers, and some lettuce. And help you get the word out about your extra."

"Thanks." Teo bent, picking peppers rapidly and slipping them into Wayne's other bag. "If anyone killed Métier, it was Noriega's wife, Elena. She was having an affair with the sous-chef that got killed."

"Really?" Wayne's attention sharpened. "How do you know that?"

"Oh, I took a delivery to the restaurant during the day. Caught them . . . " Teo made a graphic gesture with his hands. "In the office. And François, he was a player. She wasn't the only one he was with."

"Interesting." Wayne kept his face neutral as he filed away this tidbit to tell Stevens later. He hated gossiping, but he was pretty sure Teo wasn't someone the cops would think of interviewing, and he seemed to know a lot about what was going on at Feast. "But why would Mrs. Noriega kill her lover?"

"She a proud woman. She was always . . . " Teo lifted his chin and thumbed his nose to show Elena's snooty attitude.

"So if it wasn't either of the Noriegas, who else could it be?" Wayne squatted down beside Teo, blatantly fishing.

"I liked Métier, but he was a slippery one. He was going to open his own restaurant." Teo glanced sidewise at Wayne, slipping an especially large, bright bell pepper into the bag. "He promised to pay me extra if I supplied his kitchen and cut off Feast."

"Not good," Wayne said. "That's some motive for Chef or Elena right there. Was he ripping off anything else from the restaurant?"

"Don't know." Teo's weathered mouth tightened. "But if he was willing to steal Feast's suppliers, what else might he have tried to steal?"

"And what did you tell him about growing for him exclusively?"

"Show me the money." Teo shrugged. "I gotta stay in business. And farming is a tough business."

"Amen to that." Wayne straightened up again to ease his sore back. "Now I need a minute to make a phone call." He left Teo, moving his way down the aisle of plants. Once out of hearing, he called his son-in-law's cell phone.

Wayne wasn't surprised when Stevens didn't pick up—he was probably in the middle of the investigation. He kept his words short, leaving a voice mail with the tip that Teo had passed to him and Teo's contact number to reach him for an interview. "I thought you should know that Teo's familiar with a lot of what goes on behind the scenes at Feast. See you at dinner tomorrow."

Wayne ended the call and tipped his head back to breathe in the warm, mulch-scented air and feel the sun on his face. Then he rolled his shoulders and walked back to join his friend, glad he'd done what little he could to help find the killer at Feast.

Esther

Esther Ka`awai sat in her teaching room, supporting herself on a small, round pillow in order to sit cross-legged in spite of arthritis in her knees and hips. She held the large *ipu* gourd poised in front of her, ready to begin the *oli,* the opening chant of the dance.

Three of her best dancers, dressed simply for practice in pareus knotted above their breasts, held the opening pose of this dance: one knee cocked, arm held high and extended, pointing upward with fingers flat, the other hand on hip.

Esther opened her mouth and called the chant, her voice vibrating with the powerful Hawaiian words. Beginning the song, she brought the large, seasoned gourd down with a sharp reverberation and beat the strong percussive rhythm that animated the dancers like an electric current bringing them to life.

Esther's whole body was suffused with energy as the dancers dipped, spun, turned, and stamped, their feet striking the floor with the firm crisp steps characteristic of the *ai kahiko*, the ancient style of hula that was all she taught in her halau. As Esther continued the *mele*, keeping tempo with the *ipu*, she pictured the costumes she'd dress them in for the famous Merrie Monarch hula contest on the Big Island: stripped ti leaves with bright yellow and red fabric underneath, traditional chief's colors to highlight her halau's elite standing.

Esther felt a sudden shiver, as of a cold wind passing over her. It raised the tiny hairs on her arms in "chicken skin." A "knowing" was coming.

She steeled herself to receive it.

Her mind's eye filled with a picture of bent-over, lashing palms. Waves pounded the land, and a boat heeled over and swamped in her vision.

Esther stopped the chant and set the *ipu* on the floor. She closed her eyes and lifted a hand to rub them. "Take a break."

Esther would never forget that other great storm, Hurricane Iniki, which she'd known would come many years ago—her foreknowledge had been unable to help so many who were affected by it. Her "gift" of knowledge still often felt like a curse.

Her *alaka`i*, leader of the dancers, dropped to her knees in front of Esther. "Are you all right, Mama?"

Esther sighed and opened her eyes to smile at her daughter's concerned face. Lehua was aging gracefully, keeping her slim figure, and her thick waist-length black hair was threaded with only a few strands of silver. Esther could still see the beautiful girl she'd been, even though Lehua was the mother of a grown son.

"I will be. Give me a moment. I have to pray."

"You have a knowing?" Lehua still looked worried. She laid the back of her cool hand on Esther's sweating forehead. "Is it bad?"

"Leave me alone, and I'll know soon enough." Esther's tone was harsher than she meant it to be.

Lehua rose quickly and clapped her hands to the other dancers. "Come. We'll get *Kumu* some nice cool lilikoi juice." The women exited her teaching room, and Lehua shut the door behind her.

Esther comforted herself with a long look around the cool, dim studio. The walls were lined with hand-woven lauhala matting, providing a layer of both insulation and decoration here in damp, cool Wainiha Valley on Kaua`i, where Esther had lived her whole life.

The floors were smooth and springy for the dancers, recently refinished in light bamboo flooring by her grandson Alika and clear of any covering so as not to impede their movement. The floors glowed golden in natural light falling through high, narrow louvered windows.

One whole wall was lined with instruments of music and dance and formed an arrangement pleasing to Esther's eye: poi balls in a row, *uli uli* rattles with their bright yellow and red feathers, bamboo *pu`ili* sticks, a graduated row of *ipu*, and a shallow shelf lined with large spotted cowries and smooth black *ili ili* lava stones used for percussion.

On the opposite wall was a long piece of tapa cloth she'd made with her students, hand-stamping patterns with traditional inks they'd made together.

As always, the reverent, peaceful environment of her teaching space calmed Esther. She smoothed the folds of her daily muumuu, a simple garment she'd made herself in a cheerful red aloha print, and set her hands on her knees.

"I am yours, Lord," she said aloud. "Speak to your servant as you see fit."

Esther shut her eyes.

At first there was nothing, and she felt relieved—just the warm red of the inside of her own eyelids, the soft sensation of her breath. But then she felt the knowing again, a certainty of approaching danger that tightened her chest with anxiety. That sensation was followed by flashes of vision: whipping palm trees, bolts of lightning, a power pole going down in a flurry of sparks—and then Lei's face, contorted with pain.

The perspective pulled back, and she could see that Lei was hunched over, arms encircling her round, tight belly. She was sweating, her mouth drawn. Outside the window of the room she was in, the storm broke like a horror movie with the sound turned off.

Esther gasped, opening her eyes. "Oh, no!"

Esther scrambled up off the pillow and staggered as she felt a wave of dizziness. These spells had been happening more and more when she forgot to take her time and mind her balance. She stumbled toward the old-fashioned dial phone in the corner of the room and fumbled for the small, spiral-sided black address book beside the phone, flipping the pages to Lei's number.

Esther found the number, and then her finger paused. What would she say to the young woman God had brought into her life, given her to watch over, so many years ago? That Lei would go into labor in a storm? What did the vision really mean?

More importantly, Esther had been praying for weeks for Lei and Michael's child's Hawaiian name, an important gift they'd asked her for as the baby's godmother. So far no name had come. The couple didn't know if the baby was a boy or a girl, and Esther didn't, either, though she often did by now.

The Holy Spirit simply hadn't revealed it yet. It didn't necessarily mean anything bad was going to happen. Sometimes she didn't receive a child's name for days after its birth.

Esther needed more information before she alarmed Lei and Stevens unnecessarily. The fact that she still didn't have the name didn't mean there was a problem with the baby.

Did it?

"Please, Lord. Protect them. These children don't need any more trouble."

She'd call Lei later, when she knew more. There were still three weeks until the baby was due. When she felt calm again, Esther turned away from the phone and went to the doorway of the studio, calling up the stairs and clapping her hands. "*Hele mai!* We practice!"

CHAPTER THREE

Stevens

STEVENS DISMISSED THE CRUISER HOLDING Chef Noriega with a pat on the hood and the vehicle took off, taking the volatile restaurateur to the station for questioning. Stevens had instructed the officers to put Noriega in an interrogation room but to allow his lawyer to meet him if the man turned up.

Stevens took a minute to calm his adrenaline-charged pulse after the confrontation with Noriega. The man had kept going after his wife even when Stevens had thrown him off. His level of violence alone was enough to have him brought in for this murder.

He rubbed his aching temples. The head injury he'd sustained months ago seemed to act up whenever he got too agitated. Pain clouded his thoughts.

"You okay, LT?" Mahoe had come up behind him.

"Yeah, fine." Stevens turned with an abrupt movement. "We have a lot of folks to question. How many statements did you get?"

"Five, so far." The two moved into the shade of a spreading rainbow shower tree that contrasted vividly with, and sheltered, the elegant black-lacquered doors of the restaurant, where *F E A S T* was picked out in tall gold lettering on a red background above the entrance. "I'm picking up some really interesting rumors. Métier was a ladies' man." The young detective scrolled to his notes feature on the phone. "Three of the kitchen staff confirmed that he was sleeping with multiple women, both at the restaurant and outside."

Stevens fiddled with the steel watch at his wrist. "Dr. Gregory confirmed that the stab wound that killed him, while deep, could have been administered by a woman. And then there was that ring in his hand."

"Let's talk with Elena Noriega next. Since we need to interview her about her husband's attack anyway."

"Sounds good." Stevens's cell phone buzzed as Mahoe pushed one side of the glossy front door open, so they could enter. He checked the caller—Kathy Fraser, his ex-partner. He pushed the Silence button on the phone with a jab of guilt.

Kathy didn't deserve the way he'd been blowing her off since he'd returned from Honduras, but it was what it was. He didn't want any mixed messages with her. He and Lei were solid since his return, and the complication of his relationship with Kathy was something he hoped would disappear if he ignored it long enough.

Looking at the phone, he noticed a message flashing from his father-in-law. He listened to it as he walked through the dim interior of the restaurant.

"This is Wayne. I've got a tip from my friend Teo Benitez. He got a call from a friend who works in the kitchens where the sous-chef was murdered. Anyway, Teo farms produce for Feast, and he witnessed Elena Noriega and the victim having relations in the restaurant. Not only that, Métier was planning to open his own restaurant and steal suppliers and possibly more from Chef Noriega. I thought you should know that Teo's familiar with a lot of what goes on behind the scenes at Feast. See you at dinner tomorrow."

Stevens put his phone away thoughtfully. He'd often received good intel from his father-in-law, who, in spite of his relatively recent arrival on Maui, had quickly embedded himself in the culture of the island and was connected all over the state through his bistro.

The fact that Elena had been having an affair with Métier was big, and along with the circumstantial evidence of the ring, it could point to some jealousy-related motive. That affair, along with the French chef's plan to undercut Noriega, also provided motive for the restaurant's owner. Stevens was glad he had the explosive chef in custody at the moment.

Stevens and Mahoe walked through the main eating area, a large space with long tables already set for the restaurant's community-style dining. Spots of warm, colored light from hand-blown Venetian light fixtures created dramatic spots on plank tables, illuminating Mexican mouth-blown glassware, folded white napkins, and hand-forged steel flatware. The whole space had the feeling of a medieval dining hall, with brick surrounding the open kitchen area like a huge fireplace and antique coats of arms embellishing distressed stucco walls.

Elena Noriega had seated herself at the desk across from her husband's in their shared office. She'd tied a filmy scarf around her neck, hiding the marks of his hands, and she was tap-tapping at her laptop. She looked up at their appearance. Her eyes were puffy, her face tear-stained. "Our lawyer is going to meet Winston at the police station."

"Would you also like counsel?" Mahoe asked politely.

Stevens wished Mahoe hadn't said that. Waiting for another lawyer for Mrs. Noriega would take time they didn't have. He made a mental note to remind the junior detective of that. But Elena shook her head, then winced, touching her throat.

"No. I can make a statement on my own. But I prefer to wait until my friend Kathy Fraser is here."

So that's what Kathy had been calling about. Stevens drew out a folding chair and sat down facing Elena. "Would you mind shutting down that laptop? We're going to need to take a look at it, as well as your husband's computer."

Elena frowned, but turned off the laptop and closed it, handing it to him with poor grace. "I don't see why you need mine."

Stevens ignored that, handing the laptop to Mahoe who slid it into a large paper evidence bag. "Why don't we begin with some background questions?"

Elena folded her lips. She tweaked a tissue from a nearby box and blotted her eyes, visibly pulling herself together. "I'm waiting until Kathy gets here."

Stevens frowned. "How do you know Kathy?"

"She's one of my best friends. She did a semester abroad in college in Spain, and I met her in Barcelona, where I'm from."

"Is that also where you and Winston met?"

"Yes. He came to Barcelona to study Spanish cuisine. My father is a chef. We met through my father's kitchen."

"So how long have you been married?"

"Ten years. We moved to Maui right after we married, and started Feast."

Stevens made a couple of notes on his battered spiral pad. He needed to do a thorough background on the restaurant. "And when did your husband begin abusing you?"

Elena jerked as if she'd been slapped, then shot to her feet. Stevens's impression of her as an elegant woman was confirmed: she wore tailored black trousers and a matching scoop-neck top, with a red belt accenting her slim waist. A lush fall of curly black hair was held back from her face by a red headband. If Stevens hadn't seen her neck, he'd never believe she hadn't always been wearing the scarf she'd put on to hide the bruising. He wondered how often she'd needed such disguises.

"I—I want to wait for Kathy," she repeated. "I need a glass of water." She hurried out of the room on a waft of perfume.

"We have lots of other people to talk to." Mahoe consulted his notes. "We might as well get started. Weird that she knows your ex-partner. Small island."

"I'm sure Kathy will be a help getting Mrs. Noriega to talk," Stevens said as they left the office to interview the other staffers. But he didn't know that for sure—Kathy could be stubbornly idealistic, and her loyalties might be divided.

Jared

Jared Stevens walked up the beach at Ho`okipa, his surfboard under his arm. He shook the water out of his hair and eyes briskly. Glancing back, he grinned at one of his firefighter buddies, just taking off on a big macker of a set. Pete made the drop and pulled into the barrel, getting a good ride before the wave closed out. That had been Jared for two hours already this morning, and he enjoyed the pleasant burn of tiredness in his muscles as he roused himself to trot up the sloping yellow sand to the shower under a beach heliotrope tree.

Jared rinsed off in the cool water, aware of a couple of surfer chicks checking him out. He pretended he didn't notice. The last thing he needed was another random hookup—they never seemed to work out, ending in annoying drama. Dating on Maui was getting old after five years—the women he met were either party girls on their way to somewhere else, or older divorcées with baggage he didn't want to carry.

When he arrived at his truck, Jared checked his phone for messages, one eye on a rain shower making its rainbow-trailing way in his direction from across the ocean. His brother had called. As usual, Stevens had left no greeting. "I'm on a homicide case at a restaurant in Lahaina called Feast. One of our interviewees said you'd been out here last week investigating a fire in the kitchen that they thought might be arson. Need to discuss your findings with you."

Jared frowned, setting his phone on the passenger seat and retrieving a towel.

Now that he'd made fire investigator, replacing his friend Tim who'd returned to the mainland, Jared had a nine-to-five schedule rather than the irregular shifts of a firefighter. He loved the process of investigation—checking out the scene, using all his fire science knowledge to trace the source and course of the fire, interviewing people, drawing conclusions. It was like being a detective in a lot of ways, and sometimes the outcomes were deadly, too. His cases often crossed into working with the police department.

He had ruled that fire, which had begun with a buildup of grease in one of the ovens, inconclusive—there had been no clear ignition cause. But now, if there was a homicide, the fire might be related.

Jared wrapped a towel around his waist, dropped his board shorts and pulled up his boxers and jeans. He took off the towel and pinned it neatly to a length of line that ran across the back of his truck's extended cab. Everything had a place in Jared's truck, and in his life. Organization helped keep things under control.

Stevens had come back from his stint in Central America a physical wreck but back in control of his life. Jared had been pissed at his brother for going overseas in the first place, but by the time he returned, Jared was just glad Stevens was alive. Stevens now claimed that everything that had happened over there had been part of his recovery—he'd beaten his drinking and the PTSD that had pushed him into alcoholism in the first place.

At least his brother was sober now. Stevens's recovery had been rapid overall, but he still suffered from headaches and memory loss. Still, Stevens and Lei seemed to be back on solid ground with their relationship and excited about the coming baby. He'd worried they were headed toward being another statistic.

Jared shrugged into a Maui Fire Department polo shirt and hopped into his Tacoma. He shut the door of the truck, rolled up the windows, turned on the engine, and cranked the AC—even in the morning, the sun was significant and his cab had heated up. He called Stevens back.

"Hey, bro. Homicide at Feast?"

"Yeah. What did you determine about that fire?" Stevens, never one for chitchat, sounded distracted and in a hurry. Jared pulled together his focus.

"It began after hours in one of the stoves. Looked like a grease fire, but there was no obvious ignition source. In fact, they were lucky the whole place didn't go up. I ruled it inconclusive." Jared flipped down the sun visor, taking a quick look in the mirror to comb his short hair with a hand. "Want me to come out there? I could bring you a copy of the report, statements from the people I interviewed."

"That would be great. Thanks, bro. I'll still be here at Feast for the next couple of hours." Stevens ended the call.

Jared put his truck in gear and got on the road toward his office at the main firehouse in Kahului. In his almost six years on Maui, his goal of getting closer to his family had been achieved. He went to dinner at Lei and Stevens's at least once a week, and things with his mother were much improved. He often spent time with his nephew, Kiet, teaching him water sports. Still, a sense of something missing nagged at him.

No time for maudlin musings. He had a job to do.

Jared spent a minute greeting friends at the firehouse, then jogged up the stairs two at a time to his office, where he pulled the fire report. He made copies of it and of the witness statements. Back on the road to Lahaina, Jared checked in with the main fire chief about his current location in case of a call, then put the pedal down.

The drive along the Pali brought reflection as the views of cliffs, sea, and sky slowed his pace to that of tourists taking in the views for the first time. The two-lane road wound along the edge of the West Maui Mountains, curving along a rugged, dry coastline hundreds of feet above the ocean. Off in the distance, spume marked whales' breath and the shapes of Lanai and Kahoolawe rose like turtles right off the coast.

His life was so different now from his early days as a fire-fighter working in Los Angeles. The ocean was his playground, and its constantly changing moods never failed to lift his spirits. Fire emergencies on Maui were frequent but less severe than in California, where it was routine for hundreds of firefighters to be deployed to battle massive blazes in the summer. Here, most of the calls were small home emergencies or wind- and drought-related blazes in the open areas.

Jared pulled in at the restaurant, holding up his ID badge for the police officer guarding the door. "Fire investigator. Here to see Lieutenant Stevens." He signed into the log and headed inside Feast.

His brother was back in the restaurant's office with his partner Mahoe, a young, square-built Hawaiian. Seated at a desk across from Stevens was Elena Noriega, whom he'd met during Feast's oven fire investigation. She looked beautiful but upset. Beside her sat a stunning woman in an MPD uniform. They all glanced up at Jared as he opened the door.

"Come in. You might as well hear this," Stevens said.

"I brought the report." Jared held the folder up and advanced into the crowded space. "Mrs. Noriega. Nice to see you again. I'm sorry about the circumstances." The woman nodded, blowing her nose on a tissue. Beside her, the brunette police officer extended a hand. "Sergeant Kathy Fraser."

"Oh, you're my brother's ex-partner! Jared Stevens." He shook her hand. Kathy had a strong grip and slight calluses across her palm. This woman spent time at the shooting range, and damn, she was hot. Stevens had hardly mentioned her, though Jared knew they'd been partners in MPD's training programs for going on two years. Maybe Stevens didn't want Jared hitting on her, a situation that had gone bad on the brothers before.

"Have a seat, Jared." Stevens pulled out a folding chair and wedged it in beside him. "We were just talking about the sabotage pattern Mrs. Noriega discovered in the kitchens."

"Oh, really? That since I was here investigating your fire?" Jared opened his folder and addressed this inquiry to Mrs. Noriega.

"Yes. I think the fire was the first incident," Elena Noriega said. "Then there was the walk-in left open, the short to the air-conditioning system, the cash register burglary." She detailed the different incidents. "The police officers who responded to each incident didn't seem to put them together with the other incidents, though I repeatedly told them I thought we had a saboteur of some kind."

"That brings up my report on your kitchen fire." Jared took the copy of the report out of the folder and handed it to Stevens. "I believe you have a copy, Mrs. Noriega. The grease that combusted in the back of the stove didn't have an obvious ignition source, but it could have been started by some sort of spark. A buildup like that grease puddle is always a danger in a kitchen."

"Which is why I wish I'd talked to you." Mrs. Noriega nervously touched the scarf knotted around her throat, stroking it. "Chef makes it a priority that all equipment is thoroughly cleaned. There's no way that grease buildup happened by accident." She rummaged in the desk, coming up with a binder. "Here's our kitchen procedure manual. All the things we do to make sure Feast's kitchens are some of the safest and cleanest on the island."

"Well." Jared shrugged, smiling to take the sting out of his words. "Procedures are only as good as those following them."

"Do you suspect anyone in particular as being behind the sabotage?" Stevens took notes on his pad. "Is there any particular staffer you think has a bone to pick with the restaurant?"

"Yes. We have a blogger in our midst." Mrs. Noriega said "blogger" like it was a dirty word. "I've been trying to figure out who it is. That person is out to make us look bad."

"And I've been working on that for Elena." Sergeant Fraser held up her phone, pointing to the website on it. "The blog is called At the Feast. It's a sort of . . . diary-like blog. Very funny. It's gotten picked up by HuffPost Hawaii, too, so it's getting a lot of hits."

"It's not at all funny." Mrs. Noriega frowned at the other woman.

"Oh, come on, Elena." Fraser turned the smartphone and read, "'Sometimes Feast reminds me of a soap opera—Chef is the only person, man or woman, who hasn't slept with the Frenchman.' That's funny, right?" She looked around. "'The Frenchman' must be Métier."

A tight silence fell. Elena Noriega's cheekbones flushed as she looked down at her hands, twisted in her lap. "Ridiculous."

"Interesting that you would say so, considering I have a witness who claims to have seen you in a compromising position with Métier. On the premises, in fact," Stevens said dryly.

There was a short, charged silence; then Fraser swiveled to face the other woman. "Elena? What is Lieutenant Stevens referring to?"

Elena Noriega covered her face with her hands. "I'm so embarrassed."

"This is murder, Mrs. Noriega. The stakes are a little higher than embarrassment." Stevens leaned toward the woman, his voice low and sympathetic. "Of course you turned to other arms for comfort. Your husband was clearly abusive."

Jared had to admire his brother's interviewing technique, as Elena appeared to melt. She lowered her hands, looking up in appeal, eyes shiny with tears.

"That's it, exactly. There was no one I could turn to. François—he saw the way Winston treated me, and he'd felt the sharp side of Winston's temper plenty of times himself. But François was the only person to reach out to me, to confront me about it. He told me one day that he hated how Winston treated me." Elena turned toward her friend. Kathy Fraser's face was blank with surprise and suppressed emotion. "It was exactly like the lieutenant says. François was good to me. He . . ." Elena seemed to belatedly realize how many people were in the room, and she swiveled a wild glance around at Jared, Mahoe, and Stevens. She turned to Kathy Fraser. "I should probably have a lawyer, shouldn't I?"

"I don't know, Elena. Should you?" Conflicted emotions flickered in Fraser's dark blue eyes. Clearly she wanted to help the investigation, but this was her friend, perhaps incriminating herself. Jared could see internal struggle in hands interlaced so hard that the knuckles were white. "If you've got nothing to do with the murder, then you've got nothing to fear in telling the truth."

"Well, I had nothing to do with François's death." Mrs. Noriega turned back to Stevens and spoke clearly. "Yes, I was having an affair with François, I'm ashamed to say. But as you had occasion to witness, my husband was abusive." Her slender hands went to her throat, and Elena Noriega unknotted the scarf. Jared's eyes widened at the bruises darkening the woman's pale skin.

"I'm going to need to photograph those marks as part of our investigation. I recommend that you press charges against your husband, whatever the outcome." Stevens gestured to Mahoe, who held a camera.

"You can take the pictures, Lieutenant. But I don't plan to press charges. Winston just doesn't handle his anger very well."

Mahoe stood with the Canon and approached the desk. Fraser got up from her seat and moved to stand next to Jared as the young detective shot photos from various angles, the flash searing in the small room.

Jared felt Kathy Fraser's proximity like an electric field as she was pressed briefly against him by Mahoe's maneuvering. He needed to get her number, no question. He hadn't been this attracted to a woman in forever. He held perfectly still, suppressing a zing of reaction, as her hip brushed his shoulder.

Seated on his other side, Stevens seemed to have forgotten that his brother was there. He turned to Jared. "Well, thanks for bringing the report."

Jared stood in the cramped space. Kathy's head was level with his chin. He smelled her coconut shampoo as he inhaled. "Is there anything else I can do?"

"I don't think so." Stevens absently rubbed that watch he'd worn since Honduras against his wrist.

"I'll be right back," Fraser said to Elena. The policewoman pushed past Jared, and he grabbed the opportunity to follow her out of the office. Seemingly oblivious to him, she headed down the hall toward the restroom.

She was getting away.

He took three long strides to catch up. "Kathy."

Kathy turned, and now he was standing too close. She backed up, wiping her eyes with a hand, refusing to look at him. "What?"

"It's not your fault. You were a good friend. She was hiding the abuse from everyone." Jared spoke instinctively to the struggle he sensed going on in her.

"I wasn't a good friend. I suspected, and I never pushed her. I didn't want it to be true." Kathy leaned against the wall, pressing the backs of her hands against her eyes in a gesture both concealing and defensive.

"I'm sorry. Tough way to find out. Murder investigations have a way of bringing everything out of the closet." Jared restrained himself from touching her by clasping his hands behind his back.

Kathy dropped her hands. Blue eyes, framed by lashes spiky with tears, seemed to blaze at him in the dim hall. She squared her shoulders, tugged down the jacket of her uniform. "You don't have to tell me that. I may work on the third floor, but I earned my place there by being a good cop."

She spun on a heel and stomped into the women's room.

There was nothing for Jared to do but turn and walk out of the restaurant, disappointment sour in his throat.

CHAPTER FOUR

Stevens

STEVENS RESUMED QUESTIONING ELENA NORIEGA AS MAHOE PUT AWAY THE CAMERA.

“That blogger said the Frenchman slept with a lot of people. Were you aware of his activities?”

“I suspected.” Elena wrapped the scarf back around her throat, knotting it loosely. “I heard rumors. He always had someone on his arm. The blogger might have killed him—maybe she was one of his castoffs.”

Stevens eyed her carefully. Elena didn’t seem emotionally responsive to the fact that the sous-chef had other lovers besides her.

“I’ve been trying to figure out who the blogger is for weeks.” Kathy reentered and sat back down beside her friend. “Elena asked me to do a little digging. I’ve read all the entries, and there’s nothing that directly links back to a specific role. The blogger talks about the kitchen, working the floor, everything. I’ve run some trace software on the blog, but it’s hosted on one of those onion sites—untraceable.”

"Clever, using the darknet," Mahoe said. Stevens glanced at the young man, surprised that the junior officer knew of the network that ran under the radar of trackable web applications. "Mrs. Noriega, Lieutenant Stevens and I began interviewing your kitchen staff. Most of them were aware of the blog."

She shook her head. "I hated it. That's why I had Kathy trying to find who it was."

"Well, hopefully we'll flush out the blogger in our interviewing," Stevens said. "Tell us how the affair with Métier got started."

"Like I said before, François was kind to me. We met every week. He'd work with Chef on the menu for the week, depending on what was fresh and in season. Then, when they had that figured out, sometimes down to the day, François and I would photograph a few sample dishes and discuss the media opportunities for the week. As you know, I am the restaurant's promotional and business manager." She gestured to the corner of the office, where a powerful spotlight was clamped to the edge of a filing cabinet, aimed at an area draped in black velvet. "We'd stage the food photos over there. I'd take the photos, then post them on social media and use them in advertising. We have our own website and various social media accounts, too."

"Perhaps you could take us through the day before, step-by-step."

"Well, I assume what I do at home isn't of interest to the police." Mrs. Noriega smoothed her trousers. "I came in about eleven a.m., as I usually do. I checked in with our floor manager, Peter Claymore. He had things in hand, so I went back to the office." She described the various things she'd done. Stevens found his attention wandering. One of his stress headaches was gathering force behind his temples. "I didn't spend any time alone with François yesterday, and I left at four p.m.," Elena finished.

Kathy spoke up. "Elena has an alibi for the time in question. She was home, with the Noriegas' child, when the murder took place, if it was late at night—as it seems to have been."

"Mrs. Noriega has already been offered counsel," Stevens told Fraser sharply, annoyed with the interference. "I'd appreciate it if you weren't functioning in that role."

Bright red spots appeared on Fraser's cheeks. "Perhaps I'd be better able to help the investigation and you, Elena, if I focus on finding the blogger." She stood up. "I'll see you back at your house later."

"Don't go, Kathy!" Mrs. Noriega pleaded, but Kathy exited the office.

Stevens glanced at Mahoe. "Let's take a break. I need some water." He stood. "Do you need anything, Mrs. Noriega?"

"No, thank you."

Stevens headed out into the kitchen.

He found a glass and swallowed a pain pill over by one of the sinks, splashing some water on his face. There were still hours of interviews to go, and his energy was flagging.

Stevens hoped he'd been wrong about the interest in Kathy Fraser he'd sensed from his brother. Jared made no bones about being sick of Maui's transient dating scene, and he'd lit up like a Christmas tree at the sight of Kathy—the attraction was hard to miss, if only one-sided. Hopefully Kathy knew enough from Stevens's stories about Jared to stay away.

Stevens probed his own mind. Was he apprehensive about Jared's interest in Kathy because he, himself, was still attracted to her? He stared at the swirl of clear liquid filling his glass.

No.

He just didn't want his tomcat brother shitting in his personal sandbox. Things were messy enough with Kathy, between Lei's jealousy and the weird vibes that remained from their almost-kiss before he left for Honduras.

His ex-partner really deserved better.

Stevens's cell phone buzzed in its belt holster. He checked caller ID and answered only because it was Lei.

"Hey, Sweets." Stevens turned away from the watching eyes of the annoyed-looking kitchen helper he still hadn't had time to interview. "What's up?"

"I heard you caught a fresh one." His wife's voice sounded a little thin, as it often did due to her lack of lung space. "You missed my baby shower."

"I know." He pinched the bridge of his nose between his thumb and forefinger, willing the pain in his temples to subside. "I wish I'd been there. Were you surprised?"

"Very. Good thing Baby didn't decide to join us right there. I about had a heart attack with everyone yelling and the confetti poppers going off. Anyway, I don't want to take up your time since I know you're deep in it. I just wanted to tell you I'm on my way home—on early maternity leave. Captain Omura found me some comp time."

"Good. It's been getting hard for you to get around." He'd even had to tie her shoes for her as they got ready for work. "Everything okay?"

"More than okay. I'm looking forward to being the one to pick Kiet up after school, for once." Their son, now in first grade, was usually watched after school either by Lei's father, Wayne, or Stevens's mother, Ellen. "And I'll be able to finish the nursery. But never mind all that. What's going on with your case?" He detected a slightly frantic note in her voice. Clearly decorating the nursery wasn't as appealing as a homicide investigation.

Stevens caught the eye of the kitchen helper again. "You know what? I'll have to fill you in when I get home. See you when I can. Love you." He ended the call.

He walked toward the staffer, a slender young man with the caffe-latte skin of mixed heritage and dreadlocks decked with beads in the red, yellow-gold, green, and black of a Rastafarian. "You seem to have something on your mind."

"Indeed." The young man advanced. "Sage Bukowski. I'm a busboy and food runner." To Stevens's surprise, the young man had a well-educated British accent. He extended a hand and Stevens shook it.

"I'm Lieutenant Stevens. Sorry we're taking so long to interview all of you."

"I thought I'd make sure you knew Elena Noriega was sleeping with François, since you're interviewing her for so long." The young man slid his hands into the tight pockets of narrow stovepipe jeans he wore with a peace-sign-decorated tank shirt.

"Thanks for that. What we're more interested in right now is who else he was sleeping with." Stevens took his notebook out of his back pocket. "Got any names for me?"

Bukowski had plenty of them. "But none since he started the affair with Elena. Seemed pretty serious about that one, even if it was 'secret.'" He made air quotes with his fingers.

"What about you?" Stevens aimed his pencil stub at the young man. "The mysterious blogger claims Métier was bisexual."

"Just hyperbole." Bukowski's face flushed a little. "Métier was straight."

"How do you know?"

"Because I'm not." Bukowski winked flirtatiously. "I wouldn't have said no to a bite of French baguette, had it been on offer."

Stevens snorted a laugh. "You certainly know a lot of gossip and have a way with words. Where'd you go to college?"

"Oxford."

"So what's a highly educated young man like you doing in a job like this?" Stevens gestured to the empty kitchen.

"Kiteboarding. Maui's the best in the world for that, and windsurfing. I'm a foreign national; not too many jobs here for Brits with a degree in literature. Chef is paying me under the table—I hope you aren't going to report me."

"Got bigger fish to fry. Where were you last night between ten and midnight?"

Bukowski pushed a handful of dreadlocks out of an eye, summoning his thoughts. "I got off at nine-thirty. I went out with some friends to a bar in Lahaina." Bukowski named a place and Stevens noted it, along with his address and phone number.

"Thanks. You can go. I'll be in touch if I need anything more."

The young man headed for the front door with a wave.

Stevens headed back to the office and ran into Mahoe outside the door. They could see Elena, texting on her phone, through the window into the office. "We just want to run through Mrs. Noriega's story again, push for detail so we can verify if she had the opportunity to commit the crime—we already know she had means and motive."

"Yes." Brandon nodded. "Should we interview the rest of the staff after that?"

"We can't leave Chef Noriega waiting at the station much longer, so let's just take quick statements and make notes on who we want to follow up with for longer interviews. And I've already got one down I want to talk to more." Stevens took out his notebook, thumbed to the page. "Sage Bukowski. That kid has the gossip and language skills to be the blogger."

Caprice

Dr. Caprice Wilson poured herself a glass of bubbly water and added a slice of lime and ice cubes before settling herself into her favorite lounge chair on her little deck overlooking Hilo Bay. She leaned her head back and released a heavy sigh, letting go of the tension of a day filled with multiple consultations, a couple of therapy appointments with police officers, and an emotionally harrowing hour testifying at family court.

The wind was settling on the bay, just a slight roughness to the cool water, and late afternoon sun gleamed on the coconut palms and banyans around Hilo. The long, deep, foliage-covered ridges around the bay seemed to hold the town in a jewel-like setting. Dr.

Wilson let her eyes wander over the water, taking in a fishing boat coming in, a canoe team paddling by, the dip and swerve of a shearwater. She shut her eyes, and as they'd been doing all day, her thoughts wandered back to Lei and Stevens.

She had a little time alone before Bruce got home from work, and she patted her lap. "Hector. C'mere, my man."

The elderly Siamese was pressed up against the invisible sonic barrier defining her yard and keeping him contained. Hector turned his regal head and gazed at her from unblinking crystal-blue eyes, dark markings circling them like eyeliner. When he was ready, and not a moment before, Hector turned and paced over to her, commenting loudly on the weather (damp) and his appetite (large). After so many years together, she understood him perfectly.

Reaching his mistress, Hector jumped gracefully onto her lap, turned three times, kneading, and settled himself with a rumbling purr. Only then did Dr. Wilson's hand drift down to stroke the cat's creamy fur. Hector had been with her through so much—raising her son, Chris, a tumultuous divorce, a subsequent drinking problem after Chris left for college, and her eventual relocation to this idyllic spot on Hilo Bay that suited her new life so much better than the Hidden Palms estate home she'd built with her ex.

"I don't know why, but Lei is on my mind," Caprice told the cat, tipping up his pointed chin to look into blue eyes that always reminded her of her son. Chris was settled in California now, graduated from college, and dating a young woman Dr. Wilson hoped she'd be calling a daughter-in-law someday. "I've learned to listen to that intuition."

Caprice thumbed to Lei's personal cell number on her phone. Their relationship had evolved over the years from an early one of mandatory counseling to the friendship of colleagues who'd worked many cases together. Most recently, she'd assisted in Stevens's recovery from a disastrous stint overseas.

"Hello? Dr. Wilson?" Lei's voice sounded near and immediate in her ear.

"Hello, my dear. How are you and the little one?"

"Not so little. Let me sit down." Caprice heard a rustle and a grunt, and pictured Lei as she'd seen her on a recent visit, feet up on the coffee table, one hand on the mound of her belly, wearing the maternity "uniform" she'd come up with. "Man, I'm looking forward to this part of parenting being over. They say it's the way I'm carrying the baby that's making me so uncomfortable. It's all out in front, like a big ol' basketball, and I can't seem to get my breath, and I always have to pee. But you asked . . ."

"So everything's just as it should be, then," Dr. Wilson said.

Lei laughed. "I guess."

"How's Michael doing?"

A long pause as Lei considered. "I think he's okay. The EMDR treatments Security Solutions set up really helped. He's still sober, and he hasn't had any flashbacks involving Anchara since Honduras. But he gets headaches and has trouble remembering recent events—that hasn't really improved. He gets frustrated with not feeling a hundred percent."

"Those are the results of head trauma, as I told both of you. He needs to take it easy, be patient with himself. And so do you. That last month of pregnancy can be tough."

"I miss running," Lei said. "I'm off work for the duration. Captain Omura sent me out on leave a few days early. Cleaned out my desk this afternoon."

"Perfect. You can get ready for the baby now. Didn't you tell me the nursery still needs a few things?"

"We're keeping the baby in with us in Kiet's cradle at first, but yeah. I have to clean out the office and set it up for the baby. It's a project, but I'm not sure what I'm going to do with myself for a whole month, uncomfortable like this."

"What about swimming? Go to the ocean. Get your exercise. It's good for your body, good for the baby, and good for your state of mind."

"I've been doing that after work every day I can. But what I really want to do is have a case to work on. Something quiet."

"Lei, that's a bad idea. Your cases always seem to turn into more than what they first appear."

"That's what's so great about my job. I miss it already."

"Well, let me tell you something." Caprice stroked the purring cat, her gaze on the horizon. "The job will always be there, sucking every minute you'll give it. But you will have this season with your unborn child only one time." Caprice felt tears prickle her eyes, remembering Chris: how far away he was, how fast his childhood had gone with her working so much. "Put a pause button on and be a little restless—but be *present.*"

"You sound like a therapist." There was a smile in Lei's voice. "Gotcha, Dr. Wilson."

"So are you having a baby shower?"

"They threw me a surprise one at the station. Tiare, who's going to be my labor coach, put it together. The station is buying us a crazy expensive stroller. That's more than enough fuss for me. To be honest, my best friends are on Oahu, and they'll come see us after the baby's born."

"Marcella and Sophie, you mean."

"Exactly. Marcella's hip-deep in work, married life, and baby Jonas. And Sophie—well, if I can get her out of her computer cave, it will be a miracle. But she swears she'll come."

"So you still don't know the baby's gender?"

"We want it to be a surprise. We've got the first names picked out, one for a girl and one for a boy, but we're waiting on the baby's Hawaiian middle name from Esther Ka`awai, who's the baby's godmother. She is praying about it and waiting for it to come to her. We might know the baby's sex when she tells us that, and she's never been wrong."

Caprice smiled at the excitement in Lei's voice. "You're embarking on your biggest mystery yet. I can't help feeling a little like a proud grandma."

"You?" Lei snorted. "The youngest, prettiest grandma ever, then. Aunty is a better fit."

"Well, call me when you have any news. And seriously, slow down and relish this time. Even if you have another baby, there will never be another season just like this."

"You always have such good *mana`o* for me. Love you, Dr. Wilson."

"Don't you think it's time you called me Caprice?" Hector's deep, rough purr vibrated through Caprice's body as she stroked him. She'd asked Lei to do that before, to no avail.

"All right, then, Aunty Caprice," Lei said. "Love you. Talk to you soon."

Caprice's former client Lei Texeira, healed and matured into an incredible woman, ended the call with a soft *click*. Caprice smiled, leaning her head back against the lounger. Rarely in her work did she get to witness the kind of transformation she had in Lei and her husband, and continue to be part of it. But this time she'd been able to, and what a journey it had been. Aunty or grandma, she couldn't wait to hold their baby in her arms.

CHAPTER FIVE

C.J.

Captain C.J. Omura settled herself with a Diet Coke in the observation room. She flicked on the audio monitor and stared through the one-way mirror at Chef Winston Noriega, seated at the bolted-down steel interview table.

Noriega slumped in the chair and fiddled with the handcuffs in his lap. He was still wearing an immaculate white, side-buttoned chef's coat, and his burly shoulders strained the sturdy fabric as they bunched. Dark hair, buzzed short, gleamed with pearls of sweat, but that wouldn't last long in the strong air-conditioning they ran at Kahului Station.

C.J. liked these quiet moments in the observation booth by herself. She could get a sense of the witnesses, observe their behavior when they thought themselves alone, and read their expressions, body language, tiny personal rituals, and self-soothing behaviors. Truth was, she'd always been a bit of a voyeur, and that curiosity, while having its downside, had served her well in her career.

C.J. opened the zip-front leather binder she carried everywhere.

Inside, a crisp new pad of legal paper was held down by an elastic strap beside a quality silver pen, a gift from her parents, slipped into a webbing sleeve to use for note-taking. Her date book, a handheld recorder, tube of hand cream, and her second phone were secured in a zippered mesh pocket.

She checked the phone and read a text message from a familiar number. *Meet me after work.*

C.J. frowned, then remembered not to wrinkle her forehead. Her mother, a noted beauty even at sixty, had passed on a whole list of appearance rules she followed. Omura adhered to most of them, though she'd rebelled against her mother's dictums in most everything else. She texted her lover back.

You don't tell me what to do.

A beat went by. Then, Sorry, gorgeous. Will you, pretty please with kisses on it, meet me after work at our special place?

She grinned. Since you ask so nicely . . . yes. Wear something dangerous.

Consider me your pirate for the night. I'll shine up my peg leg.

C.J. smiled again, thumbs flying. I'm more in the mood for something criminal this time. Think handcuffs, nightsticks, and the back of a paddy wagon.

Cuff me and throw away the key, Captain. I've been bad, came back to her. I'll provide the nightstick for some hard time. I'll even wear orange for you, baby, though it's not my best color.

C.J. snorted a chuckle even as her heart rate shot up. He was irrepressible, naughty, and nothing she threw at him ever got him down. Their relationship was inappropriate and would never go anywhere; but he made her laugh, and that didn't happen often enough.

Not to mention, the sex was *amazing.*

C.J. wiped the smile off her face and flipped the phone over as Lieutenant Michael Stevens opened the door of the interview room. "Hey, Captain. Did Noriega call for his lawyer?" Stevens asked.

"No. I heard one was on the way at the wife's request, but he never requested it, so you can proceed. Any new developments?" C.J. said.

The tall lieutenant entered, shutting the door with a quiet *click* behind him. "Noriega's wife confirms she was having an affair with the victim." Stevens pushed rumpled dark hair out of his eyes. C.J. had always appreciated Stevens's ruggedly handsome appeal in an aesthetic way. Dark circles of fatigue or pain under his crystal-blue eyes only made them bluer, and his rangy body exuded power and a lithe grace.

She'd had a fantasy or two about him in her lonely bed back in the day, when it seemed like he and Lei would never tie the knot; but as time went on, C.J. worried about them in a way that annoyed her. Thank God she'd gotten Lei home and on maternity leave before some disaster happened to her favorite detective in her ninth month. Lei was a magnet for trouble, attracting wackos and vendettas in a way that defied statistical odds.

C.J. cared too much, felt the dependency of their little family in a way that made her second-guess herself, and Stevens's bruised-looking aspect irritated her because of that. "Did you have a headache today?" she snapped.

"None of your business, sir," Stevens said evenly. "Did you want to catch up on the case or not?"

C.J. bit back a retort. She tapped her nails on the worn counter. "Report."

"We took initial statements from all the restaurant staff we could round up. Got multiple motives for Chef Noriega and his wife: she was having an affair with the victim and he was abusive. The vic, Métier, was stealing recipes and more from Feast, planning to set up his own, competing restaurant. And there was a pattern of sabotage happening in the kitchen." Stevens described a series of "accidents" and petty theft, flipping through his notes. "There's also a blogger lampooning the place on a regular basis."

C.J. frowned, leaning back in the chair, tapping her fingertips together. "All this motive, and yet I have a sense you don't think Noriega did it."

Stevens shrugged. "It was a stupid murder. Meaning, no effort was made to conceal the body or mitigate the consequences to the restaurant. Chef Noriega has an anger problem and abuses his wife. Seems like he'd commit a different kind of murder than a cold-hearted stab to the back. I think Chef might have confronted Métier and killed him much more face-to-face—strangled him, hit him on the head, beat him to death. But a stab in the back with one of his best knives?" Stevens shook his head. "Doesn't play for me."

"Where's Mahoe?" The enthusiastic young Hawaiian, injured on a case a few years ago, was another subordinate who weighed on C.J.'s mind more than she would have liked.

"Filing the evidence. The most interesting thing we picked up at the scene was an engagement ring in the victim's hand."

"That *is* interesting." C.J. sipped her Diet Coke, narrowing her eyes—but that made wrinkles, so she opened them wide instead. "What do you think it means?"

"He was getting ready to pop the question to someone. The vic slept around at the restaurant, but we couldn't identify any particular woman he might have been wanting to marry except Elena Noriega, who, in her interview, showed no sign that she was in love with Métier. She was in need of consolation, and he provided that—according to her, all the affair was to her." Stevens hitched his belt up on his narrow waist. He still hadn't regained all the weight he'd lost during that Honduras fiasco. "Maybe he was trying to steal her from Noriega along with the chef's recipes. But if so, I'd bet money she didn't know he was going to pop the question to her."

"So it could have been some spurned lover that stuck him in the back?" C.J. took the small tube of expensive hand cream out of her folio and rubbed a dot into her hands.

"Right. Only we couldn't shake loose anyone specific who cared that much about him."

"Maybe Noriega will know, or you'll find something at his residence."

"Yes. Mahoe and I are going to do the search after this interview."

C.J. turned to look at Noriega. The chef was flipping a coin between his fingers, one of those tricks where it seemed to be walking, over and over. "I want you to get to interviewing him before a lawyer shows up."

"I have enough to charge him. We could keep him in custody," Stevens said.

C.J. shook her head. "No. We'll shake loose more by letting him go. All you have on him so far is circumstantial, anyway."

"But what about Elena Noriega? He might go home and beat her. She refused to press charges on him, but I'm filing those on her behalf, since I observed him choking her." Stevens sounded frustrated. "It will take what it will take for her to wake up and smell the coffee about the abuse." C.J. had little pity for those she considered doormats. "We can't hold him without something solid. It will just bite us on the ass if we do."

"I also thought you should know Elena Noriega and Kathy Fraser are close friends. Elena called Kathy out for moral support when we brought Noriega in."

"I'm sure she will be a help to the investigation as long as she can keep up with her regular duties. Kathy's a solid investigator."

Stevens ducked his head affirmatively. "I'll find Mahoe and get to it, then."

C.J. turned her phone off and stowed it. Yeah, she'd lose all credibility if anyone knew she was sleeping with one of her detectives. Might even get consequences from the chief if he ever got wind of it. Maybe that was part of what made her affair so much fun.

That, and the way he made her laugh.

C.J. put the evening's future activities out of her mind, refocusing on what was happening in the interview room as Stevens and Brandon Mahoe entered.

Brandon

Brandon Mahoe turned on the video equipment at Lieutenant Stevens's nod. His partner and mentor seated himself in front of the witness with a handheld recorder and a pad and pen. Brandon's heart thumped so loudly that it seemed like Chef Noriega would hear it. In spite of the high air-conditioning, sweat gathered under the arms of Brandon's best aloha shirt.

Chef Noriega was a celebrity and a known asshole. The man's heavy-lidded stare tracked him as Brandon made sure the camera was aimed properly and the sound adjusted. He felt a little like a cockroach with a boot nearby—but somehow he had to get past that. LT was counting on him to take the lead in the interview today.

Brandon wiped his hands unobtrusively on his jeans and sat down next to LT. "This interview is being recorded, and you have the right to remain silent, or the right to an attorney if you choose to have one. Anything you say here may be used against you in a court of law. Do you understand these rights?"

Chef Noriega inclined his head the barest amount, still staring Brandon down.

"Where were you last night, between the hours of nine and midnight?" Brandon restrained himself from wiping his hands on his jeans again.

"I was at the restaurant. As you know perfectly well." Noriega began flipping a quarter between his fingers, pointedly ignoring Brandon. A schoolyard bully he'd grown up with had played with a coin like that. The boy had done all kinds of tricks with it, even pretending to pull it out of Brandon's ass, making everyone laugh.

Brandon felt his neck flush. *That was then, this is now.* "Who can verify that you were at the restaurant?"

"Anyone you ask. So do I have an alibi for the exact time of Métier's murder? No." Noriega set the coin down. He leaned forward, gaze boring into Brandon's, a feeling like being probed by a high-powered light. "But I didn't do it."

"You sure seem to have a lot of motive," Brandon stated.

"Like what? That man was a little brother to me."

"That's not what the witnesses we interviewed said. Care to change your statement?" Brandon stared right back. "In fact, we have at least two good reasons for you to have killed him."

"Like what?" Noriega laced his fingers on his belly, his body language challenging.

LT stirred beside Brandon. "The detective here has given you a chance to revise your statement about the victim being like a brother."

"Well, he was. At one time." Noriega looked down, plucking at a loose button on his sleeve. The handcuffs clinked. "I think you're biased toward me because of the way I discipline my wife."

"Discipline?" Brandon felt anger flush his whole body now. His dad had beaten his mom when he was a kid, and she'd had to leave him because of it. Brandon had never been sure which parent he was angrier at until right this moment, and now he knew. Rage tightened his voice. "You think it's okay for a man to choke his wife? That's discipline?"

"Elena understands." Noriega made a flicking gesture. "She knows the rules. Why am I talking to *you,* anyway?"

"Maybe you need a taste of what your wife goes through." Brandon surged up out of his seat, lunging for Noriega. LT caught him by the arm and hauled him back into his chair. His red-fogged vision cleared as he was restrained by his superior.

"Chain your pit bull," Noriega said. "I can file a complaint even with these on."

"Back it way up, Mahoe. Calm down." Brandon could hear surprise and concern, as well as rebuke, in Stevens's voice.

Brandon schooled his features into a blank mask and folded his arms on his chest, staring at a speck of gecko crap on the wall just above Noriega's head. He sucked one of those relaxation breaths Dr. Wilson had taught him in the mandatory counseling sessions he'd had some years ago when injured on a case.

"Sorry about that, Chef. Mahoe here is still learning the ropes, gets a little enthusiastic sometimes. Back to his question though—were you and your wife having difficulties?" The LT was using the incident to move in on the witness. Brandon had always admired how Stevens seemed to turn whatever happened in interviews to his advantage.

"Don't see how that's relevant," Noriega growled, flipping the coin again.

"I only ask because of something Mahoe was indicating—motive. Were you aware your wife was having an affair with the victim?" LT's voice was silky with fake sympathy.

"What?" The quarter dropped from Noriega's fingers onto the table with a metallic *clink* as he jumped to his feet, face purpling with rage. "I'll kill that bitch!"

Now Brandon had a good reason to jump out of his chair and wrestle Noriega back into his, clipping the man's handcuffs to the table. "Glad we got that on tape, Lieutenant."

Noriega seemed to realize that wasn't the best thing to have said. He settled back as far as the cuffs would allow. "No. I didn't know that my whore of a wife was sleeping with Métier, though plenty of others were."

"So you don't deny killing Métier for having sex with your wife?" Stevens cocked his head.

"What? No. I mean, yes! I deny it!" Blood suffused Noriega's face again. His blood pressure looked problematic. "What the hell kind of question was that?"

"I'm sorry. I must be the one confused." The LT steepled his fingers, tipped his head forward and frowned as if puzzled. "I just heard you say, and let me get this straight . . ." He looked down at his notes and read flatly, "'I'll kill that bitch.'"

"You know what? Maybe I will have that lawyer now." Noriega glared at Brandon since Stevens's eyes were on his notebook. Brandon glared right back.

"Oh, that's a shame. We were actually going to let you go. Pending assault charges on your wife, of course. But it would be so helpful if you could point us at another suspect. Any other suspect. Right now all we have is you, and you know what they say: 'The husband always did it.'" Stevens's lips twitched humorlessly in a parody of a smile.

Damn, the man was good. Brandon remembered the very first big case he'd worked with the LT—stolen petroglyphs that had led to murder. That case had been so nuts. Yeah, he'd got a beat down on that one, but it had only made Brandon more determined to be a good cop. LT had been there for him ever since. Never in too much of a hurry to talk, coaching him through all the steps to prep for his detective exam. LT had even suggested Brandon continue with school, which was why he was close to graduating from University of Hawaii with a degree in criminal justice. That would help him move up in the MPD, and he'd learned a lot that helped him on the job now. He owed LT big-time, and days like this, Brandon knew he still had more to learn from his mentor.

"Okay, then." Noriega blew out a breath. "I knew Métier was working on something behind my back. Trying to snake my suppliers, steal my recipes. I even think he was the one sabotaging the kitchen. All this might sound like I had even more motive to off him—but I didn't kill him. I had a plan to deal with him. I have more friends on this island than he knew about; various people came to me about him, and we made other agreements.

"I was planning to fire Métier at the end of this month, when his contract ended, and pull the rug out from under him. Had it all lined up: getting his business loan canceled, the space he was going to rent would no longer be available. And my suppliers?" Noriega shook his head. "I paid many of them for next month's produce while it was still in the ground. It's killing me financially, but I also couldn't afford to let Métier get his restaurant going."

Stevens frowned. "Interesting. We'll need to verify all that. And I still don't hear another idea of who might have killed Métier."

"My wife," Noriega said with perfect composure. "Now that I know she was sleeping with the Frenchman, it makes perfect sense. Elena's a jealous woman, and François was a slut. Perhaps he tried to break if off with her."

Brandon frowned. This man went from threatening Elena Noriega to throwing her under the bus at the first opportunity. Marriage looked like a little slice of hell. He'd never fall into that trap.

"You mentioned that you knew François was sleeping with a lot of people. Anyone special?" LT was fishing for whom the ring could be for.

"Maybe. There's a waitress we have. Kitty Summers. They went home together after a lot of shifts. I didn't keep track of Métier's habits, besides telling him he'd better not cause drama at Feast, get those chicks jealous of each other. Looks like he didn't listen to me."

Brandon wrote the woman's name down, and LT went on. "So can you think of anyone else who might have motive to kill Métier?"

"The blogger. I followed that blog, and whenever Métier was mentioned, there was always a tone to it. Like the blogger was bitter. Whoever it was described Métier as 'the Frenchman' on a good day, and 'that psycho Frog' on others."

"Seems pretty thin."

"You asked." Noriega shrugged. "I'm damn pissed that François got himself killed in my walk-in. Wrecked thousands of dollars of food. We'll have to be closed for a couple of days at least. I have to hire a new sous-chef. And now this." He held up his hands, jangled the cuffs. "This, I'll never forgive him for."

"The man is dead," Stevens said. "Seems like that would be punishment enough."

Noriega slitted his eyes but didn't respond.

The LT pinched a finger and thumb on either side of his nose. His eyes were shut as if in pain. "Mahoe, do you have anything else for this witness before we show him to the door?"

Brandon couldn't come up with anything. He stood and took out his handcuff key. He leaned down next to the chef and whispered in his ear, "Don't lay a hand on your wife. We're watching you."

Noriega snorted as Brandon undid the cuffs.

"Stay in town," LT said as Brandon turned off the video. "You'll be answering to assault charges from the DA on behalf of your wife in the next few weeks—and keep your hands off her."

Noriega stood up without speaking, tugging down his jacket. He glared but kept his mouth shut as he headed for the door. Brandon followed the man out and down the hall, escorting him out of the building. Noriega pulled a phone out of his pocket and had hardly dialed it when a gold Lexus SUV drove up. Keone Chapman, that pretentious *haole* lawyer, was behind the wheel. He gestured for Noriega to get in, and they drove off.

Brandon went back into the station. He found Stevens at their office, turning off his computer and picking up his jacket.

"I need a break," LT said. "I'm going home for a couple of hours. I'll text you when I'm on my way to the victim's address. Meet me there for the search. And get these notes typed up, will you?"

"Sure, LT." Brandon took Stevens's notebook. "Do I need to go to the captain with this?"

"Nah. I briefed her before we went in to talk to the chef, and she watched the interview. Grab something to eat, and I'll see you in a few hours."

Stevens headed out. Brandon sat down and opened the case and computer files. He'd get food when he was caught up. If he ever caught up.

Stevens

Stevens wove down the narrow road bordered in lush tropical growth as he headed toward home. His blood quickened thinking of Lei. He loved her pregnant: small round breasts full, her belly an inviting curve. Once he'd decorated it with shaving cream in the shower, making a smiley face with her popped-out belly button as the nose.

Yeah, that had been fun . . .

Stevens pulled the old Bronco up to the gate of their compound and punched in the code. He waited for the gate to retract and drove inside. That gate, the ritual of opening and closing, highlighted how much home and family were set apart from the darkness he walked through during the day. He shook his head to clear it of morbid thoughts as he pulled up to the house.

Keiki and Conan, their Rottweilers, greeted the vehicle with their usual enthusiasm. In spite of his fatigue and headache, he paused beside the truck to pet them.

"Good girl." He squatted and rubbed Keiki's chest. The elderly Rottie leaned her broad square head against him. The trust and love in her posture gave his heart a twinge—her muzzle was thick with white hairs. Conan nosed at her impatiently, and Stevens rubbed the younger dog's ears with his other hand. "Gluttons for attention, you two."

"Daddy!" Kiet barreled down the steps and hit Stevens from the side, tipping him over into the pea gravel of the walkway.

Stevens gave an exaggerated groan. "Officer down! Call a medic!"

His son laughed, trying to tickle him. They tussled, making so much noise that Conan barked with excitement.

"I'll have to get the hose out to calm you boys down," Lei said, from the top of the porch.

Stevens glanced up at her and broke into a grin. "What the heck is that thing you have on?"

"A maternity bathing suit." Lei tugged at the seat of the polka-dotted garment. "The office girls gave it to me at the shower. I was just trying it on. What do you think?"

She struck a pose. Kiet covered his mouth with his hands, giggling, as Stevens tried to keep a straight face. Lei carried the pregnancy way out in front, and the suit, a bright orange one-piece, was trimmed in ruffles. Stevens sat up, capturing Kiet's head under his arm and giving the six-year-old a knuckle rub as he grinned at his wife. "It's cute, Sweets."

"No, it isn't. I look like a beach ball." She tugged at the ruffles. "This is *so* not my style."

"Beach balls are cute, aren't they, little man?" He let the wriggling Kiet out of the headlock.

"Mama does not look like a beach ball. She looks like a giant hot air balloon!" Kiet's favorite storybook featured hot air balloons, his current obsession.

"That's it. I'm going back to my bikini." Lei flounced into the house.

"A giant orange pumpkin with spots!" Kiet said as they walked up the stairs, the dogs flanking them.

"No, son. Your mama looks beautiful," Stevens said loudly, noticing that the bedroom door was ajar. She was probably in there changing, and hearing every word. "Not long before your brother or sister joins us, and she'll be right back to normal."

"Nice save, honey. But I heard *you,* little man." Lei reappeared at the bedroom door in the short plumeria-print muumuu she'd taken to wearing around the house. "And I can still catch you and throw you in the bath." She darted out and chased Kiet, shrieking with laughter, down the hall to the bathroom.

Stevens, grinning, went to the fridge and opened it, taking out an O'Doul's non-alcoholic beer and popping the top. He still felt an occasional tug of longing for that evening drink, but so far he had been able to redirect or modify old habits. He heard a rush of water and murmur of voices as Lei turned on Kiet's bath.

Stevens smelled something good and peeked into the oven. Teriyaki chicken rarified the air with the scent of ginger, soy sauce, and garlic. The rice cooker bubbled, and a salad was already made. Lei reappeared, cheeks flushed, hair a frizz.

"I'm sorry you had to see me in that thing."

"Wouldn't have missed it." He hooked an arm around her neck and drew her in for a kiss. "You look . . . what do they call it? Blooming."

"'Ballooning' is more like it. Kiet called it right." She hugged him, though, snuggling close under his arm. He brought a hand down to rub the hard bulge of her belly pressed into him.

"I think I like you home. Barefoot. Pregnant. Fixing me dinner." He kissed the top of her head, tightening his stomach for the punch she gave him, a playful blow he'd been expecting—and that turned into a leisurely exploration. She ran her hands over his abs as he caressed her belly. They kissed.

"I'm breathing better," she said against his mouth. "Baby moved around again, and now I've got room for my lungs."

He slid an arm around her. "Hmm—does seem like it's further down since this morning."

"Yeah. I now constantly have to pee, not just most of the time. But I hope that means things are progressing."

A stab of apprehension and excitement tightened Stevens's guts. They were as prepared as they could be, except for the nursery area, which hopefully she'd have time to work on now that she was home. Both had gone to the childbirth class held at the hospital, and Lei wanted to have the baby natural.

"I'm healthy and strong. Women have been doing this since the dawn of time. How hard can it be?" He remembered her confident declaration at the class, and the tittering of more experienced mothers. It had given him a shiver—but Lei *was* strong, one of the bravest women he knew. If anyone could do this, she could. Besides, Lei had Pono's wife, Tiare Kaihale, as her labor coach and doula. Nothing would dare go wrong with Tiare in charge.

"I need a shower. This is just a pit stop; I have to go back out. We're searching the victim's house." Stevens gave her tummy a final pat. "Told Mahoe that this old man needed a home-cooked meal."

"You should have invited Mahoe over—you've got that kid picking up all the slack. Dinner's almost ready." Lei bent over to open the oven and poke at the bubbling chicken. "Get your shower. This will be on the table by the time you're done."

"Yeah. Like I said, I could get used to this." He gave Lei a light swat on the behind and went to their bathroom.

STEVENS WAS ABOUT to sit down when his father-in-law arrived from his cottage next door. Wayne's craggy face lit with a smile at the sight of Lei carrying the chicken in a glass pan to the table.

"My favorite, Sweets," Wayne said. "And I didn't have to fix it. That's always a treat."

Ellen, Stevens's mother, followed Wayne, her arms wrapped around a big paper bag. Stevens came around the table to greet them.

"Hey, Wayne. Mom." Stevens kissed his mother's cheek, pulling her in for a hug. She was looking good, her blond hair touched up, her skin smooth and fresh. She smiled, blue eyes bright.

"I'm so excited. I can't stop buying stuff for the baby." Ellen spotted Kiet, sitting at the table already, and caught his eye. "But I never forget my best little man." Stevens let go of his mother's slender form, and she hurried over to hug Kiet. "Brought you something fun. You have to wait until after dinner, though."

"Oh, good," Kiet said. "Is it Legos?"

"Like I said. After dinner."

"All we need is for Jared to show up." Stevens heard the familiar beeping on the wall alarm that told them someone had punched in the code. "Speak of the devil. Did you call the whole family?"

"Guilty. I wanted to kick off my maternity leave with a family dinner," Lei said. "I knew you couldn't stay long, but I hoped we'd all be here."

"I smell teriyaki chicken," Jared announced when he entered. He held up a metal pan. "I brought dessert. One of the guys down at my station made a mango cobbler. Really huge, so I stole some."

"Excellent." Lei gave Stevens's brother a quick hug. "Glad you could make it on such short notice."

"I always make time for a noteworthy occurrence, like a night you cook dinner and the smoke alarm doesn't go off," Jared teased.

"You mean my cook timer?" Lei said. "Gotta make sure that annoying thing doesn't need batteries."

In moments they were all seated around the picnic-style dining room table Stevens had built.

Wayne cleared his throat. "Grace?"

They held hands and bowed their heads around the table. Stevens relished the feeling of Lei's hand in his on one side, Kiet's small one on the other, and all of their close family gathered in their home. Moments like this didn't come often enough with everyone's hectic schedules.

"Heavenly Father, thanks for these blessings we are about to receive," Wayne prayed. "Help us use this food to make us strong. Bless my daughter's hands that fixed this, and may your spirit join us as our honored guest. Amen."

"Amen," they all echoed. Stevens noticed that Ellen and Wayne were still holding hands as Lei got the chicken pan, large salad, and bowl of rice moving around the table. He caught Jared's eye, and his brother raised his brows in a way that told Stevens he wanted to talk to him after the meal.

Stevens took his time eating, as the headache he'd been battling all day finally receded. He let the conversation ebb and flow around him.

"Been watching the weather reports." Wayne cut into his chicken. Weather monitoring was one of Wayne's hobbies, though there wasn't much to follow with Maui's mostly uniform patterns of sun and rain. "Looks like there's a hurricane on the way."

"There's always a hurricane on the way, during the season." Jared helped himself to seconds. "We keep an eye and ear on it, too, at the fire department. But Maui has never had a major hurricane. We're buffered by the Big Island and the smaller islands off our coast."

"Shouldn't get complacent," Wayne said. "That's when something can go wrong. Is your hurricane supply stocked up?" He aimed this last question at Stevens.

"Can't say." Stevens wiped his mouth. They kept the extra water, batteries, toilet paper, canned food, and other supplies in a metal shed in the backyard, but he knew it had been a while since they'd made sure it was usable. "Lei, maybe you could check on that when you're working on the nursery."

"Sounds good. One more thing to go shopping for," Lei said. "I'm sure the TP is shot. The cockroaches come in from the jungle and eat anything they can get into, and I don't think we put it in a plastic tub or anything."

"So disgusting." Ellen sipped from her water glass. "I'm amazed at the things cockroaches will eat here in Hawaii. At the Sunday school class I teach, I found they'd even gotten into the crayons. Chewed on them and left colored bits of poop all over the cupboard!"

"Gross," Kiet said. Stevens smiled at his son; the boy was using his knife and fork like a champ.

Dinner wound down, and Stevens helped clear the table, waving off dessert. "Unfortunately, I have to get back to work—we caught a fresh homicide today, and you know the twenty-four-hour rule." He kissed Lei and Kiet as they sat at the table. "Don't wait up for me, Sweets. Mahoe and I have a lot to do." He headed for the door.

Jared set the cobbler on the table and chased after him. "Gotta speak with you privately, bro."

"What is it?" Stevens continued out to the Bronco, opening his door.

"I want Kathy's number," Jared said.

Stevens paused, then turned, frowning. "You don't get to screw around with her, bro."

Red suffused Jared's neck. "It's not like that."

"Yeah? How is it, then? The way you 'liked' Stephanie McCormick? And Jessie Saldana?" Stevens named friends his brother had dated in LA who'd ended up crying on Stevens's shoulder when Jared dumped them. "She's my ex-partner. My officemate. I can't have you shit where I eat."

"I thought that might be your attitude. Makes me wonder if you aren't eating a little of that yourself."

Stevens felt hot rage flush his body as he spun toward his brother. On top of the issues he'd had with Lei about Kathy, it was too much. "You didn't just say that."

They glared at each other, gazes clashing. Stevens felt the need to hit Jared vibrating along his arms. *Family is overrated. Brothers in particular.*

Jared dropped his eyes. "Shit. No. I didn't just say that."

Stevens let out his held breath. "Good thing, too."

"That was a long time ago, Mike. I've changed."

"You've been here five years, bro, and all I've seen that whole time was the three-bang rule." Jared's habit of sleeping with women three times before disappearing was something of a legend.

"This is different." Jared's jaw bunched. "I guess I'll have to prove it."

"Yeah, and you'll have to get her number some other way, too." Stevens jumped into the truck and fired it up, then drove out of the compound without looking back.

CHAPTER SIX

Brandon

BRANDON WALKED BEHIND LIEUTENANT STEVENS toward the upscale condo complex in Lahaina where the victim had lived. Darkness rendered the building dramatic, lit by spotlights on a fancy ivory-and-plum color scheme. Palms in huge planters marked an entrance between two of the buildings. Brandon admired the sandstone walkway that led to a trickling fountain of a mermaid pouring water into a small, lily-studded pond. Beyond the buildings, a large pool, lit from below, glowed space age blue.

Stevens checked his phone for the victim's apartment number. "Looks like it's just ahead."

"This guy was living large," Brandon said as they ascended a short flight of stairs that split at the entry into two units. He was still struggling with his upcoming thirtieth birthday, and Métier had been thirty-two. "He wasn't a lot older than me."

The LT didn't reply. He'd procured the key from the body, but he knocked on the door.

No answer. He knocked again. "Open up. Maui Police Department."

Still no answer.

"No one at the restaurant thought he had a roommate, male or female," Brandon said, as the LT slid the key they'd taken off the victim's body into the shiny, lacquered black door and pushed it open. The living room was spacious, half of it sectioned off into a loft, where Métier's office area was accessed by a metal spiral staircase, leaving a high-ceilinged living room area. Sliding glass doors opened onto a patio overlooking the glowing blue pool and an ocean view.

"Where'd he get all the money?" Brandon set down his crime kit on a granite counter leading into the kitchen. He snapped on his gloves. "The vic must have been loaded."

"Appearances can be deceiving. We have to find out who his next of kin is—they will be getting all this." The lieutenant went ahead of Brandon and quickly checked each room. "Always make sure the residence is clear, Mahoe. Who knows? He might have had a friend here or something."

"You mean a woman."

"You sound jealous of this guy, Mahoe." The LT fixed Brandon with one of those hard blue stares that seemed to laser his soul. "You may have been close in age, but from what I can tell, Métier was a jerk. You're solid. Just keep doing what you're doing—you're already a success." Stevens clapped Brandon on the shoulder. "Take the bedroom and bathroom. I'll take the kitchen and office. We can both do the living room. Let's start here since this is where we are."

Brandon nodded. He searched rapidly, pulling books off the dark wood shelf and flipping through them, shoving them back in. He appreciated the LT's words, but it was hard to feel like a success when he didn't even have a girlfriend and lived with his mother, trying to save up for a down payment on his own place someday. That goal felt next to impossible on Maui, with the island's inflated prices.

He flipped open a glossy art book, and frowned in surprise as hundred-dollar bills drifted out of it. "Got a cash stash here."

"He was funding this new restaurant with something," LT said from across the room, where he was checking around the entertainment unit. "He didn't make enough as a sous-chef to afford an apartment like this, let alone to open a competing restaurant."

Brandon squatted, picking up the hundreds and stuffing them into an evidence bag. He almost slipped one into his pocket reflexively. *Who would ever know?*

He would know, and so would God. He didn't need a penny of this guy's dirty money. Brandon labeled the bag and set it by the door. He moved on, lifting the pebbled black leather couch cushions quickly. The sound of Velcro ripping up on one of them was loud in the room. He spotted an unsecured corner of black fabric over the boxy structure of the couch, and found a small safe nested inside.

"Hey." Brandon gestured for the LT. "Looks like some kind of strongbox or safe here." It weighed a ton, and LT helped him lift it out.

"Gonna have to take this to the station to get it open." Brandon fiddled with the dial-style combination locking mechanism.

"Well, he definitely had a stash of some kind going on," LT said, rising. "Maybe we'll be able to find the combination somewhere."

Brandon moved off into the bedroom with his kit. The room was large, dominated by a bed covered in black satin. The doors of the closet were mirrored. Another mirror hung over the bed, and a third one was inset in the padded satin headboard, bringing Brandon to a halt.

Images of Métier bringing hot women here for sex filled his mind. Brandon scowled, his hands fisting. The guy was dead, and Brandon was alive. He'd meet someone special someday, and hell if he'd make a performance out of their private moments like this sleazeball had.

Brandon photographed the room briefly and walked across the silky gray plush carpet to the bed. He pulled out the top drawer of the roomy nightstand next to it.

A collection of sex toys and bondage equipment filled the space. Probably not worth bagging and bringing in, but the props were highly realistic. He stirred them with a finger, glad he had gloves on, and pulled out the next drawer.

Masks, feather boas, spandex and leather costumes, both male and female, filled the drawer, each one in a plastic bag neatly labeled. Brandon grinned at the cop costume—the pair of handcuffs looked real, but the blue satin man thong wasn't going to leave much to the imagination.

Métier probably had a camera somewhere to record the activities. Why get all crazy and dressed up if there wasn't an audience? Brandon took out a small flashlight and shone it along a collection of tribal masks set on a narrow shelf that ran around the room at shoulder height, giving an impression of a watching audience. Directly across from the bed, he found the camera, a small round lens planted in the eye of one of the masks. The camera was attached to a narrow wire that fed into a hole in the wall.

"Hey, LT!" Brandon called.

"Yeah?" Stevens's voice drifted down from above. He must be in the area of the loft office.

"Can you check if there's a black cable leading into the floor, coming from the computer?"

A few minutes went by, then: "Yeah. Looks like it goes into the floor."

"I think the victim might have been making porn in here," Brandon said. "If so, that could be some important evidence for us to review."

"I'll give that to you to go through when we gain access to it. I'm a married man with tender sensibilities."

"Aw, damn, LT, really? You gonna make me watch the vic's homegrown porn all by myself?" Brandon grinned as he checked under the bed. Nothing there but a dried-up condom. He opened the closets. Rows of expensive-looking clothing and designer shoes. "That was the big news in here. Guy was quite a player from the looks of it—in more ways than one."

"Maybe that's what got him killed." Stevens appeared in the doorway, carrying a computer. "Thing's password protected, so we'll have to take it in for Jessup to crack."

"I'm moving on to the bathroom." Brandon followed the lieutenant as he added the computer to a growing pile of items to carry out to their vehicles for processing. "Did you find anything else interesting up in the office?"

"Yeah. The name of Métier's financial adviser and an estate lawyer. That should help us find the source of his funds, and maybe his next of kin."

Brandon was heading for the bathroom when they heard the sound of a key in the lock. Brandon pulled his weapon, slipping behind the doorjamb, as Stevens did the same, standing beside the front door. The door opened with the kind of loud, confident click and shove that told Brandon the young blond woman entering expected to be alone. She jumped and dropped a large canvas bag at the sight of the LT holding his weapon.

"Oh my God!" The woman's hand came up to her throat. Wide blue eyes, waist-length ripple of hair, skimpy outfit, long tanned legs—probable girlfriend. "What are you doing here?"

"Lieutenant Stevens and Detective Mahoe of Maui Police Department." The LT holstered his weapon and showed the badge on his belt as Brandon held up his ID. "Who are you?"

"Kitty Summers." The woman's eyes filled and she covered her mouth with a hand. "This is about François being killed, isn't it?"

"Yes. We were going to find you to talk with you about the murder, but since you're here, why don't you have a seat? Brandon can take your statement," the LT said. "I'll finish the search."

Brandon's mentor was trying to get him to take the lead on investigations more and more. He squelched intimidation at the woman's total hotness and smiled, gesturing to the living room seating area. "Please. I'm sorry we surprised you this way."

He followed her down a step into the slightly sunken living room, admiring her slim curves in an aqua-colored miniskirt and halter top. He'd probably get to see a lot more of her in the videos on that computer. He felt a guilty flush at the nasty thought.

She looked around at the books, not as neat as they'd been before. Bright red accent pillows had fallen off the couch, and Brandon picked one up off the floor after Summers retrieved the other two, smacking them into the corners of the couch in a way that told him she was annoyed by the disarray.

"I should have expected this. I guess I just didn't realize you'd get here so fast." Summers sat on the loveseat across from him and crossed her legs. Her feet were bare, and her toenails hot pink—she must have slipped her shoes off at the door, as was done in Hawaii.

Summers reached for a tissue from the box on the coffee table, dabbing her eyes, but he hadn't seen any moisture in them.

Brandon took out his phone and thumbed to the voice memo, setting it between them on the coffee table. "Okay if I record this? It often helps us get all the information we need in one interview."

"Okay. Do I need a lawyer or anything?"

Brandon smiled reassuringly. "This is just an initial statement, but of course that's always your right." He waited a beat, but she didn't respond. He flipped open the spiral pad he liked to use for notes—he hoped it conveyed his seriousness to witnesses. "So. How did you know the victim?"

"We worked together at Feast. He was my boyfriend." Summers cast her eyes down and dabbed again—she was trying to muster up some tears. They heard scraping and clanking sounds. LT was searching the bathroom, opening cabinets and shutting drawers.

"Were you exclusive?"

"I had a key to his apartment. That's pretty exclusive."

Summers fiddled with the little purse she'd carried in. She retrieved a stick of gum, putting it in her mouth. "I'm trying to quit smoking." Her expression was defiant as she chewed, the gum making a moving wad in her cheek beside plump pink lips. "I was the only one who had a key."

"So you knew about his . . . habits."

"What habits would those be?" Summers chewed harder. The gum bunched her cheek.

Brandon cleared his throat. Was she kidding? "We have statements from several witnesses that he slept around at Feast. That he was a player."

"I knew that. But we were moving forward." Summers grabbed the throw pillow, wrapping her arms around it, hugging it. "He loved me. I know he loved me."

Brandon waited a beat, but Summers bent her head so her hair fell forward to hide her face. "So were you working the night he was killed?"

"I was. I had the later shift, came on at seven and worked past closing. I can't believe he was dead in that walk-in. I must have passed it a hundred times that night." Finally, tears brightened her eyes. She was the picture of bereaved, wringing slender fingers to go along with that woebegone face. "He was going to ask me to marry him."

Brandon was glad Stevens had come to join them, sitting down next to him on the sofa. "This is interesting, Lieutenant," Brandon said. "Apparently Miss Summers was about to get a proposal."

"So how did you know that?" LT asked.

Summers shrugged, and her eyes skittered away. "We'd been talking about marriage. He was . . . nervous that night. Keyed up. Told me he had to talk with me after work. That's why I was surprised when he never came to my place. I went home and waited for him there until I finally fell asleep around midnight."

"So you didn't call his cell phone?" Brandon had bagged the

phone found on the body, scrolling briefly through it at the scene. He remembered seeing her name on the Recent Calls list.

"I did call. He didn't pick up. I figured something had come up."

"Did you have any other signs that he was going to propose?" LT asked.

"We had decided to be exclusive. He said he had to—tie up some loose ends, as he put it. I thought that meant breaking it off with—others." She looked down modestly. "And I spotted a ring. In his pocket."

"Since you were moving forward as you say . . . did you know who else he was tying up loose ends with?"

"I don't know. But I did know we weren't exclusive until recently."

"So when did things change for the two of you?" Brandon leaned forward, hoping to show sympathy with his posture and clasped, dangling hands.

Summers flicked her hair back and sighed. For the first time Brandon saw real emotion in her brimming eyes. "I missed a period. It turned out to be nothing, but it pulled us together. He told me things were going to change between us." The tears, now that they'd gotten started, were really going, slipping quietly down her cheeks. "He was such an amazing man." She dabbed her eyes.

"Hmm, yes," Stevens said. "Is there anyone who can verify that you didn't enter the walk-in after nine p.m.?"

"Maybe our floor manager, Peter Claymore. We were jammed. He was moving wine, and we had some tables we were working together."

"So what did you come to the apartment for today?" Brandon asked, noting the manager's name. They had an interview scheduled with him the next day.

"I was picking up a few things. Personal things." Summers ducked her head again. Probably had wanted to remove the sex toys and other paraphernalia before they were seen.

"Were you aware that Métier may have been recording your . . . intimate moments?" Stevens asked, brows knit in concern.

Summers's gaze flew to the computer, on the floor beside the front door. "Uh. Yes. These videos were for us." Again, the wide defiant stare. "I'd appreciate having them back."

"Well, we aren't sure who's going to inherit all this," Brandon said. "Could be they would get the computer. Any idea who his next of kin is?"

Summers's eyes flashed with anger. "I get those recordings. They were private!"

"I understand, Miss Summers. Right now the computer and its contents are evidence. We'll get back to you on who gets what. In fact, we're just finishing, but we can't let you take anything out while the apartment is an active crime scene." The LT stood. "So you don't have an alibi for the time of the murder?"

"I would never—I loved François!"

"I take that as a 'no.'" Brandon rose to his feet as well.

"A hundred people saw me working. Would anyone swear I never went into that walk-in? Probably not. But I didn't do it." Kitty Summers stood, smoothing her miniskirt. "I want those videos. They're mine. And . . . the other stuff, too."

"We'll be in touch," LT said. Brandon herded Kitty Summers gently out the door. He shut it behind her.

"Do you think the vic was proposing to her, LT?" Brandon bent and picked up the heavy safe.

Stevens picked up the computer. "I don't see it. I'm guessing Métier was the type who'd want to marry someone who enhanced his status or brought something to the table. Summers knew about the ring, though, and she *was* telling the truth about being in the videos. I'll put money on that."

"Not a bet I'd take," Brandon said. They sealed the door with crime scene tape and headed for their vehicles.

"You did all that casework while I took a dinner break—so I'll take these items to the station and log them all in to evidence. You hang out with Jessup now and again—can you let him know we have a computer for him to work on?" Stevens hefted the computer into the backseat, and Brandon set the safe beside it.

"Sure. I hang out with the kid on occasion—if you call getting my ass handed to me at World of Warcraft 'hanging out.' Murioka is way too good." Brandon swiped an arm over his forehead. "I'm more worried about getting this safe open. Did you find a combination in the office?"

"No. I plan to call and set up an appointment with the financial planner and estate lawyer with the info I found. Maybe they will know something. We still haven't got a next of kin to notify. Did you see any names in his phone?" Stevens stowed the evidence bags beside the safe in the backseat.

"It was password protected. Gonna have to have Jessup unlock that, too. You sure I can go home?" Brandon was reluctant to leave. His mother, a nurse, was working graveyard tonight. Nothing and no one waited for him at home but a frozen pizza and *The Wire* on Netflix.

"Yeah. Go get some rest. We've got another long one tomorrow." Stevens slammed the door of the Bronco with finality and drove away.

CHAPTER SEVEN

Dr. Phil Gregory

DR. PHIL GREGORY OPENED HIS closet and looked at the row of aloha shirts neatly arranged in a rainbow of colors.

He was feeling green today.

He riffled through the various choices. "Honey, where's my green shirt with the honus on it?" The shirt's background, ocean-colored, set off sea turtles done in purples and yellows, a particularly eye-catching design. The turtles, with their curious expressions, helped him find answers.

Leslie Tanaka sat up in bed, stretching slender arms high. She wore a pink sleep tee with Tweety Bird on it. She shook her head. Her jet-black hair, cut with its edgy knifepoint angles, fell effortlessly into place. "I think that one's in the laundry room."

"Thanks for washing it for me."

"You didn't get blood on it this time, thankfully." She flopped back down. "We're backlogged, aren't we?"

Phil came around the bed and leaned over to kiss her. He still couldn't believe she actually loved him—he was the luckiest man on Maui. "Take another hour. The dead won't complain."

Leslie reached up to touch his face. "Yeah, but the living will. You're so good to me."

"Ha. It's mutual." Phil left her with another kiss and went to the laundry room. Their house was a new ranch in Waiehu; he liked how close it was to the morgue and to the ocean. He never got tired of listening to the sound of the surf wafting across the edge of the golf course the house faced. With solid jobs, they'd been able to buy it during the depressed real estate market, and he was still pinching himself that he'd achieved his dreams: living in Hawaii, doing a job he enjoyed, spending every day with the woman he loved.

Phil shrugged into the honu shirt, pleased to see that it was hanging a lot better since he'd amped up his workouts and cut out convenience foods—not easy at a job where he basically never left the building. Leslie, without ever saying a word, had rubbed off on him. She cooked nutritious meals, packed lunch for both of them, and used the gym in the hospital building daily.

He wanted to be worthy of her—not that she'd ever indicated he wasn't, but he didn't like the way his paunchy gut looked next to her slim figure. Plus, the bachelor diet of pizza and beer was just tired.

This morning he had a meeting with Lieutenant Stevens and Brandon Mahoe about François Métier's post. He'd begun it last night but hadn't quite finished—he'd had hula practice.

Another Leslie idea. Phil grinned. It was so crazy, a *haole* guy like him with the *kane* hula group, and klutzy, too. Good thing his *kumu* was understanding.

Phil returned to the bedroom. Leslie seemed to have taken him at his word and had gone back to sleep, so he shut the door carefully and went into the kitchen.

After a quick breakfast of fruit and yogurt, he picked up the lunch Leslie had prepared for them the night before and got on the road to the hospital.

Morning on Maui was glorious. The sun broke over the

shoulder of ten-thousand-foot Haleakala like a lance ripping the blue fabric of sky to emit the gold of angels passing. Palms swayed along the congested road leading into town, and even with the bumper-to-bumper morning commute traffic, Phil got a glimpse of canoe paddlers in Kahului Harbor and the latest cruise ship, decked with lights, at anchor.

The morgue was quiet. "And I'd be worried if it wasn't," Phil said aloud as he hit the iPod he used to pipe music into the open work area with its shiny metal tables. Hawaiian slack-key guitar began a mellow backbeat to his day as he stowed their lunches in the little personal fridge near his and Leslie's office area.

He donned his apron, choosing the yellow smiley face one today, and then went to the bank of refrigerators.

François Métier looked the same as he had yesterday—bluish from exsanguination, the cause of death Phil had recorded officially on his report. He finished dictating his notes as he closed the chest incision.

A buzzer sounded, and he glanced up. Lieutenant Stevens and Brandon Mahoe were framed in the glass of the door leading into the sally port. The tall lieutenant wasn't looking that good. His color was off and he looked tired, even though it was only eight a.m.—but then, he'd been recovering from that disaster in Central America. Considering what could have happened, Phil was glad the man was back at work at all. He and Lei were some of Phil's favorite people.

Phil hurried around the end of the table to open the door for them. "Hey, guys. Wish I had some coffee to offer you."

Mahoe's brown eyes had gone to Phil's apron, already a little smeared from leaning over to get a particularly stubborn stitch through Métier's chest incision. Skin could be tougher than people knew. Phil rubbed the spot but made it worse with his bloody glove.

He gestured with his black-threaded needle. "Come on in. I'm just finishing up with your boy."

"Nice to see you looking so healthy, Dr. G," Stevens said.

"Thanks. How's your wife?"

"Rough night last night." Stevens pushed his hand through his rumpled hair, moving it off his forehead but mussing it further. "She had a lot of those false labor pains, and her back was hurting. We were up a lot. But it's okay—she's out on maternity leave now, so she gets to take a nap if she needs to." He laughed ruefully. "I wouldn't mind a nap myself."

"I can run to the cafeteria for some coffee, LT," Mahoe said. The square-faced, earnest young Hawaiian looked a little ill; clearly not comfortable with the sights and smells Phil took for granted.

"That would be great," Phil said. "Grab me one too, will ya? Black."

Stevens nodded at Mahoe. "I'll take cream and sugar in mine today," he told the young man. "Thanks."

Mahoe left for the hospital's cafeteria on the first floor, and Phil gestured to the body. The two of them approached Métier.

"I don't have anything too surprising to say about your victim," Phil said. "As you might have guessed, cause of death is exsanguination due to a stab wound."

"Hmm." Stevens made a note in a spiral notebook with its stub of pencil tied on with a bit of string.

"He had some epithelials under the nail on the hand that was holding the ring," Phil said. "It's going to take a while to do DNA processing on the sample, and it's so small I'm concerned there won't be enough tissue to process. But that could at least show who he was with recently. As a chef he'd have been washing his hands frequently in the kitchen during food prep, so perhaps the DNA belongs to his killer."

"Good. I'll put a rush on that at the lab," Stevens said. "Anything else?"

"No. This is the body of a healthy thirty-two-year-old male in excellent physical condition, dead of unnatural causes." Phil sighed. "If we'd found him sooner, we might have been able to harvest some of these beautiful organs."

"No one ever thinks he's going to die." Stevens met Phil's eyes. "I know better, especially after my stint overseas. And—of course I'm an organ donor."

"Well, I hope never to meet you on one of these tables." Phil fussed with removing some instruments from the autoclave to hide his emotion. Stevens had come way too close to death last year for his peace of mind.

"I'll second that," Stevens said.

Mahoe appeared at the sally port, and Phil buzzed him in. "Black for Dr. G, cream and sugar for LT." The young detective handed them each covered cups of coffee from a cardboard carrier.

Stevens's gaze rested on the victim as he sipped his brew. "Anything about the knife wound that we didn't already cover?"

"That chef's knife was so damned sharp that it severed a major artery and dropped him like a rock." Phil grimaced over his black coffee—he couldn't afford the calories the way he liked his coffee, and black took some getting used to. "The thrust didn't require a lot of strength, but this person knew just where to hit him—or was very lucky. Slid that blade right between his ribs. Stabbings are often messier; take more hits to kill. The vic takes a while to die and can sometimes get help. This stab was quick, clean. Surgical, almost. I'll fax over the report when it's done, per usual."

"Thanks, Doc." Stevens lifted his coffee in a wave, and the two left.

Phil put his hands on his hips, surveying his little kingdom. "Let's finish this," he told Métier, and picked up his needle and thread.

CHAPTER EIGHT

Lei

Lei surveyed the guest room/office, the third bedroom of their modest house, and rubbed her aching lower back as she looked at the daunting amount of furniture. A filing cabinet, desk, office chair, dresser, and a twin bed would all have to be relocated or given away.

She just wasn't willing to do it. Truth was, she didn't want to pack this room up and turn it into a nursery—she and Stevens needed somewhere to get away from the family noise to work, and also a place to put guests who visited from the mainland or another island.

Better to just keep the baby in their room in the cradle and then move the child into the bedroom with Kiet when he or she was old enough to sleep through the night. Until then, if one of them needed extra rest, they could crash in the guest room.

"Thank God," Lei muttered, decision made. "I didn't want to do that chore anyway."

She went to the bathroom again, addressing the persistent feeling of needing to pee. She spoke to the bulge straining her T-shirt. "I'm turning into one of those people who needs to wear Depends, Baby. I don't know how I'm going to get through another month."

Lei was washing up when she heard the beeping that let her know someone was typing in the code for the front gate. "Good. Tiare's here."

Out in the driveway, Pono's tall, statuesque wife hopped down from the jacked-up purple truck that Lei's partner usually drove.

"What're you doing driving Stanley?" Lei called from the porch as the Rottweilers' barking changed to ecstatic whining as they caught Tiare's scent—she always found time to give them treats and pets.

"Ha! Pono told me you called the truck that. My car's in the shop, so I dropped him off today." Tiare grinned at Lei as she scratched behind Conan's ears. "What is that rag you're wearing?"

"Stevens's shirt. With yoga pants." Lei wound her hair up, tying it in a knot. "You should have seen me in that maternity bathing suit the office girls bought me—yikes! Kiet said I looked like a hot air balloon."

"You're actually not that big." Tiare ascended the porch steps, intelligent brown eyes assessing. Long black hair in a braid the width of Lei's wrist brushed her back over scrubs she wore from a shift at the hospital. She frowned and put her hands on her hips. "The baby's dropped since yesterday."

"I know." The women hugged briefly, and Lei led the way inside. "They say first babies are late, but it's hard to imagine going another three weeks like this."

"Well, you probably will. And that last month is a killer. Don't let anyone tell you different. But it's good I came by to review the birth plan, just in case."

"Yeah. Thank God the captain sent me out on leave yesterday. I keep running to the bathroom, and my back is so sore."

"Let me give you a little massage. Give you a feeling of what we'll do when you're in labor. Get on the couch and rest your arms and head on the back, and I'll give you a rub."

Lei knelt on the couch and put her head down on her crossed arms on the high, padded back. Tiare was able to come close and rub Lei's aching lower trunk easily. Lei sighed at the strong, gentle touch of her friend's hands. "That feels so good. So, how hard was the extra training to be a doula?"

"It's challenging, but I've loved adding labor coaching to my résumé. I've been able to deliver several babies myself, but I'm not a midwife, as we talked about before—I'll just be your coach. I can spot when medical intervention might be needed since I'm an RN, and since you're using the hospital's birth center, everything's going to be really safe." Tiare kept up the deep, gentle rubbing. "When you're in labor, we'll massage you like this between contractions if you feel like it. The key to progression is staying relaxed, just submitting to the process. I'm not gonna lie. It will hurt like a mofo—but natural childbirth is what our bodies were designed to do. And, girl, I'm so excited to meet this baby, I might as well be the mama." Tiare set the side of her arm on Lei's back and drew it slowly down with a wide, deep pressure. Lei groaned at the wonderful sensation. "You ever get a lomilomi massage before?"

"Never had any kind of massage before." Lei kept her eyes shut. She'd never liked being touched by anyone but Stevens, but this was different. Her body had stopped being her own when Baby took up residence, and it was doing the pregnancy beautifully without her anxious mind's help. It would doubtless do the birth just fine, too. Thinking about the coming birth as an athletic event —one she was training for—helped Lei feel confident. Physical things she could do. Pain, she was familiar with. "I've been doing that prenatal yoga routine on the video you gave me every day."

"What about cardio?"

"Can't run, obviously. But I've been swimming four times a week. I plan to go daily now that I'm homebound."

"Excellent." Tiare straightened up. "I need a beer. It was a long day at Maui Memorial."

"Of course." Lei hauled herself to her feet. "But, as you know, we only have the fake stuff. I'm not drinking, Stevens isn't, either, and I just prefer to keep temptation out of the house."

"Good enough." Tiare dug around in the knapsack she'd brought in as Lei popped the top on an alcohol-free beer. "Let's go over the list of items you need to buy."

"Perfect. I have to go shopping to restock the hurricane supplies—my dad says there's a watch. If it hits, it'll be in a couple of days."

"Maui keeps getting lucky—not like the Big Island and Kauai."

"Well, we have all those other islands buffering us here in the middle of the chain. Hopefully we just get a little rain." Lei handed Tiare one of the beers, and they sat on the couch to review the birth plan and shopping list.

Finally, Tiare put a hand on Lei's abdomen. "Let me feel around, check the position." She did so. "Good. The head's down and well into your pelvis—a big change of position since yesterday. Could be that backache is low-level contractions. Don't get your hopes up, but this one could come sooner than three weeks." Tiare took a stethoscope out of her bag and applied it. "Good strong heartbeat. Let me just get your blood pressure—though you don't seem to be retaining too much water, I still want to keep an eye on that."

All Lei's readings were normal, and finally Tiare put her equipment away. "So did you have any questions? Anything from doing the class, or about the plan we made?"

"No. Just—I wish Esther Ka`awai would call us with the baby's Hawaiian name. Apparently she's never been wrong about the sex of a baby, either, and I'm getting antsy to know."

"Having that lady on our team, praying, is some powerful medicine right there."

"Yeah. But I'm wondering how to keep Stevens busy during

the birth. I want him there, but I don't want him getting agitated—if he can't handle it, it's going to throw me off." Lei rubbed her hands on her legs. "I worry that he'll get upset if I'm in pain. He used to get all crazy anytime I was doing something dangerous."

"So how did he do during the class?"

"Quiet." Lei sighed. "He's different since his head injury and that trip overseas. He just seems—like he's not all there. Sometimes he's a million miles away in his mind. Other times he's overreactive, like it's all he can do to just handle the feeling of clothes on his skin. We're doing good, considering. I know he's super happy and excited about the baby—but he was really serious and quiet during the labor and childbirth class. I could tell it was hard for him."

"Well, we can always kick him out." Tiare had the whitest teeth, and a dimple next to her mouth when she smiled. "Birthin' babies is women's work, anyway. Pono was a wreck all through my pregnancy and got so freaked-out during the deliveries my midwife made him do push-ups—for a half hour—until he could calm down enough to be any sort of help. Frankly, I could have done without him in the room just fine—but it was good for him to know just how much work it took to have our kids." Maile and Ikaika, their children, were now high-achieving, soccer-loving middle schoolers at Kamehameha Schools.

"We'll just have to play it by ear. I could be worrying too much. Everyone who's ever worked with Michael says he has a cool head for intense situations, that he's rock solid in an emergency. And for us that's been true—I'm the squirrely one. So this is one more thing I'll try not to worry about. Good to know you'll kick him out if it gets to be a problem."

"Yup. Executive doula decision."

The two hugged, and after Tiare left, Lei felt at loose ends. She threw the ball for the dogs and went out to the aluminum shed in the backyard where the hurricane supplies were stored.

She slid the door open with a squeal of corroded metal and peeked inside.

It smelled musty from the lawn mower, parked at the front of the shed and covered with moldy grass cuttings. Lei squeezed past the mower into darker depths, where heavy-duty metal shelving held a row of gallon jugs of water, a lantern with fuel, boxes of candles, a stack of unopened barbeque lighters, a Coleman stove, and rows and rows of cans along with closed pails of dried food she'd ordered from an online supply. The damp of Haiku, a rainy part of Maui, had contributed to decay, which Lei spotted on the packaging of the stack of toilet paper. She checked inside the pails. The dried food was intact, but several of the canned foods showed rust, and the water was probably bad.

Lei made notes on her phone, where she'd added things to buy for the hospital trip and outfitting an infant. The baby shower had yielded a few of these, but she wanted to pack a diaper bag with the right essentials to take to the birthing center.

Heading back to the house across the stretch of lawn interspersed with fruit trees, Lei enjoyed the sight of their solid, sturdy, fireproof little house with its stucco exterior and the dark red metal roofing that imitated Mediterranean tile. They'd built something lasting here on Maui, both personally and in the community. It would all go on for a while without her.

She had other important work to do.

Lei smiled and picked up her pace as she walked to her truck. At least she had room to breathe now, whatever else the shift in the baby's position meant.

CHAPTER NINE

Stevens

STEVENS AND MAHOE STOOD ON the doorstep of a tidy ranch house in one of the newer neighborhoods of Kihei, an area on the south side of Maui. Stevens swiveled to take in the sight of a new Kia SUV in the driveway, along with a child's plastic wagon and a kid-sized basketball hoop. Mahoe knocked as Stevens counted four pairs of slippers beside the welcome mat: large, medium, and two small.

Peter Claymore, Feast's floor manager, was a family man.

"Hello, detectives." The man in question stood in the doorway. Five foot ten in height, one sixty in weight, blond with blue eyes, Claymore had one of those faces that registered as attractive and pleasant without being noteworthy.

"Lieutenant Stevens and Detective Mahoe. Thanks for seeing us." Stevens and Mahoe displayed their IDs.

"Of course. Come in." Claymore waved them in, opening the door wider so they could come into the foyer. "Thanks for coming by the house. Once I get to the restaurant, it's pretty much a whirlwind. The kids are at daycare and school and my wife's at work, so we can have a decent private conversation."

"I know the feeling. Got a six-year-old at home and we're about to have another." Stevens followed the manager into a sunken living room carpeted in industrial beige, littered with Legos and toys.

"So you understand. Sometimes I go to work to mellow out, and it's not like Feast is a relaxing workplace." Claymore lifted a pile of laundry off the couch, transferred it to the floor, and gestured for them to sit. "Terrible thing, what happened to François."

They settled themselves, and Stevens glanced at Mahoe, signaling him to lead. Mahoe took his phone out.

"Would it be all right to record this interview? Helps us keep track of all the moving parts of the investigation," his young partner said.

"Sure." So far Claymore seemed at ease. He gave his tan chinos a little tug and sat on a large ottoman facing them. "How can I help the investigation?"

"We're interviewing everyone who works at Feast," Mahoe said. "Strictly routine. Everyone gives a statement. So what can you tell us about the evening of Métier's death?"

Claymore cast his eyes up and to the left, recalling events. "Busy night. But then, they all are, at Feast. We were running our asses off until nine. Kitchen closes at nine-thirty, and we really only had a few new dinners to serve after nine p.m., so as you probably already figured, the food got put away a little early and no one went into the big walk-in after about nine-fifteen."

"Did you see anyone go in there after eight p.m.?"

"No. I've been covering for our sommelier, who's been out with a sinus infection. I was walking around with a selection of brandies and cognacs on the floor from eight on. Didn't spend much time behind the line that night."

"Tell us what you know about François Métier," Stevens said.

"François?" Claymore pushed a hand through thinning sandy hair. "Let's see. Talented with food. And the ladies, as I'm sure you've already heard. Stood up to Chef, which isn't easy to do. Some might say he was a snob, but I'd call him confident. Knew his place in the world and didn't question it."

Stevens's brows went up at this astute description. "Was there anything specific that gave you that idea about his confidence?"

"It was how he carried himself, spoke, and dressed. I could tell he came from money."

"Was this ever confirmed? That he came from money?"

"Yeah. Overheard him on the phone with a financial adviser, talking stocks. His address was a ritzy building, and he drove a Beemer. None of that came from his sous-chef pay, that's for sure. I liked him. Not everyone did."

"You mentioned women." Mahoe was getting better at spotting an opening and slipping into it. "Can you tell us if there was anyone special in his life?"

"You mean other than Mrs. Noriega?" Claymore's pale blue eyes crinkled at the corners. "You know about that, I hope?"

"We do. Anyone special other than her?"

"Kitty Summers was angling for more. I heard from some of the guys that the two of them had some sort of home porno business going. Seemed beneath François, but . . ." The manager shrugged. "No accounting for taste."

"Who was he sleeping with at the time of his death?" Stevens asked.

"I'd say Mrs. Noriega for sure. Possibly Kitty, too, though I could tell he was trying to cut her off."

"Why would he do that?" Mahoe asked.

Claymore pursed his mouth. "Kitty's a clinger. She's a perfectly capable woman, smart and good-looking—but doesn't believe in herself. One of those women who defines herself by her looks and connections. I'm always having to sort out problems involving her, both with customers and other staff." He shook his head. "She's annoying as hell, quite frankly. I've written her up twice: once for major mess-ups with her tables, and another time for missing a shift. Third time's the charm and I can show her the door."

"Did you see Kitty anywhere near the walk-in the night of the murder?" Stevens said.

"No. Like I said, I was out on the floor even more than usual."

"You seem to have a grasp of human psychology."

"Got a bachelor's in psych." Claymore grinned. "Useful in my management work."

"Anything else you can tell us?" Mahoe had been making diligent notes in his little spiral notebook as well as recording the conversation.

"I don't think so. I was as shocked as anyone when I heard François had been killed."

"And where were you between nine and ten p.m.?" Stevens slipped it in with a man-to-man twinkle that implied they couldn't possibly suspect him of anything.

"On the floor, as I said. You can check with the wait staff," Claymore said. "I don't think I went behind the line more than twice after nine p.m. Was working the floor with the dessert wines, as I told you."

"You seem like someone who knows all the players at Feast. Who do you think killed François Métier?" Stevens leaned forward with a sincere demeanor.

Claymore stood to his feet with a pleasant smile. He brushed a few Cheerios off his slacks. "I'm smart enough not to speculate about something I know nothing about. Will that be all for today?"

Out at their vehicle, Stevens turned to Mahoe. "I think he suspects someone."

"We just have to get him to talk, then," Mahoe said.

Stevens shook his head and fired up the Bronco. "Nope. He won't say anything."

"How do you know?"

"Years of experience. Guy like that has got a lot to lose with that nice little house and a family. Which makes me think he suspects Chef Noriega."

Kathy

Kathy looked down at her phone as it dinged. At a red light, she read a text from Stevens as she drove back to the station from a recruiting fair at the University of Hawaii, Maui campus.

Got a possible for the blogger at Feast. I'm swamped—can you interview Sage Bukowski for me? Attached was the witness's last known address.

Paused at a light, Kathy voice-texted back.

"Sure. Glad to help. Headed out to find him now."

Kathy put the address into her phone, and headed out of Kahului toward Lahaina.

Elena had refused to let her come over to the Noriegas' house last night.

"Was he angry about going in to the station? Did he hit you?" Kathy couldn't help asking.

A tinny laugh from Elena. "Of course he was mad, but I'm fine. Just tired from all the drama. I'll see you tomorrow."

Kathy frowned through the windshield, hoping like hell that was true.

Her phone buzzed like a fly in a bottle, sliding down the plastic of the seat in its agitation. Hoping it was Elena; Kathy hit the Bluetooth in her ear. "Hello?"

"Hello? Kathy? This is Jared."

Her brain took a few seconds to process the warm baritone voice—*good-looking firefighter guy. Stevens's brother.* She had an impression of his penetrating gaze in the dim hall outside the restaurant's bathroom and remembered her need to flee.

"Jared." Kathy's heart rate spiked. "What's going on? Something happen to Lei or Stevens?"

"No, no." Jared laughed, self-deprecating—but there was nothing humble in the man she'd met yesterday. He'd seemed competent, confident—and if she'd read him right, used to having women fall all over him. "I was calling for—um. To get to know you better. Wanted to see if we could get a coffee or something."

Kathy focused on the road, her hands tightening on the wheel. She felt a wave of heat prickle her chest. *He is asking me out. Stevens's brother is asking me out.* She felt off-kilter, though she shouldn't—she'd felt his interest at the restaurant.

Truth was, Jared reminded her too much of his brother. The thwarted feelings she'd had for Stevens were finally, mercifully, gone—leaving awkwardness and an emotional minefield between them.

"How'd you get my number?" The question came out sharper than she'd meant it to.

"I asked around—we have a few friends in common. I meant to ask you for it when we met, but you ran off. Sorry if this is a bad time." His tone had cooled.

"I don't know if it's a good idea for us to go out." Kathy cleared her throat. "I mean, I work with your brother."

"So?" Jared sounded defensive, but like he was trying to make light of it. "It's not a marriage proposal. It's just coffee."

Kathy gave an embarrassed burp of a laugh. "I just didn't expect this call. You've caught me on the road to Lahaina, and I'm just—whatever. Sure, we can do coffee."

"Going to Lahaina? Something to do with the case, I take it?" Interest brightened his voice.

Kathy was relieved they were moving past the stilted conversational beginning. She could tell Jared what she was doing; he was a part of the team, if only peripherally. "Yes, this is related to the Feast case. We have a lead on the blogger. Stevens asked me to interview him."

"Wish I could be a fly on the wall for that. I read those blogs—hilarious. Unfortunately, I have a nasty fire out in Huelo to investigate, in the opposite direction." A pause. "So, coffee. Are you going to be back in Kahului this afternoon?"

"I should be."

"Let's meet in Wailuku at that coffeehouse on Main Street. It's got atmosphere."

"Not a Starbucks fan?"

"Not so much. And they're always mobbed. I was hoping for a little peace and quiet to talk more privately."

Kathy felt that prickle of heat on her skin again. She wasn't sure if it was anticipation or nervous dread—she'd heard stories about Jared's dating habits, and not just from Stevens. "That should be nice. I'll text you when I'm back in the area," she said stiffly.

"Sounds good. Have fun de-blogging the restaurant."

"Ha, good one."

"Yeah, I'm known for a funny now and again. See you later." He hung up briskly.

Kathy navigated the last of the turns on the road they called the Pali. The series of sinuous curves, framed by views of cobalt ocean and glimpses of Kahoolawe and Lanai, was usually one of her favorite drives. Today she couldn't get into it.

Jared asked me out. Would that be weird with Stevens?

Definitely. He wouldn't want his promiscuous brother messing around with someone on his team. But it wasn't up to him.

"I'm a big girl and I can handle myself," Kathy said aloud. "Hell if I'm going to be another notch on that guy's belt." Even so, she felt a quiver, wondering what Jared would be like in bed. Probably amazing. "Shit. It's just coffee after work."

The GPS directed her to a turnoff at the beginning of Lahaina and to a run-down, triple-decker building. Deep in the shade of huge mango trees that thrived in Lahaina's hot climate, the faded turquoise apartment building was fronted by a cracked concrete parking lot that smelled of rotting garbage overflowing a nearby dumpster.

Kathy straightened her uniform, checked her weapon, and locked the Rogue. She ascended a flight of worn metal stairs on the exterior of the building and knocked on a door sporting several pairs of rubber slippers on a pineapple-embossed welcome mat.

"Hey." Sage Bukowski opened the door without checking the peephole, swinging it wide in the trusting gesture of one who's never faced an enemy at the door.

CHAPTER TEN

C.J.

C.J. LIKED TO BEAT HER team to the conference room. It kept her in the driver's seat, and commanding a station of mostly male, testosterone-driven cops made staying in that seat extra important. She hadn't gotten to the rank of captain by batting her eyelashes, and she never let them forget it. She sat down at the head of the table. Usually there was some eager beaver, often Jessup Murioka or that crime scene intern from UH, who wanted to schmooze her by being early.

C.J. glanced at the clock. The team meeting to review the Feast murder was scheduled in ten minutes. She created a little work area by booting up her laptop, opening her zipped-up organizer, and popping the top on a fresh Diet Coke. These mundane activities gave her a private moment to mull over last night's events.

Her lover had surprised her, and she was still deciding if she liked being surprised.

They'd met at the Maui Beach Hotel, a three-star in the center of Kahului whose main attribute was convenience. Per their usual arrangement, he'd gotten there first and paid for the room in cash.

Unlike team meetings, getting to their liaison first sent a needy message—and C.J. wasn't going to be needy. With him, or anyone.

He'd texted her the room number. Ready to do some hard time, Captain.

She'd smiled at that as she'd changed out of her uniform into a simple sheath dress with some very not-simple underwear on underneath. At the hotel, C.J. had tapped on the door, feeling a pleasant buzz of anticipation. Yeah, handcuffs tonight. *For him.*

Her lover opened the door, and he was only wearing a towel. She felt her mouth go dry at his size and muscularity—his magnificent pecs were level with her eyes.

"You're a little late." His deep voice always snagged on her nerves.

"And you are—yummy." C.J. put her mouth on his nearby chest and bit gently.

He'd hauled her into the room, slammed the door, and blew away her carefully constructed fantasy with one of his own.

"Ahem, Captain."

C.J. started. Jessup Murioka, looking sheepish, waved, and she realized she must have missed the first time he called her name. She'd been too busy staring into space with a grin on her face.

"The meeting's in ten minutes." She speared Murioka with an impatient glance, then looked at her laptop, which had finally finished booting. The paperwork was overwhelming in her position, and the only way she kept on top of it at all was to multitask. "You're early."

"Yes, sir." The kid was eighteen, but his voice was still off, going high and reedy now and again, as if he were still in junior high. He'd had a recent growth spurt, and his Adam's apple worked as she glanced at him, neatly dressed in a button-down and khakis, a nice change from his school uniform. He was keeping his black hair high and tight, too, and not for the first time, C.J. was glad she'd taken the risk two years ago to accept him as a technology intern. Murioka had overhauled much of the antiquated tech in the building, and continued to stay on, paid a pittance, as he worked on a degree at UH Maui.

"I just thought I'd tell you I cracked the vic's phone and computer. There's some interesting material on there." And damn if the kid didn't blush.

Must be porn.

"Bring some way to view the material to the meeting."

"I also got the safe open."

"What's inside?"

"I didn't look. I'm not a detective."

C.J. had to find a way to keep Murioka after he graduated. She'd have to find some creative way to carve enough money out of her budget to increase his salary. "Good work. Bring the items to the meeting."

"Yes, sir." He spun on a heel and left.

C.J. tipped back her chair and tapped her fingernails together. The day she'd decided to be addressed as "sir," she'd still been a lieutenant, commanding the tiny, now-defunct Haiku Station, when she'd realized that (a) she hated how being called "ma'am" made her feel old, and (b) the fewer reminders of her gender when commanding men, the better. A woman who insisted on being called "sir" had caused some waves at first, but C.J. had checked with ACLU to make sure she had a right to use "any appropriate title affording rank."

"The shame. No grandchildren," her mother had mourned. "No one would have a ballbuster like you."

C.J. had used a bad word to her mother's face that time, and they hadn't spoken for a whole week.

She liked being called "sir" and had no intention of having children. Watching Texeira waddle around the station pregnant had sealed that decision. Messy, drooly, distracting little things, they loved to put their sticky little hands on her clothes and cause workplace absences. Her mother would have to harp on her brother for babies.

C.J. sipped her Diet Coke as the team trickled in: Stevens first, looking better than yesterday, if still a little off-color; Mahoe, his square face chapped from shaving; Murioka, carrying a computer tablet on top of the safe.

And her lover brought up the rear. He winked from behind Murioka, grinning. "Good morning, Captain."

C.J. dropped the pen she was holding and had to chase it around under her chair, getting her surprise under control. Nope. She was sure now that she didn't like surprises. This was a great example of why it was a bad idea to sleep with coworkers. He'd winked at her! She was going to have to take that out on his hide.

C.J. sat upright and tapped the pen on the table to bring the meeting to order. "This case is taking a lot of heat, and bringing in Chef Noriega for an interview is getting some backlash. I got a call from the mayor this morning about our station 'harassing' his favorite chef. Report."

"Yes, sir," Stevens said. "Before we get started, I thought I'd make sure it was okay to have Detective Torufu help us. I need the extra manpower, he offered, and he's between big cases. We have so many people to do follow-up interviews with and so much evidence from the scene to process, we could use a hand."

"Fine," C.J. barked, not making eye contact with anything but her computer screen. Abe Torufu was a decent detective, great at his bomb squad duties, and damn good in bed, too. She was in danger of liking him too much. "Where are we after the first twenty-four hours?"

"Mahoe? Can you do the tracking on the board?" Stevens asked. Mahoe got up to cover that chore as Stevens reviewed progress: trace and evidence from the body, initial statements taken at the restaurant and several interesting follow-ups scheduled, the interview with Chef Noriega, the search of the victim's residence, and their impressions of Kitty Summers, erstwhile girlfriend.

"You need to find out who that ring was for," C.J. said to

Stevens. "Anything more on whoever was sabotaging the kitchen?"

"Noriega thought Métier was doing it as part of his exit strategy. It will be interesting to see if anything further occurs with Métier out of the picture. I'd say if there are no further incidents, it's safe to assume the victim was responsible."

"Well, Chef Noriega has some powerful motive." C.J. gestured to Mahoe. "List the motives we already know Noriega has." Mahoe did so, forehead knit as he printed industriously on the board.

"We have absolutely no physical evidence tying Chef to the crime," Stevens said. "Nor anyone else, for that matter. As you pointed out, Noriega has powerful friends, and though he's a violent man, a stab in the back doesn't seem his style. He says he had a plan to deal with Métier. Seemed almost annoyed he wasn't going to be able to execute it with the man dead."

C.J. nodded. "Mahoe, make another list for Elena Noriega. Motive is jealousy of his other lovers, with perhaps the ring as a catalyst. Or same as Chef, she feels betrayed by his plans to compete with Feast."

Mahoe wrote as fast as he could.

"Still nothing linking her to the victim." There was a glint in Stevens's eyes that told C.J. he was enjoying his moment as devil's advocate. "But I have hopes for that DNA trace Dr. G found under his nails."

"And there was nothing on the knife?"

"Nothing but smears."

C.J. swung her foot. The Jimmy Choos she'd slipped into that morning had a tiny strap that was killing her ankle. "I want to know who Métier was proposing to. Find his next of kin and his best friends. Hopefully his phone or that safe will have more for us. Murioka?"

Jessup cleared his throat. "Yes, sir. I got into his phone and the lieutenant can have it." The kid pushed the evidence-bagged phone to Stevens. "I also broke into the computer. Lots of files that might be of interest. I made a copy of the hard drive last night and loaded the whole thing onto this tablet." He turned the tablet so the team could see. "Lots of videos on here. They seem to be the victim and . . . his girlfriends." Murioka pushed a button, and one of the videos began to play.

"Looks professional," Stevens said. A title, *Fellatio with the Frenchman,* came up. "This is a lot more organized than I expected."

A production company was listed. "Pause the video!" C.J. pointed to the company name. "Follow that up."

"Will do." Stevens made a note. "Let's roll this a minute, see what's on there."

"I imagine fellatio with the Frenchman is what's on there," C.J. said. "And I don't need to see that. Your team can go over the content of the laptop back in your cubicle." She was highly aware of Torufu's gaze from across the table. "Murioka also got the safe open. Who wants to do the honors?"

"I've got gloves in my back pocket, along with explosives detection paper," Torufu volunteered.

"We don't think explosives are a concern, but it can't hurt to swab first," Stevens said. C.J. inclined her head in agreement. Abe snapped on gloves and walked around the table to stand at the corner nearest her, where Murioka had set the heavy-looking metal cube. He bent, inspecting it.

She tried not to notice the way his shirt tightened across his massive back. Abe had kept himself in shape ever since his football days with University of Hawaii, and she hoped he always would—not that they had a future or anything.

Abe took a sealed plastic packet out of his pocket. "Never know when you'll need these." He swabbed around the door of the safe with a chemical-soaked cotton pad. Held it up. "No evidence of explosives. How do I get this thing open, kid?"

"I contacted the safe company and got the combination,"

Murioka piped. “It’s dialed in already. Just push down on the handle.”

The safe was set on its back wall. Abe took hold of the handle after pushing it down and lifted the door open. Stevens, Mahoe, and Murioka all surged to their feet, clustering around to peer in, but C.J. refused to lose her dignity. “What’s inside?”

Abe reached in and brought out a thick wad of bundled, rubber-banded cash. “Nothing but money.” He riffled through the packets. “Looks like ten thousand a packet.”

“Bet this is the startup seed money for the victim’s restaurant,” Stevens said.

Things got a little chaotic as the team counted the cash. “Can’t imagine having money like this just sitting around,” Mahoe said.

“He had a plan that required a lot of money, from everything we’re hearing. We just need to find out where this money came from. Could point us to a different motive,” Stevens said.

“Well, without counting every bill, I’d say there’s around a hundred grand here,” Abe said.

“Enough to get his restaurant going,” C.J. pointed the pen at Stevens. “Find out where this came from. And take this down and log it into evidence. I think that does it for today. Keep me posted. Dismissed.”

“Yes, sir.” They replaced the money in the safe. Stevens shut the door and picked up the metal cube. “Torufu, why don’t you take the tablet, surf through it, and follow up with the video production company. I’ve got too many interviews lined up today to get to it.”

“No problem,” Torufu rumbled in that deep bass that always got to C.J. He took the tablet from Murioka and hung back as the room cleared. “Can I check with you about something, Captain?” He glanced over at C.J. and grinned, irrepressible, and as Murioka left, he closed the conference room door.

C.J. narrowed her eyes. They’d met socially at a wedding in Honolulu and had been meeting on the sly ever since—but he kept upping the ante. He'd been trying to take her to dinner, and now he was talking to her at work when she'd expressly forbidden it—not to mention *winking* at her, for God's sake.

"Sure you don't want to watch this with me? It could be fun." He waggled the laptop.

"Hell no. And we shouldn't be talking alone, either."

Abe's eyes flared as his temper spiked, and he stalked around the table toward her. C.J. kept eye contact and remained seated—she wasn't going to give any ground.

"You forget yourself," she snapped.

"And you *need* to forget yourself." Abe wasn't looking away either. The intimacy of gazing into his rich brown eyes was almost too much. "You always brush me off when we're alone. I decided to say something to you here."

C.J. blinked first. She looked down at her laptop, fiddling with it, as he loomed beside her chair. She wished he didn't smell like the hotel soap they'd both used early this morning.

"Fine. What do you want to talk about?" C.J. addressed her keyboard.

"When are we going to go on a real date?"

"We went out in Honolulu."

"But we don't live in Honolulu. We live here. And I want to date you—not just meet in hotel rooms."

C.J. was thankful he'd put their liaisons so graciously—there were so many other ways he could have said that. Nervous sweat prickled under her arms. "You don't know what's at stake for me."

"Your pride."

"My professionalism." C.J. looked up at him. "I'd never live it down."

A long beat went by as they stared at each other. "Do you . . . care?" he whispered. He wasn't asking about her job.

C.J. felt heat suffuse her cheeks. She shut her eyes, sagging in her chair, and covered her face with her hands. "Yes," she whispered. "Do you?"

He reached down and grabbed her by the upper arms, lifting her out of the chair like she weighed nothing. He wrapped his arms around her and kissed her with all the determination and open-heartedness that had drawn her to him in the first place.

Abe was ruining her lipstick, mussing her hair, and it felt glorious, an ardent declaration more powerful than any words. Finally he let her go, sliding his big hands down her arms to clasp her hands. C.J. felt tears prickle her eyes.

"We're going public then," he said. "Whenever you're ready, I'm ready."

"Okay." C.J. stepped back and tugged down the jacket of her uniform, finger-combing her hair with trembling hands. *Oh, my God. I'm in so much trouble.*

CHAPTER ELEVEN

Kathy

THE YOUNG MAN IN THE doorway sported a head of dreadlocks decorated with beads in red, yellow, green, and black. He wore nothing but a pair of board shorts. "What can I do for you, Officer?"

"Sergeant Kathy Fraser." Kathy held up her badge wallet. "Hi. Can I come in and talk for a few minutes?"

"Is this about Feast?" Sage Bukowski stepped back, inviting her in with a flourish. His British accent was a surprise. "Enter at your own risk." The young man preceded her into a living room crowded with kite-boarding equipment and surfboards. He cleared a couple of pizza boxes off the coffee table and a shirt off the couch. "Have a seat."

"Thanks." Kathy sat as he took the boxes into the kitchen. "Yes, this is about Feast. Just wanted to ask you a few more questions. Do you mind if I record this?"

"No problem." Bukowski smelled the shirt he'd picked up off the couch and shrugged into it. "What can I tell you?"

"Why don't you begin by telling me what your job is?"

"I'm a busboy and food runner."

"So what does that entail?"

"Clearing and setting tables. I take the food out to the tables from the kitchen when it's ready."

"Are you here on Maui on a work visa?"

Bukowski eyed Kathy warily. "I plead the Fifth on that."

She snorted a laugh. "Okay. I take that as a no. How long have you been at Feast?"

"About six months. There's a high turnover rate for my position."

"What do you like about working there?"

"Everything." The young man gestured animatedly. "The food. The ambience. The staff is great. It's a fun place to work."

"So in mentioning the staff, do you also include Chef Noriega in the 'great' description?"

"Chef is brilliant."

"Yes, he is." Bukowski was clearly wary about saying anything negative about the restaurant while being recorded. "Perhaps we don't need this after all." Kathy turned off her phone and put it away. "So where were you between the hours of eight-thirty and midnight?"

"Oh, girl." Bukowski flapped a hand. "I told the lieutenant who interviewed me—I was off early. Went out with the boys at nine-thirty."

She made a note of it—still within the window of time of death but less likely than after ten p.m. People would still have been going in and out of the refrigerator then. "Can I get a name or two to verify your whereabouts?"

"Sure." Bukowski seemed confident, and Kathy noted the names and numbers he rattled off.

"Did you see anyone else go into the walk-in before you left?"

"Hmm. I had to refill the sauces at my workstation before I left. I was doing that from about nine to nine-thirty, and it's across from the walk-in. I don't remember anyone in particular. I wasn't paying attention—I admit, I was texting someone when I wasn't filling my sauce bottles." Once again, the cocky grin.

"How about the victim? Did you see Métier go into the unit?"

"Hey, now that you mention it, I did. He went in with his main squeeze, Kitty the porn star. She's also a waitress at Feast."

Pay dirt. Kathy's heart rate accelerated. "And did you see them come out?"

Bukowski shut his eyes in concentration. Opened them again, a remarkable hazel against his caffe-latte skin. "I'm afraid not. I went to the loo to freshen up after they went inside."

"Did you see anyone else after you got back?"

He shook his head. "I'm sorry. I just couldn't tell you." Then he lifted his head with a flare of those eyes. "Yes! Chef went in. He came right back out though, no more than a couple of minutes, tops."

"Thanks. This has been very helpful. You seem well spoken. Did you go to college?"

"Oxford. English lit. The degree really does a lot for me, as you can see." He gestured to the homely surroundings.

Kathy smiled. "So you must have some background in writing."

"Just studying the way it's done." Bukowski smiled. "I follow that blog, if that's what you're asking."

"And . . . do you write the blog?"

Bukowski got up. "I prefer to be an observer. That's more my style."

"Whoever writes the blog is awfully observant."

Bukowski went behind the breakfast bar, clearly uncomfortable. "Can I get you an espresso? Don't have much, but I do have a good machine."

"No, thanks. Hypothetically then, if I were to be speaking to the author of the blog, what are some of the benefits of writing it?"

"I would imagine, hypothetically speaking, that it would be

fun." Bukowski changed out the grounds and filled the water carafe. "Whoever is writing it clearly enjoys social commentary."

"I can't wait to read what the blogger says about the murder," Kathy said dryly. "I bet that will be a real crowd pleaser."

"Actually, Métier was better alive than dead for the blogger," Bukowski said. "He generated a good deal of juicy gossip with his bedroom habits."

"I'm aware. I've been following the blog for some time. I wonder if the blogger had motive to kill Métier."

Bukowski's hands stilled on the espresso machine. "I can't see one. Did you get any hostile vibes off the blog toward Métier?"

"Gossip, cattiness, jealousy perhaps." Kathy kept her eyes on Bukowski's expressive face.

Bukowski turned on the hissing milk steamer. Probably didn't want to comment, and she didn't much blame him. He poured his coffee drink and came back to sit beside her on the couch.

"Listen." Kathy set down her notebook and pen. "Off the record. This blog has been a huge source of stress to the Noriegas. Elena, particularly."

Bukowski grinned and took a sip of the latte. Foam decorated his upper lip. "I'm sorry to hear that. Poor lady deals with a lot. But the blog has been good for Feast's publicity. There are even rumors of a reality TV show set in the restaurant."

Kathy hissed out a breath. "That's not going to fly with the Noriegas."

"You seem personally invested for a cop investigating the case."

So much for the sympathy appeal. Kathy picked up her notebook again. "Let's go over again when you saw the victim, Chef, and Kitty Summers go into the walk-in. Nail down the times."

She took notes, trying to nail down his observations, but they remained vague. "So. On the topic of Métier, and since we've established that you are a very observant guy . . . who do you think the Frenchman might have made a proposal to?"

"Ah. Now, isn't that an interesting question." Bukowski wiped his milk mustache with a flick of his finger. "Kitty was angling for more, that's for sure, and even though they had the porn thing going, I don't think he was that into her."

"Porn thing?"

"They made videos. Some professional, some for personal use." He rubbed a thumb alongside his mouth, suppressing a smile. "Kitty was a pro with those videos, both acting in and marketing them through her production company. Métier seemed to be into it for a while, but lately I'd seen them arguing. Métier was trying to get some distance, and she was on him like gum on a shoe. My impression was that she chased him into the walk-in that night."

"Thanks." Kathy noted that. "Any other contenders?"

"He was really into Elena Noriega—always fixing her little things to eat when Chef wasn't around, meeting her in the office with the blinds down. I'm not sure how much of his attachment to her was because he really cared for her or if banging her was one more way he was sticking it to Chef."

Kathy raised her brows at his crudity, and Bukowski shook his head a little. "I like Elena. The lady's in a tough spot. But there's no doubt there was a little getting back at Chef on both of their parts in that relationship."

Kathy privately agreed, but pressed on. "You sure there's no one else serious in his life?"

"I couldn't swear to it. Like I said, Métier, for all his faults, wasn't one to kiss and tell."

"Were you aware he had other secrets from Chef?"

"You mean the other restaurant? Yeah. I overheard Métier on the phone with one of Chef's farmers, Teo Benitez. From what I gathered, Teo was reluctant to sell to him and risk losing Chef's business."

Kathy jotted down the name. "Thanks so much. This has been super helpful." She stood. "We may need to come back, check on a few details."

"Of course. Happy to help." He walked Kathy to the door. "Good luck finding that blogger."

Kathy snorted—the rascal was charming, and he'd given her good intel. "Right. We'll be in touch if we need to be."

Out in her Rogue, engine idling and AC cranked up, she called Stevens.

"Hey, Kath." He sounded friendly and upbeat. Reminded her of old times, back when they'd been friends. She wanted it to be like that again.

"Hey. I got done with Bukowski. Got a pencil?"

"You know I do." He always did, that stub tied to his spiral pad. So old school. "What'd he give you?"

"Good stuff. He's the blogger, all right, though he wouldn't admit it. He'd seen some comings and goings to the walk-in." She told him the tips Bukowski had passed on, along with the extras about the victim.

"Good work. Can you take care of verifying his alibi?"

"No problem."

A brief pause. "Thanks. Appreciate your lending a hand."

"Of course. I tried to get him to stop doing the blog, for Elena's sake, but he laughed me off. Said it was good for the restaurant."

"Cocky little bastard."

"He is that. But charming."

"Okay, then. Keep me posted." Stevens ended the call.

Kathy turned the key and fired up her vehicle. She had time for some phone calls and drive-bys to check on Bukowski's alibi, and then she'd meet Jared for coffee.

Kathy's pulse picked up—if she could get past the fact that Jared was Stevens's brother, she could admit how attractive she found him.

They were so different—Stevens serious, Jared more playful—but they had in common a laser-like focus on their objectives and a selfless dedication to their work in public service, something she shared, and admired.

Kathy smiled as she pushed down on the accelerator. She was really looking forward to that coffee.

CHAPTER TWELVE

Stevens

Roland Chen looked the part of an estate lawyer: small and tubby, he was dressed in tailored slacks paired with an immaculate white shirt and jacket, and a perfectly groomed goatee framed his small, pink mouth. He took off a pair of round spectacles and polished them with a linen kerchief. "I'm horrified to hear of François's death."

"Yes, quite a shock. And especially the manner of it." Stevens, seated beside Mahoe, pushed Métier's death certificate and a warrant for his records across the finely tooled, burled koa desk toward the attorney. "We need to know the terms of his will and sources of his assets. That information could help us determine who stood to gain by his murder."

Chen replaced the glasses on his nose and tucked the kerchief back into its pocket, a snowy corner protruding in sartorial splendor. He picked up and examined the documents. "These seem to be in order. I'm just the Métier family representative here in Hawaii, a liaison for their trust." He retrieved a slim folder. "Mr. Métier did have a will."

"Trust?" Mahoe leaned forward in his chair. "What kind of trust?"

"The Métier Family Trust. François Métier was the heir. Both his parents are deceased. He was a very wealthy man."

"So what was he doing busting his butt as a sous-chef?" Mahoe's eyebrows, and his voice, had risen.

"He never discussed that with me." Chen opened the folder. "I'll have my girl make you copies of these documents."

"Thanks," Stevens said. "If you could sum up the contents of these documents in layman's terms, that would be helpful."

"Yes, indeed." Chen removed the document and used an old-fashioned fountain pen to point to the relevant clauses. "François didn't have a spouse or children, so his will was simple: his assets reverted to the trust, which is set up to pay out and benefit several charities in the event of his death without issue. Should he have married or had children, things would have been much different."

"So how big of a trust is this? And what are its sources of income?" Stevens asked.

"The trust was established in 1990 by Métier's parents. It contains holdings in French shipping, wine, and land. Métier received a monthly percentage, which I imagine is what he was living on at a bit higher level than the average sous-chef."

"Who's in charge of it?" Stevens asked. The lawyer's secretary had arrived. She took the papers, leaving the room.

"The trust has a board of directors. Now that the last direct member of the family has died, it is set up to become a nonprofit that generates money to support the chosen charities."

Stevens sat back and frowned. "So there's no financial benefit to anyone by Métier's death."

"Well, he had a life insurance policy, too. All of this was set up by his parents—François showed little interest in anything other than his quarterly payments. I had my girl make a copy of the policy for you. It was smaller. Only a million and a half. Beneficiary was his cousin, André Métier, only surviving relative. He also lives here on Maui."

Stevens felt the hairs rise on the back of his neck. "Do you have an address?"

"There is one on the document, but I don't imagine it's current. I heard the young man is big into kite-boarding and windsurfing, and that can be a transitory lifestyle."

"Anything else you can tell us that could shed light on who might have wanted to kill Métier?"

"I'm sorry. Other than the cousin, no one benefited from his death but the nonprofit and the charities under the trust."

"Can you give us a list of what they are?"

"Of course." Chen turned to his computer, tapping keys. "Most of them are in France. I'm not sure there's anything at all here on Maui."

Mahoe got up and paced a little. Stevens frowned at the agitation in his young partner's movements, the frustration in his body language. Mahoe rolled his shoulders, staring at the expensive artworks on the walls.

"Hmm, I was wrong. There's a big bequest to benefit the Maui Forest Bird Recovery Project. They're here on Maui, focusing on saving the Maui parrotbill, or *kiwikiu.* And there's another for Keiki Cupboard, an organization that gives school supplies to needy kids." Chen hit a button and the printer spit out pages. "Those are the only local ones, though."

Stevens took the pages just as the secretary returned with copies of the will and insurance policy. "Thanks so much for your time."

"Anything I can do. This was truly a tragic waste." Chen followed them to the door. After handshakes all around, they walked out of the office and down the hall of the dignified office building in Wailuku.

"So what's got you so sour, Mahoe?" Stevens asked as they got into the elevator.

"Just isn't fair." Mahoe looked sullen, his brows low and mouth tight. "This guy had it all. Looks. Women. Money, too."

"May I remind you he's on a slab in Dr. G's morgue?" Stevens hit the Stop button on the elevator. "What's your beef with Métier and this case? You gotta think about it when a case gets under your skin—it affects the way you do your investigation. Your bias shows, Brandon." His use of the man's first name was deliberate.

Mahoe sagged against the wall, crestfallen. "I don't really care that Métier got killed," he said. "He deserved it. He had too much and did nothing for anyone with it."

"Think about what you just said." Stevens caught the young detective's eye. "François Métier may well have been a self-serving dog who had everything handed to him, or there may have been more going on with who he was than meets the eye. That's not for us to judge. His life, which is all anyone has at the end of the day, was taken from him in a brutal, underhanded way that he never saw coming. A way that tells me it was a friend, not an enemy, who did him in. The worst kind of betrayal." Stevens hit the Stop button again and the elevator proceeded. "Get over it, Mahoe, or I'll ask you to step off the case and I'll work with Kathy and Torufu instead."

"No need, LT. I'm sorry. I'll get my head in the game. Just don't ask me to watch those frickin' porn videos." Red stained the tops of Mahoe's ears.

"You'll notice I farmed that out to Torufu," Stevens said with a grin. "Didn't think either of us needed to have to bleach our eyeballs after an afternoon going through all that. One more point I want to make is this: what a man's like at thirty is seldom what he's like at forty, fifty, sixty. Métier was just beginning to get traction on his dreams. He might have amounted to someone who had a positive impact. Now we'll never know."

Mahoe looked down at his feet. Stevens hoped he was getting through to his partner, but with the young man's tight-lipped expression, he wasn't sure. He clapped Mahoe on the shoulder.

"And that age thirty thing goes for you, too, Brandon. Not happy with where you are? No time like the present to change it."

Once they exited and got back on the road to the Kahului Station, Stevens addressed his partner again. "Can you put these papers in the file and run a background on André Métier, the cousin? Let's find this guy. In the meantime, I have to call the financial planner. He's in France."

"Sure, LT." Mahoe appeared to be making an effort to rally, infusing his voice with energy. "I'm on it."

Stevens's shared office with Kathy Fraser was on the administrative third floor, a spacious room that could be used for trainings. They'd shoved a third desk for Mahoe between his and Kathy's. Mahoe loaded the papers into the file's case jacket and booted up his computer. "I'll start looking for the cousin with a DMV search."

A tasteful, gaily wrapped package waited on Stevens's desk. A small tag on it declared, *Best to the family. Love, Kathy.*

Lei hadn't mentioned Kathy attending the shower and bringing a gift—she would have if Kathy had been there. He just wanted them all to be friends, but the tension between Lei and Kathy must still be there if his ex-partner hadn't attended the shower. But maybe Kathy'd just been away from the office. He could hope that was the case. After their more friendly exchange on the phone today, he was in the mood to hope. "More loot for the baby." Stevens kept his voice light as he moved the package to the floor.

"Don't know where you folks are going to put all that stuff," Mahoe remarked, eyes on his monitor. "Babies sure need a lot of crap."

"You have no idea." Stevens sat and dialed the number he'd retrieved from the victim's home office. "Hello? Is Monsieur Raveaux available?" He identified himself and the urgent nature of his inquiry.

The financial adviser came on the line after a short wait. "How can I help you, Detective?" an accented voice asked.

"Lieutenant," Stevens corrected him. "Monsieur Raveaux, I've had our office fax you the death certificate and a warrant for the records of our murder victim, François Métier. I hope you've received them?"

"Yes, we have the documents and our legal department is reviewing them. I'm happy to assist. So sorry to hear of this tragic loss."

"Thanks for your cooperation. Tell me about Métier's income. How much was it monthly?"

"He received a quarterly percentage of his investment's gains. Right now that has been particularly strong, with the rebound of the economy. I believe it's in the area of two hundred thousand U.S. dollars."

Stevens whistled. "Quarterly?"

"Yes. Quarterly."

So Métier wouldn't have had to curtail his spending long to start his own restaurant. Which meant his job at Feast had been strictly to gain experience under a brilliant chef, in order to take his recipes—and perhaps his wife? With that kind of financial clout, Métier might easily have been able to afford to lure Elena Noriega away from her abusive husband by offering her a comfy nest to land in with her child. And if Winston Noriega knew of Métier's intentions, he'd have had a motive as old as man's possessiveness.

"We are looking for reasons someone might have wanted to kill Métier. I know you may not have known him, but do you have any information that might be helpful?"

The man considered. Finally, "Yes. Were you aware of the Bukowski Group?"

Stevens's attention, which had wandered back to his computer screen, sharpened. He refocused on the yellow legal pad he was using to take notes. "That name is familiar."

"The Bukowski Group is a coalition of more distant relatives of the Métiers. They've come together to try to break the Métier Trust and claim a portion of the profits, citing an illegal squeeze out from jointly owned lands by the Métier parents. The case is still making its way through the French courts."

Stevens wrote *Sage Bukowski* on his pad and underlined it. "That's very interesting and useful. Anything else you can think of, give me a call." He left his information and hung up.

Mahoe looked over at him. "I can't find anyone named André Métier in the DMV records."

"Well, he's a French national. Maybe he's living under another name, or hasn't established residency here. We'll have to keep looking." Stevens frowned. Concentrating had brought a familiar fog of pain. "Let's take a break and get some food."

"I've got to go out to get something. Need anything, LT? I'm going to Taco Bell."

"Nah, brought something from home." Stevens waited until Mahoe had left, then closed the door of the office. He moved his office chair out from behind his desk and took two powerful pain pills, swallowing them with a whole bottle of water. He pulled one of Lei's yoga mats, tightly rolled, from beneath his desk, unrolled it, and lay down. On his back, eyes shut, he did some of the breathing Dr. Wilson had taught him, willing his mind to relax and the tension gripping his temples to let go.

He was missing some vital piece of information on this investigation. There was a thread connecting all these separate pieces, and though circumstance and motive pointed to Noriega, he still wasn't feeling it.

Someone else had slid that knife between Métier's ribs.

CHAPTER THIRTEEN

KATHY

Kathy

KATHY TESTED THE DOOR OF the office—it was locked, though the light was on inside. She dug her keys out of her purse and unlocked the door. She was brought up short by the sight of a pair of long legs in blue jeans lying on the carpet, protruding beyond the end of her ex-partner's desk.

"Stevens?" He didn't answer, but she heard a soft snore as she came around the corner of the desk to make sure he was okay.

Stevens was taking a nap, stretched out on a purple yoga mat. One arm was draped over his eyes, the other alongside his body. He must be really wiped out—she'd never seen him crash like that at work before. The brightly colored wrapping of her baby shower present was just visible beside Stevens's foot. Kathy tiptoed back to her desk and hung her backpack on the coat rack. As her computer booted up, she smiled, remembering her coffee date with Jared.

They'd arrived at Wailuku Coffee Company from their separate workplaces at five. She'd still been wearing her uniform, but had left her jacket in the car so she could look more casual. Jared met her in the line to order coffee. He'd just showered and smelled of something lemony and fresh. Comb tracks showed in his dark hair. His eyes were very blue, a shade darker than his brother's.

"Glad you could make it." He had a great smile.

"Me too. Long day. Wish I'd had time to take a shower." Kathy made a gesture to his clean shirt and wet hair.

"I had to. Tromping around through ash and debris is downright toxic. We have regulations about tracking that around outside of a burn site—and it helps to have a shower at the firehouse." He pointed to the order board. "Why don't you grab us a table and I'll order?"

"Sure. I'll have a latte." Kathy found them a corner table in the dimly lit café, enjoying the vintage Hawaiiana collectibles on the walls as she looked around. Seated, she undid the top two buttons on her plain white blouse, loosened her hair from its ponytail, fluffing it, and touched up her lipstick nervously.

Jared wended his way through the tables with the coffees on a tray. He moved differently from his brother—Stevens had a rangy grace, his strides long, carrying his arms loose. Jared moved quickly and tightly, with the panache of a matador. He set the tray on the table.

"You look amazing. What lady magic did you do since I saw you five minutes ago?"

Great way with a compliment—also not like his brother. She needed to stop comparing the two; clearly they were very different.

"Lady magic—I like that. Thank you." Kathy took her latte and he set the tray aside, sitting down with a cappuccino. "Stevens told me you were a smooth talker."

His brows lowered. "Don't listen to everything my brother says about me."

Kathy sipped her coffee. This was a chance to find out more about the brothers' relationship. She couldn't resist probing that sensitive spot a little more. "So what does he say about you?"

"I don't know. Why don't you tell me?" Jared avoided her eyes, tinkling his spoon in his cappuccino.

"All right. He says you're a player with the ladies, but he also says you're great at your job and a hard worker. From him, that's a compliment. Also told me you love cats. Collect anything to do with them." Kathy wiggled her brows playfully. "Perhaps that part was my embellishment."

"Embellish away." His triangular grin brought out strong cheekbones. He was almost too handsome. "I actually do like cats." He dug in his pocket and brought out his key ring, holding it out to her. A steel beer opener in the shape of Catwoman flaunted outrageous metal curves in his palm. She felt a tingle—it looked so sexy in his hand

What would his hand look like on her?

Kathy felt her cheeks warm. "Well, I guess she is a cat."

"Yeah. As to the player thing." Jared slid the keys into the pocket of his jeans and rubbed the back of his neck. He caught her eye. "I've just been waiting to meet the right woman."

Kathy looked at the wall, the floor, anywhere but at him. "Ha. Sounds like a line."

"Thought you might think that, and it's fine. I'm prepared to prove myself." His voice was low and sincere. She could feel his gaze on her face.

"Don't exert yourself on my account." Kathy finally looked at him then, her own gaze as tough as she could make it. "I need a man about as much as Catwoman does."

"Ha! I know that bottle opener's a little sexist, but it's sentimental. Stevens gave it to me when I was sixteen. Couple of years after our dad died. He was eighteen, had left for the Marines. He sent it to me from overseas where he found it in some trinket shop. Don't know why I'm telling you all this." Jared rubbed the back of his neck again.

"No. It helps." She had a feeling he hadn't told that story often. She took a big swig of her latte, burning her throat, and coughed.

He pounded her back helpfully. When that awkward moment had passed, he asked, "So, what brought you to Maui?"

"Oh, the usual." Kathy smiled, on more comfortable ground. "I'm from Michigan. I came here with a friend on vacation and fell in love with the weather, the beauty. I'd been working as an officer in Detroit since college. I applied online for an opening in the Maui Police Department. The rest is history."

She wasn't ready to tell him about her partner being shot in a random drive-by when they were on patrol, and how that had spurred her move. She still couldn't talk about it without choking up. She'd tell him someday, if there ever was a someday, when she trusted him.

She heard his story, complete with anecdotes about growing up with Stevens in LA, and they'd ordered sandwiches for dinner, finally leaving when the place shut down at nine.

Not a bad first date. She'd found him funny, articulate, and intelligent. They were going out again as soon as they could make their schedules work.

Stevens sat up slowly behind the desk. She peeked over at him. "Good morning, sunshine."

"How long was I out?" He groaned, rubbing his hands through his hair, leaving a disorderly mass of tufts as he got up and sat in his chair. "Mahoe should be here any minute."

"You were sleeping when I got in ten minutes ago."

"Long day yesterday. And today. Listen, I've got a serious lead on something to do with Sage Bukowski."

He was telling her about the twists in the Métier case when the door opened and Brandon Mahoe returned, carrying two Taco Bell bags.

"Brought you something, LT." Mahoe set one of the bags on Stevens's desk. "I know you didn't bring anything from home."

Stevens looked up at his protégé for a long moment. "You might end up being a decent detective after all, Mahoe." He socked the young man in the arm, making him stagger. "Thanks."

Kathy let Stevens munch through a taco before she asked, “Want me to go back out and talk to Sage again? See if he’s part of this Bukowski Group?”

“Well, given his distinctive name, I think it’s a foregone conclusion that he’s a part of the group,” Stevens said. “But I think we need more info before we talk to him, and that’s a conversation I’d like to have myself. With Mahoe.”

“Of course.” Kathy turned back to her monitor, feeling rebuffed, and addressed her screen. “Let me know if I can help on anything further.”

“Will do.” He softened his tone. “Really appreciate how you’ve pitched in here, Kath. With Elena and Bukowski.”

“Anytime.” Her shoulders loosened—he wasn’t just blowing her off. She liked that he was back to calling her Kath.

She focused on her e-mail inbox, trying not to eavesdrop, as the two men began discussing the case and Métier’s phone logs, which revealed a lot of calls to Elena but only a few names that might be male friends.

“I don’t think he confided in a lot of people,” Mahoe speculated. “He seems to have had a plan he was executing and keeping pretty secret.”

“Right,” Stevens agreed. “The captain said we needed to find out who he was going to propose to, and while we’ve now uncovered some financial motive for the mysterious cousin, we’re not any closer to knowing who that ring was for.”

Kathy’s cell rang. She pulled it from the holster on her belt and greeted the caller. “Elena!”

Both Stevens and Mahoe looked up. She stood and wended her way around the desk to step outside the office for a little privacy, aware as she did so of the trickiness of divided loyalties. “What’s happening?”

“I need your help,” Elena whispered. “I need to leave Winston. I’m afraid he’s going to kill me.”

Kathy’s heart jumped in alarm. “Where are you?” She headed

for the lounge in the corner of the floor, wanting to get away from prying ears. "Are you safe?"

"Yes. He's at work, and I am home with Nicola." Their three-year-old was a sweetheart, and Kathy loved being called "Aunty" by the little girl. "He got home from the police station last night just crazy."

"How crazy? Did he hit you?"

"Yes. He was so angry about François and me. He found out from the detectives. I swore I'd be faithful from now on, that it was never anything serious to me. He hit me, not too bad, not the worst it's been . . . but I realized, with François gone, life is short . . . he's at work now, and I'm just . . . " Elena broke into sobs.

"Pack a bag for you and Nicola. I'll get you into the Women Helping Women shelter. Just grab what you need right now, get in the car, and meet me at the Starbucks by the mall. The shelter is in a confidential location, but I'll lead you there and make sure they're ready for you."

"Are you sure he can't find me there?"

"Yes. It's a hidden site with security. It'll give you time to figure out what you want to do, at the very least."

"All right. I'll meet you in forty-five minutes." Elena ended the call decisively.

"What's going on?" Stevens stood in the doorway, looking concerned, as she returned to the office.

"Elena's finally leaving Winston. He beat her last night after he got home from your interview." Anger warmed Kathy's cheeks. "Didn't it occur to you that he'd do something like that if he found out about her affair?"

"It did. I warned him we were watching him. Damn, I'm sorry to hear that. Is she okay?"

"No, not really. I'm getting her out of there and into the shelter." Kathy brushed past him, already calling the Women Helping Women hotline as she walked to her desk.

Stevens followed as Kathy described the situation to the social worker, preparing them for Elena and her daughter's arrival. Still on the phone, she shut down her computer and packed paperwork into her briefcase. Kathy ended the call and turned to Mahoe and Stevens.

"Find a way to nail Winston Noriega," she said. "I don't care how you do it. Just get it done. That man needs to be locked up."

CHAPTER FOURTEEN

Stevens

STEVENS DROVE THROUGH THE BUMPER-TO-BUMPER commuter traffic along Hana Highway through Paia Town. He'd consulted with the captain, who hadn't wanted him to pick up Chef Noriega until they'd had an in person verification on Elena's attack.

While he and Brandon waited for Kathy to let them know that Elena was safe and settled at the shelter, they'd gone down to the lab and processed the items they'd picked up at Métier's apartment.

They'd also revisited the trace picked up on and around the body. None of it pointed to anyone in particular. The epithelial sample under Métier's nails had been too small to process. Hairs on and around the rubber mat had gone back to a variety of restaurant staff, all of who would have legitimate reasons to be in the walk-in.

Kathy had called, saying that Elena was ready to talk, and since the shelter was on his way home, Stevens had dismissed Mahoe for the night and headed out alone. Once at the modest, anonymous home housing the shelter, he'd bitten back a curse at the sight of Elena's swollen face and black eye.

"I'm so sorry. I thought warning your husband and moving ahead with charges would be enough to rein him in."

"Winston just doesn't know his own strength, and he's so stressed out right now." Elena's puffy, split lip impaired her speech.

"Pick that bastard up!" Kathy's eyes flashed as she put an arm around her friend.

"It's a separate case, unfortunately. Captain said to get him tomorrow. Do you want to file a restraining order?" Stevens asked Elena.

"And keep Winston from seeing his daughter? He'd kill me." Elena covered her mouth with a hand, blinking in distress. "I didn't mean that literally."

"Elena! You don't owe him shit. He's lost the privilege of being a parent!" He had left Kathy remonstrating with her friend, and now it was past time to get home, have dinner, and hold his wife.

The dogs greeted him, as did Kiet, and it wasn't long before he was walking through the house to Lei. She was stirring something on the stove, wearing a once-baggy T-shirt dress that now barely contained her. Her hair was twisted up in a knot speared by a chopstick. He pulled the chopstick out and growled kisses into the back of her neck, making her laugh.

"Didn't know if you'd make it home for dinner." She leaned back into him, turning her face for his kiss as he embraced her. A moment later she pushed away. "Gotta make sure the chili doesn't burn."

"Oh, my favorite of your two specialties."

Lei smacked him. "Shut up. I do three now. Remember those enchiladas I did not long ago? And, now that I'm home, I'm planning to diversify. Might challenge myself and do lasagna or something."

"A man can dream." Stevens turned, hands on hips. "Son! Time for dinner!"

After dinner, Kiet's bath, reading bedtime stories, and a little TV with Lei snuggled against him, Stevens took Lei to bed.

Making love to her at this stage was tender, awkward, funny, and still sexy as hell. He'd never get enough of her, round or slim, and their child between them made it all the sweeter.

The fragrance of night-blooming jasmine that Wayne had planted under their window wafted in on the evening breeze, cooling their bodies. Stevens propped himself on an elbow, spooned against her. He stroked the side of her belly. "Baby's quiet in there."

"Been quiet all day," she murmured. Her hair tickled his chin and he smoothed it aside, feeling a quiver of worry. Beneath his hand, her belly tightened, the silk of her skin covering muscle that had gone hard. His anxiety intensified as her breath shortened.

"Are you okay?"

"Just a little Braxton-Hicks. Been having these for a while now. Just my body getting in shape for the big event." Lei sounded sleepy and unconcerned.

Sure enough, the flesh beneath his hand went soft again. He continued to stroke, imagining touching their child's back. "You'll let me know if anything more gets going right away. Promise me."

"Worrywart. I've got this. I've been training like it's a marathon, and you know I can handle pain." That was so Lei, thinking of the birth as an athletic challenge. That explained why she'd been swimming almost every day after work and doing yoga and flexibility exercises at every opportunity.

He hoped he could handle his own shit when it came time. He'd delivered a baby while on duty one time in LA, right on the side of the road. Poor woman had been trying to take a cab to the hospital and hadn't made it. Fortunately, he'd taken a pretty comprehensive first aid course, though there really wasn't much to do but get ready to catch what was coming and hope for the best.

He'd never forget the sight of the woman's straining, red face as the baby's head crowned into view. The child had almost stuck there, but one more massive heave from the mother and a little boy had shot into his arms, slick and intensely alive.

An amazing experience. Watching his own child being born was bound to be even more so. Yeah, he could do this even if he was a sniveling coward, terrified of seeing Lei suffering, terrified of something going wrong.

He lowered himself to lie beside his wife, drawing her just a little closer against him.

STEVENS PICKED up his desk phone at work the next morning. "Captain, Mahoe and I are going out to Feast to pick up Winston Noriega on an assault and battery charge." He told her the situation with Elena. "I filed the paperwork on a prior charge, but it won't hurt to put him in jail over the weekend, make sure the wife has some breathing space. He's still our best suspect for the murder, too."

"I agree. Go for it." There was a note of vicious satisfaction in the captain's voice. "Hopefully he'll think twice about hitting his wife after a weekend in jail."

Stevens and Mahoe got on the road for Lahaina, calling for a backup unit to transport Noriega back to the station.

"I thought about what you said, LT." Mahoe's voice was subdued as they drove. Stevens glanced at his partner's face: the square jaw was set, the young man's dark eyes on the road. "You're right. I need to make some changes in my life. I need to get my own place, maybe with some other guys or something."

"And try asking out a few women," Stevens said. "You might be surprised at what they say."

"Iris in accounting is pretty cute." Mahoe stared out the window. "I'd need to go out with someone who understands the crazy hours we keep. I haven't been dating because I've been so focused on getting to detective."

"Well, watch out, or life can pass you by. If you get nothing else from this case, remember that."

Mahoe nodded.

Feast was still closed, but a staffer was polishing the brass fittings on the door when they drove up, the cruiser close behind.

Stevens showed his badge, and they were admitted into the dim interior. The restaurant smelled of cleaning products, wine, and frying garlic. The deep, rich colors of the walls and furnishings glowed as they walked through.

Winston Noriega was in the kitchen, searing a massive amount of garlic in a big frying pan. Flames licked up around it as he swirled the pan masterfully. Stevens waited until he set the garlic down, aware that a hot frying pan full of sizzling garlic could be quite a weapon. "Can you turn that off a moment, Chef?"

Noriega did so, heavy brow knit with irritation. "What is it now?"

"Winston Noriega, you're under arrest for the assault and battery of Elena Noriega," Stevens said. He gestured to Mahoe to cuff the chef.

"What the hell. That bitch!" Noriega turned to his assistant, an olive-complexioned reedy young man wearing a chef's hat. "Get my lawyer on the phone."

"Boss, I don't have the number," the kid quaked.

"In my office, top right-hand drawer. Have him meet me at the station."

Mahoe cuffed the chef, handing him over to the officers who'd followed them in.

"Take him back to holding at the station," Stevens told them. "I have a few more people I need to talk to here."

"Yes, sir." The officers accompanied the surly, muttering chef out to the cruiser.

Stevens pulled out his notepad and addressed the young man. “Where’s Sage Bukowski?”

“I don’t know. He was supposed to be in already.” The assistant’s Adam’s apple bobbed. “I gotta do like Chef said.” He darted for the office.

“Mahoe, cover that garlic. It’s giving me a headache.” Stevens looked around as the young man did so, putting a lid on the pan and making sure the overhead hood was turned all the way up. “I need to talk to Bukowski about that group he’s likely a part of. But in the meantime, let’s see if we can verify the report he gave Kathy about the people he saw go in and out of the walk-in.”

“Not many staffers around, though,” Mahoe said.

“Yeah, I guess since the restaurant’s closed, Chef didn’t have many employees working today. Why don’t you cruise through and see if you can find anyone else to question. I’ll talk to this guy here and then we’ll go to Bukowski’s.”

Mahoe nodded and set off. Stevens popped the door of the refrigerator, still barricaded with crime scene tape, and peered inside.

A low-level stench, of spoiling food and old blood, hit his nostrils. Thank God the massive appliance was still on and not at room temperature. He felt sorry for Noriega’s staff—cleaning it was going to be a bitch. Stevens headed for the office just as the assistant chef was exiting.

“I don’t believe we got yours in our first round of statements.” Stevens flashed the smile he used on new trainees to put them at ease. He gestured to the office. “Let’s go in here a minute. Tell me about yourself.” He held up his spiral pad and the stub of pencil.

“Not much to tell. Been working here six months. Name’s Felipe. Felipe Souza.” The man’s throat bobbed again. He was older than he’d at first seemed—at least mid-twenties.

“Thanks, Felipe. So what’s your role here? What do you do?”

“I was kitchen prep under François. Now I got promoted.”

Souza straightened his apron. A dull red stained his cheekbones. "I wanted to move up, but not this way."

"Were you working the night of the murder?"

"No, sir. I did stop by to pick up my paycheck that night, though, so a few people might have seen me."

"What time did you come by the office?" They were standing right outside it, so Stevens turned to look at the door of the refrigerator. "You have a clear line of sight from here. Did you see anyone entering or exiting?"

Souza tipped his chin up a little and shut his eyes as if remembering. "I got here about nine-thirty. We pick up paychecks in our individual locker boxes. Elena puts them in there so we can get them anytime." He gestured to the row of small steel lockers lining the wall beneath the window into the office. "I don't remember looking over there. I just came in and went out."

"Who might have seen you?"

"Debbie, the hostess. She said hi."

"Thanks. Anything else you think might be important to the investigation? Anything at all."

"I overheard Kitty and François arguing. They were in the pantry." He gestured to a niche-like alcove off the main kitchen. "Things were calming down after the rush. Chef was in the office. I could see his outline inside even with the blinds down. I couldn't help noticing them over there." He pointed to the alcove as his small dark eyes shifted nervously. "Kitty was begging him not to break up with her. Said he had a good thing going; they were making money, and he'd be crazy to quit their partnership."

Stevens's pulse picked up. "And what was Métier saying?"

"He was speaking low, so he was harder to hear—she was pretty loud—but I thought he said he didn't give a shit, that he was done with her."

"Did you ever hear anything about marriage? A proposal or a ring?"

"Hell no. He was holding her by the arms, trying to keep her hands off him."

Stevens flashed to the DNA under Métier's nails. It was probably Summers's. "Overhear anything else?"

"Métier noticed me and told her to shut up. Then they were both staring at me. I grabbed my check and left."

"Thanks. You've been very helpful." He noted the young man's contact information and bade him goodbye.

Mahoe returned.

"See anyone else?" Stevens asked.

"I got a statement from the exterior cleaner guy. Nothing of interest."

"Well, I just got a little lucky. Let's get over to Bukowski's and hit him up about that group trust thing." They headed out. On the way to Sage Bukowski's address, Stevens filled Mahoe in on the statement from Souza.

"I knew there was something off about that porn star," Mahoe said.

"Gotta agree with you there. Why don't you contact Dispatch, and we'll have her picked up for an interview while we do this one? Then we can pound out interviews with both Noriega and Summers at the station."

Mahoe picked up the radio and called it in.

The GPS guided them to a run-down aqua building deep in the shade of several huge mango trees. The fruity smell of fallen mangoes dotting the base of the tree was thick in Stevens's nostrils as he and Mahoe climbed the exterior stairs, footsteps ringing on metal treads.

"Sage Bukowski! Maui Police Department," Mahoe called as he rapped on the door.

No answer.

A pair of better-quality Reef slippers rested on the plain rubber mat, and Mahoe pointed down to a plain white Ford with pipe racks, a couple of kite-boards and windsurfers strapped onto them.

"His truck's in the lot. I checked his vehicle description and plate number before coming here."

They turned back to face the sun-faded turquoise door.

"Bukowski! We know you're in there. Open up. Maui Police Department." Stevens pounded this time. In the next apartment over, the door opened.

"What's going on?" A pretty young woman in a tank top and shorts poked her head out the door to peer at them.

"Police business," Mahoe said. She pouted and withdrew into her apartment.

"Try his phone," Stevens said. Mahoe flipped through his notebook and plugged in a number while Stevens tried to peek between the blinds.

They were rotated shut, but not all the way. He could see a tipped over chair and a shattered lamp on the floor through a narrow slice of view.

"We have a situation in there," Stevens told Mahoe with a sinking feeling in the pit of his stomach. They heard the distant ringing of Bukowski's phone inside the apartment. "Exigent circumstances." Stevens tried the door. It opened and swung inward with an unsettling creak.

CHAPTER FIFTEEN

Stevens

STEVENS AND MAHOE BOTH PULLED their weapons in the doorway of Bukowski's apartment. Stevens stepped in first, walking light on the balls of his feet into the living room. Signs of a struggle showed in the broken lamp and upended chair. He gestured to the hall on the other side of the attached kitchen, and Mahoe went ahead first. A bathroom and a bedroom opened off a short hall, and Mahoe poked his head into the bathroom.

"Clear," he said.

A metallic, potent smell wafting from the bedroom told Stevens what he'd see when he looked inside.

The room was simply furnished with a queen size bed, dresser, desk, and laundry hamper. Blood spatter decorated the walls in arcs of red droplets, leading the eye to the body on the bed.

Sage Bukowski lay in a pool of black blood that had soaked into the bedding. He was sprawled on the bed facedown, hanging partway off the end, as if he'd fallen there while running to escape. His face was turned to the side, eyes open, and he wore nothing but a pair of board shorts soaked with blood.

He'd been stabbed so many times that the killing blow was going to be tough to determine, but exsanguination was the ultimate result. As they stared at the gruesome sight, a large, iridescent fly drifted casually over to land on the victim's open eye.

Stevens leaned forward to inspect the body and swished it away. "Amazing how flies always manage to get in so quickly. From the color of the blood, I'm guessing this happened yesterday."

Mahoe didn't respond, and Stevens glanced at his young partner. His brown complexion had yellowed.

"Yeah. Looks like it." Mahoe gulped a couple of times. "I'll go get the barrier tape and call for Dr. G and backup." He fled.

Stevens stepped carefully over the blood trace on the worn carpet to lean closely over the body, counting the stab wounds. He lost track at twenty-two. The murder weapon, another of those expensive chef's knives, protruded from Bukowski's back, elevated and clearly stuck in a rib, protruding at an almost jaunty angle.

Unlike the almost surgical precision of the Métier killing, rage was written all over this crime scene. This was what he'd have expected from someone with Chef Noriega's temper—but why would the chef kill Bukowski? Because of the blog? Perhaps Bukowski had known more than he'd told them about Métier's murder?

Stevens straightened up, reflexively shooing the fly again. He surveyed the room carefully from his position near the body. The blood spatter was extensive, and no attempt had been made to hide or clean up the crime.

He slipped on a pair of gloves and, stepping carefully to avoid the blood on the carpet, moved to the side of the bed, his gaze drifting over the entire corpse.

One of Bukowski's hands was clenched in the covers. Near it were some smears, standing out because of their straight lines. Stevens circled again, bending to look down at them.

From above, they looked a whole lot like a *K*.

"Kitty Summers?" Stevens looked over at Sage Bukowski's slack face, feeling a pang at how young and handsome he'd been. Funny and smart, too. The kid had had a lot of potential. "Were you trying to tell us something?"

He straightened up and did a long, slow survey of the room, his gaze stopping at a woman's gold bangle bracelet lying on the carpet beside the bed.

Wasn't Bukowski gay?

Stevens pulled a pair of gloves out of his pocket, padded carefully over, and picked up the bracelet in his gloved fingers, peering inside for an inscription. *Happy birthday, Kitty! Love, Mom and Dad* twined around the inside in delicate script.

"Mahoe! Bring my kit!" Stevens yelled.

"Doc's on his way. I'm on it, boss!" Stevens heard the clatter of the young man's feet on the stairs for a second time as he ran to obey.

A few minutes later, they were both combing through the room, dropping markers at spots to take blood samples from later, and Mahoe was handling himself well by keeping focused on the task. Backup arrived, and Stevens set them to securing the area and canvassing the rest of the building for information on who might have visited Bukowski—this murder couldn't have been quiet.

He also called in an urgent APB on Kitty Summers.

"So, didn't Kathy interview Bukowski yesterday?" Mahoe asked, picking up a hair near the body with a pair of tweezers and sliding it into a small evidence bag.

"Must have happened that evening." Stevens photographed the bloody markings near the man's hand. He frowned as he shot the hand, the bunched covers, the wobbly *K* done in blood. How would the dying man have had the presence of mind to pull that off?

Dr. Gregory arrived with Dr. Tanaka. Today's shirt was purple with cartoon rainbows. Stevens felt a smile tug at his mouth in spite of the circumstances. "Where do you find those atrocities, Dr. G?"

The doc's eyes swept the room. "eBay, mostly," he said absently, scanning the scene. He approached the body. "Someone wanted this guy good and dead. Went all Dexter on his ass."

"Not pretty. Everything's pointing to a porn star waitress he worked with at Feast. But why is another story." Stevens filled the medical examiner in as both he and Tanaka moved forward to investigate. "I haven't touched him. There was plenty to keep us busy just looking around the room here."

"Got a little tissue under his nails." Dr. G picked up one of the hands, shining a penlight on the fingertips. "Maybe he got a sample of the killer for us."

Tanaka, her elegant form graceful as a dancer's, bent and opened a kit. She slid on plastic bags to cover the hands. "We'll pull what we find and have it sent to Oahu for DNA testing."

"There wasn't any useful trace on the other body. Let's hope we get lucky with this one," Stevens said. "Just doing a visual, what do you think time of death was?"

"Sometime yesterday evening or later." Dr. Gregory dropped the man's arm. "Rigor is almost gone. Happens faster in this heat."

The ME and his assistant dusted the handle of the murder weapon for prints. Dr. G removed it with a grunt. "Stuck in the bone."

He handed it to Stevens, who bagged it. Dr. G rolled the body with Tanaka's help to check liver temp. Stevens scanned the front of the body. "Several of these strokes went all the way through."

"Like your other body," Dr. Gregory said. The ME continued to prep the body for transport as Stevens and Mahoe did a quick search of the room.

The radio on Mahoe's hip crackled to life, apprising them that Kitty Summers had been picked up at her apartment.

Stevens straightened up from looking under the bed, arching with his fists on his lower back to stretch his spine. A brief flash of

Lei doing the same thing, the curve of her belly echoing the arc of her back, distracted him. *Protect them, please, God. Don't let anything go wrong.* "Nothing more this scene can tell us at the moment. Let's go grill Summers and Noriega."

CHEF NORIEGA WAS PACING back and forth in the interview room when they arrived. Keone Chapman, his lawyer, set down the digital tablet he'd been working on and rose to his feet.

"You took long enough," he greeted Stevens and Mahoe. "I was going to lodge a complaint in another five minutes."

Stevens ignored this as Mahoe turned on the recording equipment and Mirandized the chef after he sat down at the table. Stevens studied the man, his gaze wandering over the powerfully built chef with his air of barely leashed aggression.

Noriega had dark circles under his eyes, and the knuckles of his right hand were bruised and scuffed. He'd hurt his hand beating his wife. Anger tightened Stevens's gut.

"Where were you last night?"

"At the restaurant," Noriega said.

"Can anyone verify that?"

The chef just snorted. "I was doing some reduction sauces for when we're open again. I had two helpers." He gave names and Stevens noted them.

"What is your relationship with Sage Bukowski?"

"Sage?" The chef's eyebrows lifted, intelligent brown eyes going wide. "What's he got to do with anything?"

"Just answer the question," Mahoe barked.

"He's an okay runner and busser. Does his shifts as scheduled. Gay, and a gossip. Thought he might be the blogger, but I didn't have any proof or I'd have fired the guy," Noriega said.

Stevens resumed the thread. "So when did you get off work and go home last night?"

"I got done at nine and went home. I went straight home last night as soon as the kitchen closed down."

"So you could beat your wife?" Stevens locked eyes with Noriega in a hostile stare.

"No comment," Keone Chapman answered for his client.

"What are you holding me here for?" Noriega snapped.

"Assault and battery."

"Elena won't press charges."

"She doesn't have to. We're bringing them against you for her."

"I want to see the arrest warrant," Chapman said.

"It's pending. We're holding you until your arraignment Monday, when you can see about bail."

Stevens rose. They weren't getting anything more out of Noriega with Chapman muzzling him, and if he'd been at Feast all evening, he couldn't have killed Bukowski. Elena had already told Stevens that Noriega had come home at nine-fifteen p.m., when their fight had begun. "Have a nice weekend."

He left Chapman trying to soothe the enraged chef.

Stevens poked his head into the observation room, where Captain Omura was tapping on her phone. "That was brief and not amazing," Omura said.

"Sorry, Captain, but he's got an alibi. We need to check it, verify the trace from the room and the body. That's what will win this case."

"Well, bring in the porn star, then." She made a shooing motion.

Stevens turned to Mahoe. "Book Noriega into jail and put Summers in the interview room."

"You got it, LT." The young detective hurried off.

They were about to close this case, and Stevens needed to be at the top of his game. He headed for the break room and found it mercifully empty. He poured himself a cup of thick coffee and took a couple of ibuprofen—the headache was back.

Stevens shut the door of the break room and did some stretches, working the muscles of his side and back, where his gunshot injury had left stiffness and scar tissue. He hung his head upside down for a few minutes to get circulation going, a post-traumatic brain injury strategy his doctor had suggested to increase alertness. Fifty jumping jacks and another fifty push-ups later, he felt ready for the next interview.

Kitty Summers was already seated with her lawyer, Davida Fuller, a strong litigator. The athletic attorney looked stylish in a black jumpsuit with a massive turquoise necklace. She stood as he entered, reaching out to shake his hand in an overly hard grip. "Lieutenant Stevens."

"Ms. Fuller. Nice to see you again," Stevens lied. "Detective Mahoe, have you apprised Ms. Summers of her rights?"

"I have, Lieutenant."

Stevens checked that the recording equipment was on, then, waded in. "So. Kitty. A lot has happened since we met you in the victim's apartment a few days ago."

"Really? What kind of a lot?" Kitty blinked wide blue eyes. She wore a simple chambray sundress and little makeup, going for an innocent look, but no bra—those round, pointed tits couldn't be real. "I was just minding my own business when your officers busted into my apartment and brought me here . . . for what?"

Stevens ignored that. "Tell us, for the record, about your relationship with François Métier."

"We were lovers. Going to be more than lovers." Kitty eyed Stevens defiantly. "He was going to ask me to marry him." Summers's bravado was unconvincing.

"And you knew this—how?" Stevens leaned forward.

"I saw the ring. On the day he was killed, actually. I knew he was just waiting for the right moment to ask me."

"Ah. Are you sure it was you he was getting ready to ask?"

Summers flushed and glanced at Fuller. "Of course it was me."

"Interesting. Because we have information from reliable

sources that Métier had his heart set on someone else and was breaking up with you—in spite of your mutually lucrative porn business."

"You don't have to answer," Fuller told Summers. "Just say 'no comment.' They have to prove their case with evidence."

Stevens pressed on. "Where were you yesterday evening?"

"At work." Kitty fiddled with a charm bracelet on her wrist.

"I thought the restaurant was shut down?"

"My other job. Video production."

Stevens felt Mahoe give a little jerk beside him. He'd give him a lecture later about reacting visibly to a suspect's disclosures.

"Acting or producing?" Stevens said.

"Both. We did some of both yesterday."

"Seems like you were really brokenhearted over Métier's death," Mahoe said. "Must have been tough to get back in the saddle with another man so soon. In a manner of speaking."

Fuller frowned at Mahoe. "Your sarcastic attitude does you no credit."

"The videos are work," Summers snapped. "Not a relationship. Not like with François."

"So who were you with? And during what hours?"

Stevens jotted down the names and times. Summers could have had time to go stab Bukowski. "So how well did you know Sage Bukowski?"

"Sage?" Kitty raised her brows. "Not well. He's that busboy and food runner with the dreads, right?"

Stevens narrowed his eyes. "He's the blogger who wrote about Feast. And he certainly knew a lot about you."

Summers shrugged. "Oh, he was the blogger? I enjoyed following it. And if he called me a porn star now and again on the blog…Well, it's true." She examined her nails.

"So you two never had a problem with each other?"

"No."

"So what was your gold bracelet doing near his bed?"

Summers looked up, completely blank. "What?"

"Show us this item," Fuller demanded. "And why were you in Sage Bukowski's place, anyway?"

"Because we found him murdered today," Stevens said. "With the same kind of weapon that was used on Métier." Both women gasped. Stevens gestured to Mahoe. "Bring the bracelet and photos in from evidence, please."

"Right away, LT." Mahoe left.

Stevens stared at the two women, waiting for one of them to attempt an explanation. The bracelet, so conveniently inscribed, seemed like overkill paired with a K written in blood, but this interview was the only place to start to find answers—and as he'd told Mahoe, most times the obvious was the obvious.

"I didn't do anything." Summers lifted her hands in a "surrender" gesture. "I barely knew the guy. I swear."

"So why did he spell out the letter 'K' in blood on his sheets?"

The color drained from Summers's face. She looked ready to keel over. Davida Fuller grasped the woman firmly by the shoulder. "I'm directing my client not to answer any more questions. This interview is over."

"We're done when I say we're done," Stevens said. "Kitty Summers, you're under arrest for the murders of François Métier and Sage Bukowski. You had the means, motive, and opportunity to do these murders."

"Circumstantial," Fuller argued. "The bracelet could have been planted."

"And the victim writing your client's initial in blood?"

Silence from Fuller, then: "Lots of names begin with 'K.' And it could have been done postmortem, by another party."

"I didn't do it!" Kitty shrieked. She covered her face and began to sob. "Why would I kill either of them?"

"We can think of lots of reasons," Stevens said. The door opened, admitting Mahoe. The junior detective tipped the bracelet out of its evidence bag onto the table, and it spun in a little circle before coming to rest.

"I left that bracelet in my locker at work and I haven't seen it in days. I have no idea how Sage Bukowski had it." She hunched over, covering her face again. "I can't believe this is happening."

"Where were you last night? Take us through it step-by-step. Again." Stevens was relentless. Summers was an actress, after all, and histrionics were bound to be part of her repertoire. The scene had looked staged to him, but until he had a way to rule Summers out, he had to follow the evidence.

Fuller blocked his further questions doggedly, and finally he directed Mahoe to put Summers through the booking process into the county jail until her arraignment.

"Get me out of here!" Summers wept to Fuller as Mahoe put cuffs on her and led her out by an elbow. "Please, do something."

"You'll be fine. We'll get you out on Monday," Fuller assured her. Mahoe shut the door, and the sounds of her sobs were cut off.

Stevens was alone with Fuller. The attorney narrowed her hazel gaze at him. "Kitty is a lot of things, but she's not a killer. I'll tear a hole in your case so wide you could drive a Mack truck through it."

Stevens leaned back, widening his chest and crossing his arms so that his muscles bulked up. Fuller mirrored his posture, and damn if she didn't have some fine arms. He felt a reluctant smile tug up one side of his mouth—Fuller was earning his respect.

"That's between you and the DA, Ms. Fuller. I like Summers for it. As I said: means and motive on Métier. A witness saw her begging him not to break up with her, and another witness saw them go into the walk-in. She could easily have stuck him in the ribs from behind and wiped the handle. Sage Bukowski, now, that was a brutal slaying. Lotta rage behind it, total loss of control. Good luck getting her out of this." He stood, picking up his notebook. "See you in court."

"Yes, you will." Fuller followed him out, walking to the front of the building as he headed upstairs to his office.

Kathy was at her computer, looking serious. A huge bouquet of roses took up one corner of her desk.

"Whoa." Stevens leaned over for a sniff. "Got an admirer?"

"Is that so strange?" Kathy snapped.

"Not at all." Stevens continued to his desk. "Just haven't seen such a big 'morning after' bouquet like that on your desk before."

"Wasn't a morning after," she muttered. "We haven't even kissed."

Stevens booted up his computer. "Forget I said anything. I'm just putting my foot in it. You deserve some fun and happiness."

"Glad you think so. Since it's your brother who sent the roses."

Stevens turned to fully face Kathy. Her dark blue eyes blazed at him from across the space between the desks. "Yeah. Jared sent the flowers. We're dating and it's not going away. Get used to it."

Words jostled behind his teeth, but Stevens bit them all back.

There was nothing he could say that would go over well. Truth was, he'd said his piece to Jared. If his brother had made a move and Kathy liked him, great. And if Jared broke her heart and made things tougher in his office . . .

"Hey, that's great." Stevens infused his tone with warmth. "Jared's a good guy. And if he doesn't treat you right, I'll kick his ass."

Kathy smiled. "You won't have to. I can do my own ass-kicking."

CHAPTER SIXTEEN

WAYNE

Wayne

WAYNE DROVE OUT TO TEO'S farm the following day, noticing the increasingly gusty wind and gathering clouds. That tropical depression was definitely on its way.

His friend had a crew out harvesting. Workers in wide hats and long sleeves bent over, weeding and harvesting though a sprawling patch of summer squash, the plants' palmate leaves flecked with white like paint.

"Hey." Teo pushed his ball cap up and wiped his gleaming forehead with his arm, leaving a streak of iron-rich red dirt. "Come to see what I've got?"

"Yeah. Looks like squash. I can make that work."

"For starters. Follow me."

Wayne had to stretch his legs to keep up with the shorter man as he moved rapidly down the heavily mulched path between rows. "So you doing okay with Feast not ordering anymore?"

"Yeah. I picked up one of those farm-to-table grocery delivery box services," Teo said over his shoulder. "They're coming by every time I call and taking all I give them."

"Nice. Such a cool way for people to get the best produce coming right to their homes. We get a lot of fruit a couple times a year out at our place; wonder if they'd be interested in picking up from us? We can only eat so many avocados and oranges."

"Sure. I'll give you the number."

Teo led Wayne to the section devoted to string beans. "Got some nice multicolor beans ready. They look good in a chilled salad."

"I'm all over it." Wayne shook open his canvas harvesting bag and Teo helped fill it.

"Your son-in-law never contacted me," Teo said.

"Really? I told him you'd be a good person to talk to."

"Well, I'm worried about my contact at Feast, Felipe Souza. I wouldn't call him a friend, but I know him fairly well, and the kid is really rattled by what's happening over there." Teo's strong brown hands moved at twice the speed Wayne's did, reaching in to pluck yellow, purple, and green string bean pods from among the vines. "There's been another body?"

"Yeah. Sage Bukowski. My son-in-law told me." Stevens had called him briefly with that update to the case. "He was a busboy at the restaurant." Wayne shook his bag to help the beans settle further in, enjoying the familiar tug of pleasure that the rich smells of earth and growing things brought him. He had a small plot going at the house, but since starting his restaurant, he hadn't had time to develop it any further. He kept it planted in lettuce and tomatoes for home use.

Ellen liked to garden, too. Often when she came over, she'd go out and weed, water, or harvest. He smiled, remembering her slender figure, sun bright on silver-blond hair as she sprayed the plants with a hose and turned to laugh at something he'd said. He wasn't sure when their friendship had begun to change, and he wasn't sure if his growing feelings were reciprocated. But she'd been the one to keep hold of his hand at dinner the other night…

Teo's voice pulled him back to the present. "Well, Felipe knew

Sage pretty well. Sometimes Bukowski would come with him to pick up vegetables for the restaurant, and they were tight, from what I could tell."

"Probably really upsetting to hear his friend had been murdered," Wayne said. The hot sun on his head made him wish he'd remembered a hat.

"It's more than that. I think Souza's hiding something. Maybe he knows something about who did it," Teo said.

This caught Wayne's attention fully. He glanced at his friend's sun-seamed face, shaded by the bill of his worn hat. "What makes you think so?"

"He's always been the one to keep me up to speed on what's happening over at that restaurant. Yesterday he came by. Chef wanted some fresh garlic, which I had. But Felipe was just not right. Totally shaky. Seemed like he couldn't even remember his own name."

"Huh." They'd reached the end of the row and switched to the next one as Wayne filled his second bag. "I'll call Stevens and remind him to contact you and pass this on."

"Yeah. Felipe's a good kid."

"You know, when was this?" Wayne realized he'd heard about the second murder late in the evening, and from what he could tell, the body hadn't been discovered until yesterday afternoon.

"Yesterday. But before lunch."

"Thanks for telling me."

This meant Souza could have seen the body before it was discovered, or known something about the murder—or maybe he was upset about something else entirely. "I'll call Stevens as soon as we're done picking."

Wayne ended up with a bag of summer squash, some of the remaining fresh garlic, and a big haul of beans. He lifted a hand in thanks to Teo as he headed to his truck, speed dialing Stevens.

"Hey, Wayne. What's going on?" Stevens sounded distracted, as he often did when Wayne contacted him at work.

"Remember I told you about my friend Teo Benitez, the farmer?"

"Uh—yeah."

"Well, he told me hasn't heard from you yet."

"We have to prioritize our interviews, and I think we covered the information he might have had another way."

"Not what he said to me about Felipe Souza this morning." Wayne told his son-in-law what the farmer had described. "And if Teo was right about the time, the young man was all shaken up *before* the body was found."

Wayne knew he had Stevens's full attention by the sharpening of his voice. "We have someone in custody for the murder, but we could definitely use more information of any kind. I'll follow up with your friend right away. Thanks for the tip."

"Good. Glad I could help." Wayne hung up and got into his truck after stowing his haul. On the way to his restaurant, he called Lei. He'd been checking up on her at least once a day. "Hey, Sweets," he said when she picked up.

"Hi, Dad." She sounded cheerful. "Whatcha doing? And before you ask, nothing's happening."

"Oh, good. Too soon, anyway." Wayne throttled back behind a slow-moving rental whose driver was rubbernecking for a view of whales in the foamy, wind-whipped ocean. "I'm just heading back from Teo's farm with a great selection for the menu. Want me to bring something home for you guys?"

"Always. What you got?"

"Multicolored green beans that I'm making into a chilled salad. Garlic, summer squash."

"Dad, you know I love anything I don't have to cook. Ooh." She grunted. "Baby just gave me a nasty kick. Good to have some movement, though. He's been really quiet the last day or so."

"I gotta tell you." Wayne ran his free hand through his hair, smoothing it back from his forehead. "I'll be glad when this part is over and the kid is out with the rest of us. This waiting is really getting to me."

"You and me both, Dad. Well, I'll look forward to whatever you bring home. I'm just stashing the new hurricane supplies. Did you hear anything more about it on the weather report?"

"Good news. It's been downgraded to a tropical depression." Wayne navigated the last stoplight in Kahului and turned right onto the Hana Highway, headed for the restaurant. "Supposed to hit later on. A lot of wind and rain at this point, but nothing too serious. Seems like the weather's already begun, though."

"No hurricane is good news. Well, now we're stocked up for this season, anyway. Gave me something to do since I'm not remodeling the office into a nursery."

"You're never short on things to do, Sweets. See you tonight." He ended the call and said a prayer that things continued well with her and the baby.

Lei

Lei finished stacking the last of the square gallon jugs in the shed with the rest of the hurricane supplies, a familiar ache tightening her lower back as she hefted the heavy plastic containers. She was relieved that the hurricane had been downgraded, but a little skeptical—it was smart to be as prepared as possible.

She threw the ball for Conan, Keiki leaning against her leg. The younger male Rottie still needed a good deal of exercise to settle during the day, but just the motion of throwing the ball set off a series of twinges through her abdomen.

"I need to get into the ocean. I'm so uncomfortable today," Lei told the dogs as she headed into the house. She was glad to have them there to talk to during the day now that she was home. The breathlessness was gone, but that symptom had been replaced by a constant sense of heavy pressure down below, and she wasn't sure which was worse.

She'd had a mellow morning, taking Kiet to school and restocking the hurricane supplies. Now there was another chore to do, one that gave her a mix of apprehension and excitement: packing her hospital bags.

She'd already washed the linens and set up Kiet's old wooden cradle in the living room. The beautifully carved cradle was something Kiet's birth mother, Anchara, had left him—and it felt good to think of it holding another baby. Anchara was an invisible sweet ghost Lei had made peace with by including her frequently in talks with Kiet and reminders like the cradle.

Relieved to be in the coolness of the house, she called Marcella as she filled a glass of water and went to the office, where she'd stashed the infant and birth supplies.

"Hey, girlfriend," her friend said jauntily. "All ready for the big day?"

"Getting there. I guess. If anyone can ever be ready for a thing like this." Lei stood over the pile of gifts from the baby shower at the station. She knelt and extricated the new diaper bag, the phone to her ear. "Getting our stuff packed, just in case."

"Been feeling okay?" A note of concern in Marcella's voice. "Any spotting? Contractions?"

"Yeah, a little of both, but since I'm a first timer, I don't really know what to expect. I think everything's fine." She traced the curve of her belly. "The baby has been quiet the last few days."

"When's your next wellness checkup?"

"Monday. Still three weeks until the due date."

"Well, keep me posted. Jonas can't wait to meet his baby cousin." At some point in their friendship with each other and Sophie Ang, they'd decided they'd be unofficial sisters since they were all only children. The arrival of Marcella's baby, Jonas, nine months before had drawn the three of them closer, but it wasn't Sophie that Lei called at times like these—it was Marcella, already married and a mother. Sophie would be nervous as hell talking about these issues.

They chatted about Marcella's FBI work as Lei sorted the green and yellow baby clothes she'd washed, the tiny diapers, a bottle and formula in case of breastfeeding problems, a rubber pad for changing. Her own bag for the hospital was a gym duffel, and she filled it with changes of clothes for herself and Stevens, socks, more cloths, and a rubber pad, ear syringe, scissors, a scented candle, and an older iPod loaded with soothing music.

Lei wrapped up the call. "That tropical depression is moving in, and I need to get to the beach before the weather shuts it down. I'm so hot and sore today."

"Sounds good. Let me know as soon as things get going. I want to be on a plane to come support you."

"Thanks, Marcella." A wave of gratitude swept over Lei as she ended the call—she had wonderful friends. She'd come such a long way from the isolated, damaged woman she'd been nine years ago.

"Bags are packed," Lei told Keiki, who'd followed her to the doorway of the office. Keiki hated storms, and she seemed to be able to sense the change in barometric pressure. Her warm brown eyes tracked Lei anxiously as she pulled herself up from the floor with the aid of the office chair. "Off to the beach."

Ho`okipa was too rough for swimming today, so she drove on by. The wind smacked Lei's truck, making it shimmy a bit, as she drove past the famous beach break. Palm trees bent and whipped in the wind, and storm clouds boiled low on the horizon. Hardy surfers, undaunted, were working the good-sized surf churned up by the approaching storm. Maybe this wasn't the best idea, the water was sure to be rough—but her body craved the weightlessness of floating.

Lei parked at Baldwin Beach Park a few miles farther down the road. That long stretch of beach had a sheltered cove at one end, which she enjoyed now that she was so ungainly. She let the

Rottweilers out of the back of her truck on their leashes. She'd already changed into her bikini with her flowered muumuu on over it, so she headed straight for the water.

The ocean was an inviting cool aqua in spite of the overcast, threatening conditions as she walked through the sand to the calm bay where she liked to swim at one end of the beach. The place was almost deserted due to the storm, so in spite of the leash law, she let the dogs off and threw a stick for them to tire them out, finally tying them up to a large hunk of coral.

Her aching, uncomfortable body became weightless, supported by the salty ocean, and the relief made her groan with pleasure. Lei lifted her feet off the bottom and simply floated for long moments, her belly a mound above the surface, arms spread, her face to the cloudy sky as she relished the sense of no pressure anywhere on her overtaxed body.

The wind batted at her, spattering a little whitewater into her mouth. That storm was increasing. Sputtering, she turned over and began the series of laps she usually did. Her belly might slow her down, but her arms and legs were still strong. She churned along, getting her heart rate up but supported by the cool water.

Lei hadn't been swimming long, her arms churning and legs kicking, when a tremendous cramp squeezed her midsection, stealing her breath.

Unable to do anything but gasp, Lei instinctively rolled onto her back to keep her face out of the water, her arms clasping an abdomen that had gone steel hard. Waves splashed into her open, panting mouth as she tried to stay upright and get through the unexpected contraction, but it didn't let up in a few seconds like earlier ones had.

This one went on and on.

Lei blew shallow breaths, contorted around the spasming muscles. This couldn't be the real thing; it was too soon—but she'd never felt anything like this before. Her legs involuntarily drew up against her belly. She tried to straighten them, to feel for the bottom with her feet. Extending her legs increased the pain, but she persisted—and still couldn't find it.

Don't panic. Just float. You couldn't sink right now if you tried. Get through this and then swim to the beach. Just relax. Fighting it will make it worse.

The voice in her head spoke in Tiare's authoritative tones, calming her. Lei shut her eyes and just floated, her arms and legs relaxing as she kept her face above the water.

The endless cramp finally let go. She lifted her head to see that she'd swept out considerably from the beach. Her gaze found the yellow lifeguard tower. She only had to wave for help for it to come to her—but she didn't want that drama. She wasn't in trouble yet. This was no problem. She swam farther than this every day.

Lei rolled over and went into a gentle breaststroke, worried she'd set off another contraction with too much vigorous activity. She'd almost made it to the beach when the next one hit, a breath-stealing, powerful squeeze that wrung a gasp from her. Fortunately, her feet were touching the ground, and she moved them gently along the sand bottom as she did her Lamaze breathing, arms moving in slow strokes.

The contraction eventually let go. She hadn't moved too far out this time, and she gently swam the remaining distance to shore.

A sense of urgency to get home filled Lei, but she tried to think it through. Everyone said first babies took forever. There was no emergency here. Still, it would be good to be safe in her home, and maybe the contractions would back off if she rested.

She staggered up the beach, wobbly from the extremity of only two of the cramps. Retrieving the dogs, she made it to the truck before the next one hit.

This time she could see what the contraction was doing to her body as she clung, panting, to the open tailgate. Her belly changed shape, becoming almost triangular, ridges of powerful muscle doing their job and drawing her abdomen into a focused peak. The dogs jumped into the truck bed as Lei clung to the vehicle. She hung her head between her arms, leaning forward and breathing through it until, a full minute later by her count, the vise finally loosened.

"Holy crap. That's intense," Lei panted, straightening up to look at the dogs' worried faces as they peered down at her. "But this is a first baby. I'm sure we have plenty of time."

Lei slammed the tailgate and got in the vehicle. She'd just drive home slowly. She could do this.

She got on the road for Haiku, fairly empty of traffic due to the storm, which had now decided to dump buckets of rain. With her windshield wipers flapping at full speed, Lei put in her Bluetooth and called Stevens. He didn't answer, and she wasn't ready to leave him a message until she talked to her labor coach. She ended the call and rang Tiare.

"Hey, girl." Tiare's mellow alto voice immediately calmed Lei's jangled nerves.

"Hey. Can you meet me at the house? I think I'm in labor."

"What?" Tiare's voice sharpened. "Sure it's not just Braxton-Hicks?"

"No." Lei didn't have time to explain as another contraction grabbed her in its fierce fist. She panted, emitting an involuntary moan as she put her blinker on and pulled over onto the grassy shoulder.

Lei leaned her head on the steering wheel, steeling herself and holding her breath instinctively.

"Don't grit your teeth. That sends a message to your autonomic nervous system that you're in distress, which only makes you tighten up more—which makes it hurt more. Open your mouth slightly. Put the tip of your tongue on the roof of your mouth then keep your jaw loose. Breathe in through the nose, out through the mouth, nice and slow. Focus on counting to keep your mind calm." Tiare's strong voice coached Lei through it. Finally she got on the road again.

"This is so much more intense than I thought." Tears prickled Lei's eyelids. "I'm scared."

"You're going to be fine. Now go lie down. More activity could get things going more, and this is early. It might just be false labor."

Lei couldn't bring herself to tell Tiare she was driving home from the beach. "Okay."

"I'll be over in half an hour or so. I just have to wrap up some things here at work." Tiare ended the call.

The drive from the beach to Haiku usually took twenty minutes, but with the rain, whipping wind, and four contractions that Lei had to pull over for, the drive seemed endless by the time she finally made it through the gate.

Relief to be home warred with worry about what was happening as she let the dogs out and gave them fresh water.

A hot shower. Now, that would feel good.

Their shower was oversized, and she had a small plastic bench in there already because she'd enjoyed sitting to wash as her pregnancy progressed. Now that bench was perfect to cling to, hot water pouring down her back, as she endured another contraction.

They did not seem to be slowing down, instead lasting longer as she took to counting the seconds—well past a minute in duration.

It was okay that this was happening. She was fine. Healthy and strong. The baby was only three weeks early and would be fine, too. It would be okay if this was it. She could do this. Tiare would be here soon. There was no room in her mind or her body for any but these simple thoughts.

Getting out of the shower, Lei donned the flowered muumuu she wore in the house and called Michael's cell. It went immediately to voice mail—he must still have it off—but it was time to leave a message.

"Honey, I'm in labor. I think it's the real thing. Tiare's on her way over. Don't worry. I'm okay." Tears started again. She wasn't okay. She was scared and already overwhelmed. "I just thought you should know. Call me."

She called Marcella and left a similar message. And then she staggered into the bedroom and fell onto the bed, squeezed by the strongest contraction yet.

CHAPTER SEVENTEEN

Stevens

STEVENS EYED THE FILIPINO FARMER as he shook Teo Benitez's hand, noticing the hornlike quality of the man's calluses. Benitez was sensibly dressed in baggy canvas cargo pants, a long-sleeved cotton shirt, and a worn logo cap. His seamed face was the color of well-rubbed oak, and he seemed such a part of his farm that he might have grown there among the lush lettuces where they stood.

"Thanks for taking the time to talk to me. I understand from Wayne that you have some information you think might be helpful in solving the cases involving Feast."

"I do. Come where we can sit down." Benitez led Stevens down the row of lettuce and across to a prefabricated shed with an additional stretch of roof added to form a shaded area. A picnic table with built-in benches provided a break area. They sat. Benitez picked up a battered Thermos, poured coffee into the lid. "Coffee? I can find a cup somewhere . . . "

"No thanks." A particularly strong gust of wind hit them, rattling the shelter. "Seems like the weather's coming in." Stevens took out his trusty spiral pad.

"Yeah. That tropical depression is supposed to hit this afternoon. We're harvesting everything we can—the wind and rain is bound to beat down the plants." Benitez drank from the metal cup, wiped his mouth. "Something's off with my contact at Feast. Felipe Souza."

"Wayne told me you were concerned about his behavior. Tell me more."

"He was just off. Staring into space. Had the shakes. Didn't respond when I called his name." Benitez described Souza's behavior on the day of Bukowski's murder. "When I heard about another guy at Feast getting killed, I thought he might know something about it. Would explain why he was so upset."

"Thanks." Stevens noted the comments in his pad. "How long have you known Souza?"

"Six months? Maybe a year? He's not from here."

"Oh, yeah? Where's he from?" Stevens thought back to the young man's olive complexion and dark hair. He looked Latino, but the name could be from anywhere.

"I tried speaking to him in Spanish. I'm Filipino and half Mexican on my mom's side, and we spoke some Spanish at home. Felipe didn't have any Spanish but I could tell he understood me, which was weird. He said he was first-generation Mexican but his parents didn't speak Spanish at home."

"So what was odd about that?"

The farmer shrugged. "I don't know. He's a good kid, but he's hiding something."

Like maybe that he was an illegal. "Well, I'd like to talk with him. I do have a DMV address, but those are often out of date. Do you have an address for him?"

"Just his phone number. I text him when I need him to come bring produce to Feast. I've seen his place, though, and I can tell you where it is. It's a big house with a lot of renters, where he has a room. It's on Prison Street." Benitez texted the number and description to Stevens's phone.

They stood. "Thanks for your persistence in getting this information to us," Stevens said. "I really appreciate it."

"No problem. Hey, want to take some summer squash home to the family?" Benitez gestured to a large cardboard box. "Those are my weird ones. I donate them to the food bank."

Stevens reached in and pulled out a yellow squash with a bizarre bulge in one side, another shaped like male genitalia. He chuckled at the sight. "Yeah, these are funny-looking. I'll take home a bag, thanks."

Benitez filled a paper bag with squash, and Stevens made his way back to the Bronco, already calling Mahoe.

"Got a hot tip. We need to interview this guy about the Bukowski murder."

"On it, LT. I'll meet you there."

Brandon

Brandon stood and hooked his shoulder holster off the back of his chair, buckling it on.

"Break in the case?" Sergeant Fraser looked up from a stack of reports she was going over.

"Just another interview. Kitty Summers is looking good for it, and we have her in custody." Brandon didn't voice his doubts as to Kitty's guilt. She was a bird in the hand, after all, and as the LT often said, "Usually the obvious is the obvious."

"When you have a chance, tell Stevens Elena is doing well at the shelter and has changed her mind about pressing charges on Noriega. She wants to go ahead with it now, and she's done a temporary restraining order, too."

"Good. Hate wife-beaters," Mahoe said. "My mom used to get smacked around. If my dad weren't already totally AWOL, I'd be thinking about giving him a bit of his own medicine."

"If only it were that easy."

"Yeah." He waved at the pretty sergeant as he shut the door behind him. On the drive to Lahaina, he considered his feelings about his father.

The man had left no forwarding address when he abandoned them, and his mother had been so relieved to be out from under his fist, she hadn't tried to get child support or anything else for Brandon or his sisters.

Learning to "serve and protect" by being a police officer, part of a larger *ohana* at the MPD, had helped whittle down the chip on Brandon's shoulder—he didn't feel so frustrated all the time. Even if he wasn't always happy with his own life, he helped others—and having Stevens as his mentor these last five years was almost like having a father he could respect.

He'd begun to make the changes he'd told the LT that he would: asking that hottie Iris in Dispatch out to lunch and calling a realtor to see if there was anything on the market in his price range. He now had a date with Iris, and the realtor, for next week. He grinned in anticipation and pressed down on the accelerator.

Felipe Souza's house was one of those old plantation homes crammed into a tiny lot on a side street in Lahaina, built onto in the days before permitting new development became such an issue on Maui. The termite-riddled structure filled the entire lot, and one of Lahaina's old mango trees spread over it to provide umbrella-like shade. The house was painted bright teal, the sloppily applied paint contrasting with a dull red tin roof. Loose chickens scratched around a rickety porch bordered by a ragged ti-leaf hedge.

Stevens was already waiting for Brandon, leaning against his vehicle, filling out some paperwork on a clipboard. He stowed the papers and locked his vehicle as Brandon parked behind the Bronco.

"Just gonna ask this guy where he was and why he was so upset on the day of the Bukowski murder," Stevens said. "Hopefully we'll get something more to confirm Kitty Summers as the doer."

"Gotcha, LT." The evidence at the scene had been awfully convenient. Brandon walked up the worn treads of the wooden porch behind Stevens. A warped screen door gave into a living room, where he could hear the blare of a television talk show. The smell of pickled mango preparation tickled his nose.

Stevens knocked. No answer. He knocked again. "Hello? Anyone home?"

A petite Filipina girl, pretty, wearing a sundress with a rice-sack apron tied over it, came to the door wiping her hands on a dishtowel. She smelled delicious, the sour of vinegar contrasting with the sweet of mango juice. Mahoe's mouth watered as he and Stevens held up their badges. "Is Felipe Souza home? We need to ask him a few questions."

"Sure." The girl spun on her heel and bellowed into the depths of the house. "Felipe! Cops here to talk to you!"

"Shit," the LT muttered as they heard the patter of running feet. "Run around the back and head him off, Mahoe!" Stevens yanked the screen door open and charged into the house, shoving the girl aside. Brandon spun and vaulted the low railing of the porch, barreling around the side of the house. He leaped over a rusty bike and scattered squawking chickens, ducking under a line of laundry flapping in the wind.

Felipe Souza had made it out of the back of the house. He was hauling ass down the dirt alley, arms and legs pumping. Brandon dug deep to his high school football days, when he'd been the one to bring down many a quarterback making a run for it. He was no distance runner, but he was a champ at sprints, and time in the gym on the treadmill kept him in good shape. He put on a burst of speed and hit Souza from behind with his shoulder. The man flew forward with a cry to sprawl in the dust of the alley.

He was putting cuffs on Souza when Stevens jogged up. "Nice work, Mahoe."

Brandon helped the witness to his feet and dusted him down. Dirt rose from the man's T-shirt to tickle Brandon's nostrils. "Dumb move, Souza. You must know from watching cop shows that running never works. You can't get away, and it makes you look suspicious as hell."

"What were you thinking, man?" Stevens said. "We just wanted to ask you a few questions."

Souza shook his head. Tears tracked through grime from the road on his cheeks. Guy looked guilty as hell. They walked him back to the house, where the Filipina girl was standing at the back door, her mouth hanging open.

Stevens tossed Brandon the keys. "Put Souza in the back of the Bronco. I want to see what's in his room."

Souza came to life at this. "You can't go in there without a warrant!"

Stevens wheeled to pin the young man with his gaze. Brandon knew firsthand how intimidating that blue stare was—enough to shrivel your balls. Souza looked away first. "You saying we need a warrant? What're you trying to hide?"

"Nothing," Souza muttered. "Got my rights, is all."

"We'll see about what rights you've got. I'm getting an illegal alien vibe, and I'm hardly ever wrong on those, am I, Mahoe?"

"Your alien radar is exceptional, LT."

"Besides, the landlord can let us in if he or she has concerns about criminal activity." Stevens turned to the young woman. "Miss. Who's the landlord here?"

"Me. I mean, it's my family's house. I live here and manage it. Phillie Bayang." She extended a hand to Stevens as Brandon marched Souza around the side of the house to the Bronco.

Brandon unlocked the vehicle and frisked Souza. He removed a cell phone and a pocketknife, then put the young man in the backseat. Souza sagged, resting his head on the back of the seat. Brandon locked him in, then went around and opened the vehicle, putting the key in to crack the windows and making sure the wire grille Stevens had installed was locked in place. After checking that the childproof lock was engaged, he trotted back around the house.

The LT had already gone inside, so Mahoe took a moment to scan around the yard for anything out of place. In the corner of the lot, against a low concrete block fence, a portable metal fire pit was still smoldering—and the smell wasn't wood.

Brandon frowned. He walked over to check it out.

Souza, or someone else in the house, had been burning clothes in the pit. Only a rag of blue jeans remained, caught near the metal lip. Was that a dark stain on the swatch of fabric?

Brandon's pulse picked up.

Using a stick, he edged the cloth farther away from the hot ash. He gave the remnants a stir, uncovering a tuft of unburned T-shirt material. He needed to fetch his crime kit.

Stevens reappeared in the doorway, holding up a passport. "Check this out. Felipe Souza is really André Métier."

C.J.

C.J. picked up her zipped portfolio and headed for the observation room, calling the district attorney, Pete Hiromo, as she did so. Stevens and Mahoe were bringing in a hot new suspect on the Feast murders, and not a minute too soon. The mayor was breathing down her neck about police harassment of his favorite chef.

Hiromo on his way, C.J. settled in to the dim confines of the booth and switched on the audio feed.

Felipe Souza had asked for a lawyer right away, according to Stevens and Mahoe. The suspect was unimpressive: a weedy-looking young man, olive complexioned, with dark circles under his eyes and a prominent Adam's apple. He plucked at his handcuffs.

While they waited for Souza's public defender, Stevens and Mahoe were currently logging in the evidence they'd found: a passport that identified Souza as André Métier, François Métier's only cousin, the beneficiary of millions in life insurance—and some burned cloth that had tested positive for blood.

C.J. rested her chin on her hand, gazing into the interview room at Souza's face. He lifted his head, looked around. Hollow-eyed and hopeless, maybe even sad. Yes, his was the face of someone with a guilty conscience.

Ms. Fogarty had drawn the short stick to get the case, apparently. C.J. snorted at the sight of the public defender's outfit as the young attorney entered the interview room. Per usual, the blond hoochie had shoehorned herself into a skirt that hardly covered her ass. She walked like a duck, her knees together, over to her client and sat down next to Souza/Métier.

Fogarty introduced herself, and C.J. turned off the intercom—only nothing happened. The voices piped in from the other room continued. She jiggled the switch—damn old equipment was broken. "I'm here to make sure your rights are being respected. Tell me what happened," Fogarty said.

"I was in my room. Listening to some music. And then Phillie yelled that the cops were here to talk to me. I . . . I ran."

"Why? If you did something, I need to know."

C.J. frowned. She could leave to avoid hearing this, but what was the harm? The team couldn't act on any information gained this way anyway. She fiddled with the knob and it spun freely. She wondered if they could hear her too.

"I'm traveling under a false identity. I didn't want them to find out," Souza said.

"Ah. Are you an illegal alien?"

"Well, yeah. My visa expired two months ago."

"Good. We'll confirm that's why you ran. You didn't want to

get deported. You just panicked. Anything else I should know? I can't help you if there are any surprises."

C.J. was surprised by the blond attorney's sincere, no-nonsense delivery. Maybe the chick had more going on between her ears than pedicures and spray tans.

"I'm related to the victim. The first victim, I mean. François was my cousin."

Fogarty leaned in to the young man's face and asked, "Did you kill him?"

"No!" Souza recoiled. "No!"

"Did you have motive?"

"I think they will say I did. I get some money from his passing." Some money, ha! C.J. felt her palms prickling with frustration. The kid wasn't even being straight with his attorney. This interview was bound to be a waste of time. Hopefully the trace would tie to him and bring this case to a close.

"Please just stay quiet and respond with 'no comment' until we can see where they're going with this interview," Fogarty directed.

"Okay." The suspect's voice was soft in the tinny feed. C.J. picked up the phone and called maintenance to report the speaker malfunction.

The door of her cozy hideout blew open. Stevens stood framed in the opening, the muscles of his arms bunched with tension as he braced on the doorway. His eyes were wide and his face pale. "Captain—Lei's in labor. I had my phone off and didn't know. I have to go."

C.J.'s heart lurched in response to his distress. She hung up the phone. "Isn't it too early?"

"Apparently not. I just got her message, and it started a few hours ago. When I called back, she couldn't talk. Tiare confirms it's the real thing."

"Of course—you go. Mahoe and I can handle this."

Stevens gave a brief nod and spun on his heel. She heard his footsteps running down the hall toward the front entrance. He'd left the observation room door hanging open.

The baby wasn't even born yet, and her two favorite detectives already had their hearts on the line. *Please, God, don't let anything go wrong. I need my people whole and happy.*

C.J. got up and shut the door. Not a thing she could do to help, and if anyone could crank out a baby natural, it was Lei—the woman was fit, healthy, and no stranger to pain.

C.J. shuddered at the thought of labor. "God forbid I ever get in that situation, but if I do, give me drugs," she muttered. "Better living through chemicals. Guess that makes me a coward."

She was okay with that.

Fogarty and Métier had wrapped up their little powwow while C.J. was talking to Stevens. She was just in time to see Fogarty go to the door and call that they were ready for the interview.

C.J. tugged down her uniform jacket and allowed herself a small, tight smile. Those two were going to get more than they bargained for—she was going in.

Stevens

Heavy forty- and fifty-mile-an-hour gusts hit the main town of Kahului, shaking the Bronco like a chew toy, but it didn't really start raining until just north of Paia. Visibility was so poor that Stevens hunched close to the steering wheel, driving as fast as he dared through a premature dusk flashing with bolts of lightning. The roar of rain and wind drowned out the pounding of his own heart as he sped down the normally picturesque coastal road.

He'd told Tiare he'd meet them at the hospital. Tiare had said no. Lei was only dilated at four or five, probably had hours to go, and might as well stay in the comfort of home with the weather so bad. That didn't make sense to him at all.

Hospital.

Now.

Where Lei could be safe.

He would just make them go. He'd carry Lei out to the truck and put her in. Screw Tiare and "stay home where it's relaxing." He was about to have a heart attack just from the idea of what was happening, let alone the storm—and what if the weather got even worse?

Stevens's hands went clammy, and he hyperventilated at a mental picture of driving his laboring wife through a tropical depression to get to the hospital.

Maybe an ambulance would be better . . . Yeah, ambulance. That was the way to go.

He was so amped from adrenaline that it was hard to focus on the road, but the conditions forced him to. He wove around blowing palm fronds and through broken branches. The familiar drive felt never-ending and surreal in the severe storm conditions.

Stevens finally reached the compound, vaulting out of the Bronco and up the stairs into the house as the gate rumbled shut behind him. In the entry by the front door, he shook the rain that had instantly soaked him out of his hair and toed out of his boots.

The house was dim, the lights low. He smelled something—incense? The slack-key instrumental guitar Lei liked played, a mellow sound turned up against the rush of wind and rain on the windowpanes.

That's right. This was all about relaxing and letting things happen. He was *so* not good at that. Neither was Lei. What were they thinking, having a baby at all?

Jesus. I don't think I can do this. He meant it as a prayer.

Stevens pushed a hand through his wet hair and fought an urge to turn around and leave. He could do something useful—like cover the windows with plywood. Yeah, pounding some nails in the pouring rain sounded like paradise next to what was ahead.

That's what he'd do if he couldn't get Lei to go to the hospital right away. But he had to at least go give his wife a hug.

"Man up," he muttered. Procrastinating a moment longer, he set the wet boots outside the front door on the damp, windswept porch.

The dogs were nowhere to be seen, and neither was Kiet. They were probably all with Wayne already, their babysitting plan. He glanced over at Wayne's cottage. It looked cozy and buttoned up tight, curtains drawn, but he could see a glow of lights inside.

Stevens was padding across the living room in his socks when a low cry came from the back bedroom. The sound of Lei's pain ripped across his nerves like sandpaper. He froze in the middle of the room, sweat breaking out all over him.

"Oh God," he muttered. "Oh Jesus."

Paralyzed, unable to move, he smelled the acrid sweat of fear oozing out of his pores. He heard Tiare's low, soothing voice saying something, but he couldn't make out the words. Somehow he had to get a grip and be strong for her, but running through a live-ammo firestorm was easier than this.

"Michael? Is that you?" Lei's voice calling him from the bedroom sounded shaky, scared.

Her voice released him from the spell of profound terror. He took a deep breath, blew it out, rolled his shoulders back, and strode to the bedroom door. "I'm here, Sweets."

Lei was lying on her side in the big, wide bed of their room in that flowered house muumuu. A scented candle on the side table warmed the air with soothing vanilla. Tiare stood up from where she'd been seated on the bed beside Lei, her tall, commanding presence as reassuring as Stevens had always found her.

"She's fine." Tiare spoke in that calm professional nurse voice that had probably soothed a thousand distraught relatives. "It's going a little quickly, but there's no fetal distress and Lei's progressing nicely."

"I'm not. I suck at this. It's way worse than I imagined." Lei's face was shiny with perspiration, her hair a frizzing halo. She reached for him with both hands. He knelt beside her on the floor, pulling her into his arms to hug her. He could smell fear on Lei, too, and somehow it made him feel not so alone.

For better or worse, they were in this together.

"I'm not sure I can do this. Can you do it for me?" She gave a weak giggle.

"Oh, honey, I wish I could. Honest to God." He buried his face in her hair. "You're everything to me. I'm scared as hell."

He lifted his head and gazed into Lei's big brown eyes. They filled with tears, making his own prickle. "I'm scared too," she whispered. "I was all brag. I should have known better."

"Sweets. How could you know what this is like? But we've done lots of hard things before, haven't we? We can do this together, too. Can't be worse than when the doc pulled the packing out of my infected side," Stevens said. "Or when I got stabbed. Or when you hurt your head or got hit by the car. Or when that perp bit you."

Lei smiled wanly. "It's a different kind of pain."

"You're both pretty freaked out. Why don't you go take a shower together? Chill out in there with the hot water. You can see how things are for her, Stevens. So far it's textbook, if moving faster than I thought things would go. I'll give you guys some privacy," Tiare said. She left them alone.

"Tiare's right. I felt better in the shower. Help me up. Let's at least get the stinky sweat off."

Stevens steadied Lei as she sat up and swung her legs off the bed. She'd made it halfway down the hall when a sudden gush of fluid rushed down her legs to puddle on the floor.

"Oh no!" she exclaimed. She clung to Stevens, racked by a contraction, as Tiare ran around with towels to mop up the amniotic fluid.

"I think we should call an ambulance," Stevens said over Lei's head to Tiare. His eyes felt strained and dry—they must be wide with panic. His wife leaned on his forearms, head down, breathing deeply, her spine arched by the powerful muscles at work. "I want to get her to the hospital."

Tiare straightened up, holding the towels. Her warm amber-brown eyes were calm and steady—if she was worried at all, she was damn good at hiding it. "Of course. You two are in charge. Why don't you get into that shower, and I'll call the ambulance and get your bags ready. I'm sure it will take them a little while to get here in this weather."

"Sounds good."

He could see the contraction ease as Lei's breath came easier and her hunched back straightened out. She finally stood upright, pushing her hair back with a trembling hand. "Whew. Big one."

"You did great." He gave Lei a brief squeeze, his arm around her shoulders. He was nervous, but not as worried as before—they were going to the hospital, where there would be drugs and doctors if needed. "We're just gonna get that shower Tiare recommends and get you cleaned up. She's calling the ambulance and getting us organized. Everything's under control." He was speaking to himself as much as to her.

In the bathroom, Stevens turned on the water and helped Lei undress, making sure the water was a good temperature as he quickly stripped and joined her. Lei sat on the bench as he soaped up, all business, relieved that they'd be out of the house soon.

The power went out with a little *pop*, and the bathroom went dim and gray.

"What the hell?" Stevens rinsed off the last of the soap and handed the bar to Lei. "Let me see if a breaker blew."

He grabbed a towel and threw it around his waist, heading into the living room where the breaker box was, dimly aware of Tiare behind him in the kitchen—and as he looked out the big picture window, he saw one of the massive eucalyptus robusta trees right outside their compound, a nasty invasive that didn't have enough of a root foundation for its tremendous height, begin to topple.

Tiare arrived to stand beside him and gasped, covering her mouth with her hand. They watched the catastrophe unfold in slow motion. The tree seemed to be fighting to stay upright, weaving back and forth, its branches catching on the trees beside it—but there was open space on the side where their driveway was. Another gust hit the behemoth, and with a teeth-jarring, rending roar, the huge tree gave, crashing to the ground with a tremendous thump that shook the whole house.

A fallen giant lay directly across the driveway in front of the gate, sealing them in.

CHAPTER EIGHTEEN

BRANDON

Brandon

Brandon was opening the door to the interview room when Captain Omura exited the observation booth to join him. As usual, she looked beautiful and scary. The zippered portfolio under her arm meant business.

"I'll be taking the lead on this interview, Mahoe," she said.

He felt his testicles tighten. "Yes, sir. Where's the LT? I was just down at the evidence room photographing the clothing scraps to show the witness."

"He got a call. Looks like the baby's on the way."

"Isn't it too soon?" Brandon frowned. "That can't be good."

"Babies do what they want, from what I can tell. Now, from my read on Métier, he's feeling guilty and dying to confess. I want you to go on the aggressive so I can be the sympathetic shoulder he cries his troubles on."

Brandon glanced at her steely eyes and immaculate jacket with its decorative bars and knifelike pleat. "Yes, sir."

"Let's do this."

Brandon nodded, took a breath, and pushed the door open

forcefully. He was already reciting the Miranda warning as he strode in, not meeting the suspect's eyes. Instead, he went to the recording equipment switch and turned it on.

"This is a formal interview in the matter of the murders of François Métier and Sage Bukowski. Present are André Métier, who has been living illegally in the United States under the name of Felipe Souza. Also in attendance are Shannon Fogarty, attorney, Captain C. J. Omura, and Detective Brandon Mahoe. Do you understand these rights as they were explained to you?" Brandon pinned Métier with a glare.

The man nodded, looking stunned. Brandon felt a hit of power —he was in control here, running the room, intimidating the witness. The captain had seated herself, but he remained standing, leaning in on his knuckles toward Métier, eyes locked with the other man.

"Tell us what you know about the murder of Sage Bukowski."

Métier's mouth opened and closed, but nothing came out.

"We have you cold—running from police. Living illegally in the country under a false name. Burning clothes that test positive for blood. You might as well confess, tell your side of things."

"No comment," Métier quaked. Fogarty patted his arm approvingly.

Beside Brandon, the captain cleared her throat, a delicate rustle. "Perhaps our witness needs a moment to collect his thoughts, Detective. Or a glass of water?"

Métier's head moved like a Taco Bell bobblehead. "Water. Yes, please."

The captain caught Brandon's eye. She jerked her chin meaningfully toward the door. He couldn't believe it—one minute he was going after the witness, on the aggressive as she'd told him, the next he was the water boy? Brandon muttered a curse and grabbed the door handle, yanking it open. As it closed on the pneumatic hinge, he heard Omura schmoozing.

"Sorry for my detective's attitude. He's young and enthusiastic about the job, gets a little hot when he thinks he knows what's what. Now, what can you…?" Her question was cut off as the door shut.

Brandon had reached the break room, stomping with irritation, by the time he calmed down enough to think through the captain's strategy. Likely the perp was telling her everything right now. Omura had moves, all right.

Brandon needed to keep a lid on his temper—they were on the same team, with the same goal. Served him right for getting all pissed in there. He knew better. He filled a glass and hurried back.

The three at the table looked up as he reappeared. He set the water down in front of Métier, who picked it up and drank in great gulps.

Brandon leaned against the wall and folded his arms, setting his jaw in a surly line as he stayed in character. Métier avoided his gaze and picked up the thread of whatever he'd been telling the captain.

"So I thought my expired visa had been discovered because of the investigation. I just panicked when I heard 'cops' were at the door looking to talk to me."

"You know that running just makes people look guilty." Omura smiled. Brandon had always found her smile chilling.

"I'm sorry for the hassle." Métier finished the water and set the glass down.

"So other than my client inadvertently looking guilty because he ran, on what basis is he implicated in these recent murders?" Fogarty asked.

"Ah, yes." Omura pretended to consult some notes in her zip-up binder. "I'm sorry, I'm filling in at the last minute for Lieutenant Stevens, who was called away on a family emergency. Detective Mahoe, perhaps you'd like to share why you were questioning this witness."

"Definitely." Brandon stood away from the wall and pulled out a chair, sitting forward to address Métier. "We have a witness who let us know that you were, quote, 'not yourself' on the day of Bukowski's murder—and at a time when the body hadn't been discovered yet." Brandon let that sink in. "What do you know about Bukowski's death?"

"No comment." Métier fiddled with the water glass.

"All right." Brandon leaned back. "Let's talk about motive. Back to the first victim, your cousin. Who you stood to inherit millions from in the form of a life insurance policy." The public defender's eyes widened—Fogarty hadn't known that. "Why were you working with him in the same restaurant, under an assumed name?"

"No comment," Métier said.

Brandon shot an annoyed glance at the captain. "Guy's too much of a coward to tell his side. That's all right. We can make this case on the evidence. Don't need a word from him, right, Captain?"

"Well, a man is entitled to defend himself. I, for one, am interested in what Monsieur Métier has to say." Captain Omura leaned forward, making a steeple with her shiny red nails. "Why don't you fill us in on why you were traveling under an assumed name? Surely your cousin knew you were working with him in the restaurant?"

"You don't have to answer," Fogarty said.

"No, I want to." Métier picked at the handcuffs, making them jingle. Clearly 'good cop' worked better to get him to talk than 'bad cop.' "François didn't know I was his cousin. We'd never met—I'm actually only his second cousin, and he's ten years older—it's all part of some trust his parents set up and I'm the last Métier relative. I went in to interview at Feast and couldn't believe it when I found out he was already working there. I mean, I knew he lived on Maui, but what were the chances?" Métier looked up at Omura, brown eyes appealing. "He was the rich cousin who had everything. I didn't want him to know I was trying to get a job there so I could be on the island kiteboarding and living in a dive. I started as a busboy, but I wasn't so good with people, so they put me in kitchen prep, too. And sure enough, I got to see that my cousin was a real asshole."

"So you never identified yourself to your cousin?" Brandon asked.

"The more time that went by, the less I liked François. I knew he'd take every opportunity to rub it in on me that I was the poor cousin while he had everything."

A pause. Omura moved in. "So you realize this speaks to motive to kill him, don't you?"

"But I didn't kill him. It was like I said—I went in the day he was killed to pick up my check. I saw him breaking up with Kitty Summers. I left. That was it."

"And why were you so upset the day Sage Bukowski was murdered?"

"I was worried that lying on my application and getting hired under a false name would be discovered and that it would look bad."

"Well, you're right. It does," Brandon said. "You had means, motive, and opportunity to do in your rich cousin who 'had everything.'" He made air quotes with his fingers.

Métier put his head down. "No comment."

"Let's move on for the moment." Omura flipped a page in her folio. "So there was no other reason for you to be upset the morning of the day Sage Bukowski was killed."

"I was stressed about the situation. In general," Métier mumbled.

"But isn't it true that Bukowski is also your cousin, if a more distant relative? And that he's a part of the Bukowski Group, a coalition trying to break the Métier trust?" Omura's voice sounded warmly curious.

"Yes," Métier whispered. "I knew about the Bukowski Group. Sage and I were close. But I had nothing to do with that. Nothing to gain by it. All the Métier fortune still goes to charities, not to me in any form."

"Except for his huge insurance policy," Brandon said sourly.

Métier just shook his head.

"I have a theory." Omura gazed at Métier with a slight smile on her perfectly red lips. "My theory is that you and Bukowski were in on the scheme together. You came to Feast to spy on Métier, gather information to be used to break the trust—and then, one day you heard that François was getting ready to get married. If he did so, your only asset, the insurance policy, would go to someone else. So right after he ditched Kitty, you followed him into the walk-in. Stabbed him. He never even knew it was you—but Sage did. We have his testimony already. He's stated that he was working at a prep station with a line of sight to the walk-in door. He saw Kitty and François go in. I'm betting he saw you go in after François, and only you come out."

"No, no. That's not what happened." Métier's complexion had gone sallow with fear.

"Don't say anything else," Fogarty warned. "They can spin theories all they want, but they have to prove their case beyond a reasonable doubt if you don't implicate yourself. You don't have to respond to any of this."

"Allow me to finish," Omura said icily. Fogarty shut up. "As I was saying, you killed Métier, an impulsive act driven by your jealousy, frustration, and greed. Bukowski saw. And he blackmailed you."

Métier jerked in his chair like he'd been poked with a red-hot pin. Brandon had to admire the captain's technique.

"Don't respond." Fogarty touched Métier's arm.

"So you went to Bukowski's apartment. Perhaps to talk, perhaps with payment he demanded or a contract handing over a portion of your insurance policy. Something." Omura flicked a nonexistent bit of lint off her jacket, her eyes fixed on Métier.

Brandon filled in. "The witness who told us about how upset

you were also told us that you and Bukowski appeared to be close. Friends outside of work. Bukowski knew you were André Métier."

"No comment," Métier said.

"All right, if that's how you want to play it." Brandon opened the file he'd carried into the room with him. The photos inside, of the burned clothing, had taken him extra time to process and print, which was why he'd missed Stevens's exit. "These scraps of material were found at your home." He slid two photos, one of the T-shirt scrap, the other of jeans, over to Métier and Fogarty. Using his pen, he pointed out the dark stains on the jeans. "Something you may not be aware of, Ms. Fogarty, was that Sage Bukowski was violently stabbed twenty-seven times. There was blood all over his room: the walls, the ceiling, soaking the bed he collapsed on. And no doubt, blood all over his murderer." He tapped the photo. "These stains tested positive for blood. We've sent samples to Oahu for DNA testing."

"No," protested Métier. His eyes went so wide, white showed around the iris. "Maybe Phillie's dad or someone killed a pig and burned those clothes in her fire pit."

"I never said where the clothes were burned." Brandon felt a heady sense of power, of being about to win. "You said they were in the fire pit. How would you know that?"

"I . . . ah. It makes sense," Métier said. "But I swear, I know nothing about it."

"Well, we sent our best crime scene guy out to go over your bedroom, bathroom, and shower. We found more blood evidence there. The samples are all going to Oahu for DNA processing, so we'll know if they match the victim soon. Within days. This is your chance to tell your side of the story."

Métier sagged in his chair and covered his face with his hands. Fogarty tugged her skirt a little toward her knees, but it didn't move much.

"I again advise my client not to comment on these matters," she said. The sideways flash of Fogarty's eyes at Métier showed she was angry. No wonder—clearly her client had kept her in the dark about his actions.

Omura closed her folio. "Your lack of cooperation is noted, Monsieur Métier. You are under arrest for the murders of François Métier and Sage Bukowski."

"I didn't do it!" Métier protested again as Mahoe came around the table and hoisted him up by the arm. "Really. I didn't."

"We don't need you to tell us anything to be able to lock you up and throw away the key," Brandon said.

"But it was Kitty," Métier said. "I swear, it was Kitty. And I can prove it to you."

Now things were really getting good. Brandon rubbed his hands together underneath the table. He caught the same gleam of excitement in Captain Omura's eyes that he felt.

There was nothing quite like closing in on prey at the end of a hunt.

CHAPTER NINETEEN

Stevens

STEVENS OPENED THE DOOR TO get a better look at the massive downed eucalyptus. A blast of cold air and blowing rain almost yanked the heavy wood out of his hands. He slammed it shut—he was lucky his towel was still on.

"We'll never get to the hospital past that tree." He turned back to Tiare.

Tiare looked him square in the eye, hands on her hips. "We're having a home birth now."

"Oh Jesus." Stevens covered his face with his hands. "Oh God. I'm so not ready for this."

"Doesn't matter. It's happening. Man up. This is not about you."

Tiare's brisk words were a bracing slap. Her gaze made him think of a warrior princess going into battle—he'd heard that ancient Hawaiian women fought alongside their men.

"You're right. What do I have to do?"

"Things are moving quickly. I actually think she's going to want to push in the next hour or so, but it's going to be very intense for that time. So I want you to go get in that shower with her and make her feel good. Safe. Loved. Rub her back and touch her, if she'll let you. I'll set things up out here. We have everything we need, and I've got plenty of experience. So you get a grip and go take care of Lei. I'm also going to try to call your brother and Pono, see if I can get through. I've been trying the phones and they haven't been working—but if I can, I'll have them come with chainsaws and try to cut that tree in case we do need to go to the hospital." Tiare patted his arm, reassuring him once again. "I'll come in when you want me, maybe when it's time to bring her to rest in bed. But keep her calm and comfortable, with the water on her back, as long as possible. The more she can relax and submit to the process, the faster and easier the baby will come."

"Okay." Stevens went into the bathroom to find Lei bent over with the force of another contraction. She'd angled the bench under the falling water and was using it for support, leaning over to hold on to it as hot water poured over her back.

Stevens could hardly believe the shape that her belly, previously such a pleasant round, had gone. It was steeply pointed. Every muscle and tendon was sharply defined along her sides. She was breathing noisily, but began a deep, low moan as he stepped into the shower beside her, forgetting he was still wearing the towel. Water promptly soaked him as he knelt on the tile beside her.

"You're doing great—almost done with this one," he said. She suddenly grabbed his hair with one hand, pulling as she moaned. Shocked by the pain of her action, he didn't fight it. Instead, bracing himself, he set one hand on her straining side and the other on the bench as she wrenched his hair. If she wanted him to be in pain, too, so be it.

The tremendous tightness finally loosened, and so did her clutching fist. His scalp burned. She opened her fingers, white with strain. The palm of her hand was filled with dark hairs.

"Sorry," she panted, collapsing to sit on the bench. "I don't know why I did that."

"I do." He fetched a washcloth and wet it under the flow of water. He stood behind her and ran it over her back in long, smooth strokes. "You wanted me to suffer, too. Don't blame you a bit."

"Can I bite you next time? I really feel like biting something." Lei bared her teeth at him. Stevens couldn't believe she was joking at a time like this.

"No." He couldn't even smile.

"Aw. I really want to bite something."

"Didn't Tiare tell you to relax your jaw?"

"Screw that."

"Okay, then. You can bite on this washcloth." He handed her a fresh one from the cabinet. She put it between her teeth, growling and shaking her head playfully like one of the Rotties with a bone.

"Turns out we aren't going to the hospital after all." He wrung out his washcloth and began a gentle massage on her back.

"We're not?"

"No. We're staying here. Tiare says we have everything we need. She thinks you're within hours of delivering the baby. Less disruptive just to do it here, with the weather so bad outside."

"Okay." Stevens was surprised that Lei wasn't more worried, didn't ask questions—but her focus had turned inward.

He saw the contraction begin, a tremendous lifting and tightening, her abdomen changing shape again. He stabilized her to stand, clutching the bench, the water pouring down on her back once more. He stroked her back with his washcloth as she breathed through it.

He tried to match her breathing and get her to slow down. "Just relax. Let it roll through you. It's like the weather, passing over the land. And the land endures." Her eyes were shut. He moved around to stand in front of her. "Open your eyes. Look at me. I'm here with you." Gently, he tugged at the washcloth in her mouth as Lei bit down on it. "Let go. Relax. Let it move through you."

Lei opened her mouth. She let go of the washcloth and went into a slower, deeper breathing rhythm with him, but her legs were trembling with exhaustion when it passed. He put his towel under her knees to pad them against the hard tile. She crossed her arms and rested against the bench until the next one.

They went through four more like that until she was shaking with tiredness between contractions, and with the power out, the water was cooling. "I want to lie down," she muttered. "I need to lie down."

"Tiare!" he hollered into the dim house. "Need help here!"

Between the two of them they walked Lei back to the big bed in their room.

Tiare had been busy. The bed had been stripped and covered with a big white sheet that crackled with plastic beneath Lei as they got her onto the bed. Candles surrounded the room, casting both light and scent in cozy pools. Tiare had closed the drapes, shutting out the sight and sound of the storm outside.

Stevens was glad, in that moment, that they'd sprung for the heavy-duty, insulated windows. He could hardly hear the lashing of wind and rain outside. They were as safe here as they'd be in any of the island's hurricane shelters—the house was solid, a concrete cube with a metal roof. Making this place a fortress had been their priority, and once again he was glad of it—glad, too, that a few years ago they'd had all of the tall robustas growing on the property completely removed.

Too bad, though, he hadn't spent the extra three grand to get the ones near the gate cleared.

These musings were banished as he helped Lei turn onto her side, her back to him. He took a moment to haul on sweatpants and a T-shirt as Tiare murmured to his wife about what was likely coming in the next few hours.

"I want you to stay on your side and just rest between contractions. They say it's the most comfortable position. Let me know when you feel like you want to push, and I'll check and make sure it's time." Tiare put her stethoscope on the mound of Lei's belly. "Everything sounds good in there. Baby's not stressed."

"How will I know it's time to push?" Lei's voice was hoarse.

"Oh, there's no mistaking it. The body just takes over at that point," Tiare said. "Here's a little water." She gave Lei a cup with a straw and helped her into a loose shirt that buttoned in front.

Stevens returned to Lei's side. "Move over. I had a long day at work. No sense you hogging the bed."

Lei smiled, and wriggled over into the middle. Stevens lay down behind her and draped an arm over her. He shut his eyes. They rested, waiting, listening to the rush of the rain on the sturdy windows.

CHAPTER TWENTY

Jared

Jared lay on his back in bed, watching the storm through the uncovered sliding glass door that faced the ocean over Kuau. Massive cloud galleons raced across the sea, trailing scarves of rain shot with lighting. Rain and wave spume made the scene otherworldly, glimpses of intense action veiled and then revealed between skeins of blowing, shroud-like mist.

"It's beautiful, isn't it?" Kathy rested her chin on his bare chest to look out the slider.

They'd been having lunch at his place, totally platonic on their third date, when the storm hit. His little table on the deck where they'd been sitting had been hit with a belt of wind and torrent of water—but Kathy hadn't wanted to go inside.

Jared loved storms, too. Kathy was so sexy as she clung to the railing, laughing into the gale. He moved up beside her and crossed an arm over her body as they stood side by side, gripping the railing. The deluge plastered hair and clothing to skin. Exhilaration brought on by the elemental forces around them made Jared throw his head back and yell.

And then she'd turned inside his arms, pulled his head down, and kissed him—and hot damn. The storm had been totally forgotten in what came next.

Jared drew her in front of him and shaped her against him from behind, propping their heads on the same pillow so they could both watch the weather. He slid his hand up and down her side, loving the silk of her skin, her elegant shape. He still couldn't believe how perfect she was.

God, he hoped she felt even halfway the same about him.

Kathy reached behind her and stroked the length of his thigh, sighing.

Yeah. He could hope.

His phone, plugged in beside the bed, buzzed with a text.

"Don't get it," Kathy murmured. "For a little while longer, I want it to be just us."

Maybe she did feel the same about what was happening between them. But with the storm, there were bound to be emergencies.

"You might as well get used to this now—I'm a firefighter. Interruptions and emergencies are going to be part of our life together." He kissed her shoulder. She turned her head to look up at him, those blue eyes hazy. He found her lips with his. "If there's a big one, they'll call me in. With this storm, there's no telling."

"I thought I heard you say that we're going to have a life together." She tugged his ear playfully.

"Hell yeah. I'm not letting you go." He pressed Kathy closer and picked up the phone.

A text from Tiare lit up the screen: Lei is having the baby. It's the real thing. A big downed tree has us trapped inside their compound. Can you round up some guys with chainsaws to get the gate open?

"Holy shit." Jared flung the covers off and stood up. "Lei's in labor and they're trapped at the house by a fallen tree."

“Oh my God!” Kathy jumped out of bed on her side, then pulled up short. “My clothes are sopping wet!”

“Stay here. You can dry them and wait for me.” He liked the thought of her in his house, waiting for him—it energized him. “I have a chainsaw out at the tool locker.”

“No. I’m not staying here. I’m coming to help.” Kathy grabbed her panties off the floor and wriggled into them. “You’re not leaving me behind.”

Jared liked that even better than her waiting for him.

The phones were down, but texts seemed to be getting through, so he texted Tiare that they were on their way and he’d try to get a few more guys to help.

Working his phone with his thumbs, calling on several firefighter buddies, Jared sneaked glances at Kathy as she dressed in her rain-soaked clothing. Her mouth puckered as she worked damp pants up long, slim legs. “Wet jeans never go on easy.”

“You sure you want to wear those? I’m okay with you going without.” Jared grinned.

“Brat. I could use one of your shirts, though.”

Jared grabbed one of his Maui Fire Department T-shirts and tossed it to her, pulling another one on himself. Kathy clipped on her bra, wincing at the sensation of the wet fabric, and he laughed. “You can leave that off, too.”

“You’re incorrigible.” She shrugged into the shirt, huge on her, and poked her head out. “Where’s the toolshed? Let’s go.”

“I like you in my shirt.” Jared pulled her into his arms for another kiss.

She pulled away eventually and smacked his chest. “Family emergency. Baby on the way.”

He put on a slicker and handed Kathy a transparent plastic poncho from his closet. They loaded the chainsaw and a couple of axes into the back of his pickup and got on the road to Haiku.

The Hana Highway was almost obliterated by blowing leaves,

branches, and torrential rain. Jared navigated as quickly as he dared, circling another fallen tree.

"I'd stop and cut that and move it if we weren't in a hurry." Jared's phone beeped with incoming texts in the console between them. Kathy picked the phone up and read it.

"Two of your friends and Pono are meeting us there. Good. We'll have help."

A route that normally took half an hour seemed to take forever, but they finally reached the turnoff for the house.

The tree was massive, with a five-foot diameter and fifty-foot length, one of those eucalyptus invasives—and it had fallen right in front of the compound's mechanized gate. Lei's partner, Pono, had just arrived. He jumped out of his jacked purple truck in a bright yellow slicker.

"My wife's trapped in there, too," he yelled across the gale to Jared. His junior high-age kids, Ikaika and Maile, hopped out of the truck's cab and trotted around to join them as he hefted an extra-long chainsaw out of his truck bed.

"How do you want to go about this?" Jared asked. "Did you call the county? They should send out their big tree-cutting rig, too."

"I tried to call them, but the phones are still down." Pono's eyes widened curiously at the sight of Kathy getting out of Jared's truck, her Maui Fire Department shirt visible through the clear plastic poncho she wore.

"Kathy was at my house when the storm hit, so she's here to help." Jared slung an arm around her possessively, and felt happy when she let it stay there.

"Hey, Pono," Kathy said.

"Hey." The burly Hawaiian clearly grasped the situation. He grinned quickly, but turned back to look at the house. "Why don't we each start a cut? Maybe do them every three feet so we can roll the sections out of the way. Bigger logs will weigh a ton."

"Sounds like a plan. I've got a winch on my pickup." Jared

gestured to the back of his truck. "I can pull out any bigger sections."

"The kids and I will trim the branches." Kathy called the kids over, introducing herself. The three of them headed away from the heavy chain saw action to chop at the branches digging into the mud and asphalt.

Jared fired up his chainsaw with a roar, feeling the urgency of their task, but also a deep satisfaction. Kathy was with him, wearing his shirt and working right alongside him, hacking away at a thick branch. He sneaked a look over at her. Hair wet, cheeks red with effort, she still looked gorgeous.

He was pretty sure he'd fallen in love.

Man, that had taken a lifetime—but not long at all, once he'd met the right woman.

Jared eventually made his first cut all the way through the massive tree. Pono had finished his, with a longer blade on his saw, and begun another cut as Jared let the straining motor cool for a moment before starting the next one.

The world around Jared closed down to nothing but the tangy smell of flying wood chips and exhaust, the roar of the saw, the buck and heave of it in his gauntleted hands, the sting of rain in his eyes. Jared felt a hand on his shoulder and cut the power, turning to see one of his off-duty firefighter buddies.

"My turn," his friend Freddie-O said.

Jared surrendered the saw. "Thanks for coming out." Releasing the heavy tool to the other man, he was surprised to find that his shoulders were tight and burning from exertion—but he and Pono had made several cuts all the way through the massive tree. "Let's start moving the sections," he told Pono.

"Ikaika!" Pono called to his son. "Take this cable and climb over the tree. See if you can find a sturdy branch to hook it on to on the other side. We'll pull the first section out with the truck."

"Sure." The bright-eyed kid grabbed the heavy hook attached

to Jared's winch. He shimmied up the huge, wet trunk and disappeared over the other side.

"Let's move a couple of these out and see if we can get them far enough away that we can get a vehicle through there," Jared said.

"Sounds good." Pono gave a brief nod.

"Got it hooked!" Ikaika yelled from the other side of the log.

"Stand way back from it!" Jared yelled. He got into his truck, surprised to find Kathy was already sitting there.

"Whatever you're doing, I'm doing," she said.

He had to kiss her.

Then he put the truck in four-wheel drive and pulled forward.

CHAPTER TWENTY-ONE

C.J.

Driving to the jail through the whipping squalls and pouring rain, Mahoe at the wheel of the cruiser, C.J. was filled with an unfamiliar excitement.

She so seldom got out of her office on a case. She'd long ago concluded that her strength as a leader lay in forging a solid team: bringing together a group of talented people, training them, equipping them, providing clear direction, and then getting out of the way to let them work.

She had a talent for bureaucracy, and she knew it.

But a part of her had missed this: heading out into a storm wearing her weapons, on an important case, just when the pot was coming to a boil.

Mahoe was a cautious driver. Went along with living with his mother and his dedication to the job. Good kid with potential—not the brightest bulb in the box, but a hard worker. She saw him making sergeant someday at the top of his career, married with a couple of kids.

The thought made her a little warm and fuzzy. She was maternal that way, not that she let anyone know.

A sheet of roofing tin bowled across the road in front of them and Mahoe jerked the wheel in reflex. “Holy crap!”

The corrugated metal hit a parked car and the alarm went off. C.J. called in a unit to secure the area as Mahoe turned the cruiser into the older jail facility in Wailuku, a low complex of metal-roofed buildings inside a fence topped with double layers of razor wire.

“Let’s see what kind of interviewee Kitty is,” C.J. said after they were admitted, following a correctional officer down a hall lit by dim emergency lighting since the power was out. “She might do better with me as bad cop.”

“I think so, from what I can tell at our other interview.” Mahoe gave her a sideways glance. “Summers doesn’t like other women and thinks she can manipulate men.”

This was a surprise—maybe Mahoe had more going on upstairs than she’d given him credit for. C.J. nodded in acknowledgment and let Mahoe request the prisoner and an interview room.

In the bare cubicle with its bolted-down table and chairs, C.J. resisted reminding Mahoe to Mirandize the suspect as Summers was brought in, looking sallow and unkempt in prison orange. Summers would never be pegged as a porn star now. Her straggling blond hair showed roots, and without makeup, she looked a homely fourteen.

She was also sporting a black eye.

Mahoe turned on a recording device after greeting her warmly and reciting the Miranda warning. C.J. was glad she’d bitten her tongue on reminding him.

“How are you holding up, Kitty?” he asked, all sympathy.

“Are you here to let me out?” Summers’s blue eyes darted toward the door. “I want to lodge a complaint. I was assaulted by another prisoner.”

"This is jail. What did you expect, a Holiday Inn?" C.J. smiled without humor. "We'll pass your concerns on to the management." Ah, bad cop. Her favorite role.

"I'm so sorry that happened, Kitty. For sure we'll let the CO know you're being harassed. We're just here to get your help on the case, though, unfortunately," Mahoe said. He had a cute face when he smiled, square and earnest, and if he dressed better, the kid wouldn't be half bad. "Some new information came in, and we have someone in custody."

"Oh, yeah?" Summers lit up, obviously thrilled she was no longer suspect number one. "How can I help?"

"Take us through your talk at Feast with the first victim on the day of the murder," C.J. said. "We found a few discrepancies between your original story and some eyewitness testimony."

"Oh. Well, yeah." Summers pushed her lank hair back behind her ears. "I've had a little time to think in here, and I want to revise my statement."

"Please. We appreciate that." Mahoe made an encouraging hand gesture.

"Okay. I wasn't totally candid earlier. François was the one doing the sabotage at the restaurant—not the cash register ripoff, though. That was someone else." Summers told them how François would get mad at Chef and "accidents" would happen in the restaurant. "François wanted everything Chef had, from the restaurant to Elena Noriega. He was obsessed."

"So tell us again about the night Metier was killed."

"François was breaking up with me. We argued. I wanted him to give me another chance, but he told me he was serious about someone else. Elena Noriega. He showed me the ring." Summers's eyes filled, and she covered her face. "I was devastated."

At last they knew who the ring was for. "And what else?" C.J. prodded, unimpressed by the woman's crocodile tears.

"I followed him into the walk-in. The door was open, but they had the plastic cold retention panels hanging over the entrance. I knew we were alone in there, and I begged him not to go ahead with it. I told him Chef would come after him if he tried to steal his wife as well as his recipes. I guess Chef did." Summers looked at them triumphantly. "Maybe Chef overheard us? I thought he was in his office, but maybe he came in and stabbed François after I left . . ."

"Hmm, seems possible. Please continue," Mahoe said.

"Well, he said he'd think about what I said. He was looking for some scallions for his sauce. I left, and I passed Chef on the way toward the walk-in. That was the last time I saw François." More tears spilled.

"Interesting." C.J. reached into her pocket and removed the device that André Métier had directed them to find in his interview earlier in the day. "This phone was retrieved from Sage Bukowski's apartment."

The color drained from Summers's face.

"Perhaps you'd like to tell us what's on this recording?" Mahoe prompted gently. "We haven't listened to it yet." A lie, but then, investigators were allowed to manipulate the truth in their quest for answers once the suspect had been apprised of his or her rights.

Summers covered her face with her hands.

C.J. thumbed to the voice memo feature. "I really want to hear what's recorded that's worth killing for."

Summers sat back. Folded her arms on her chest. "I'm done talking."

"Let's listen together, then, shall we?" C.J. pressed Play on the time-stamped, dated recording and turned up the volume.

A rustling sound. Voices arguing, getting clearer. "Please, François. I'm begging you. Don't do this." Summers's voice.

"I told you, Kitty. It's over. Show some dignity and get the hell out of here." Métier's tone was cold and haughty. "Unless you know where my scallions are?" C.J. could tell by the sound quality that he'd turned away.

There was a sudden, deep grunt—a shocked sound of pain—

and then a heavy *thud.* "You stabbed me," Métier gasped, the last word bubbling into silence. They also heard the shocked intake of breath made by Sage Bukowski as he recorded the events.

"Here are your scallions, you arrogant prick." The sound of a kick, followed by a moan. "You had it coming." Summers's voice sounded rich with vicious satisfaction.

A whispered, "Oh my God," in Bukowski's Brit accent. A rush of feet. The recording ended.

Bukowski had hotfooted it out of the doorway and back to his workstation before Summers discovered him.

Summers tightened her lips and glared defiantly. "I'm not sure what I was hearing there. A court won't be sure, either."

"Oh, I'm pretty confident we can reconstruct the events in a convincing way and match these voiceprints to you, Métier, and Bukowski." C.J. leaned forward. "Tell us about your relationship with Sage Bukowski. Again. Since your testimony was that you hardly knew the guy."

"I did hardly know the guy."

"So you didn't go to his apartment after he threatened you with this recording, and murder him?"

"Of course not."

"Well, he didn't die right away after you stabbed him. He left evidence that you killed him—your bracelet and the letter 'K' written on the sheet of his bed in his own blood. These things you already know." The color had drained from Summers's face, leaving her harshly plain in the dim glow of the emergency lighting. "And that's not all," C.J. went on. "He'd told his cousin about recording the murder and called him to come over and join him when he met with you about the blackmail. The cousin, who you know as Felipe Souza, was late getting there—which gave you time to kill Bukowski. But Souza was in time to hear Bukowski name you as the murderer."

"Bullshit. Bukowski was dead when I left. Dead, dead, dead!"

Summers screamed, cords standing out in her neck. The woman was close to coming unglued, but they had her now.

C.J. smiled—a slow, wide smile. Yes, she'd missed this part of the job.

Summers hunched forward and covered her face with her hands. "Oh God. I need a lawyer."

"You sure you don't want to share your version of the events?" Mahoe asked. "Must be so stressful carrying those memories around inside you."

"Think I don't know what you're trying to do?" Kitty sat up. Her eyes were dry, her expression defiant.

"We can show that Sage Bukowski was spying on you at Feast, gathering information for his blog. He followed you to the entrance of the walk-in, recording you on his phone for his gossip column, and inadvertently recorded the murder on voice memo. He decided to blackmail you. You went to his apartment and killed him for the recording, which, ironically, was in his back pocket the whole time. Souza found it there when he arrived too late to save his cousin. If you hadn't been so busy stabbing him, *you* might have found it." C.J. tapped her nails on her folio. "Souza found the phone instead and set you up by planting the bracelet and writing the letter 'K' with the victim's blood."

"I want a lawyer!" Summers looked up at the surveillance camera's round eye in the ceiling. "Guard! I'm being harassed by these police officers!" Summers screamed full volume. C.J.'s ears rang.

The CO appeared in the doorway. "What's the problem here, ma`am?" He addressed C.J.

"You can call me 'sir' or Captain, thank you. This witness is going back. Put her in solitary. For her own protection. Since she's been assaulted by someone in gen pop."

"Yes, sir."

Summers's eyes went wide. "Solitary?" The blond woman was hustled past them by the correctional officer.

Summers gone, Mahoe turned off the equipment. C.J. stood, brushing down her uniform briskly—just being in this room, made her feel dirty.

"We got her," she told Mahoe, and grinned. "That was fun."

Esther

Esther had decided to ride out the storm in her teaching room, the safest room in the house. Added on below the upper floor, the room was a solid heavy wood bunker with small, louvered windows set high around the ceiling to admit light and air flow—but no glass anywhere.

Esther unfolded her trusty futon mattress and toted her bedding downstairs. She set her bed up in the middle of the room on a lauhala mat. She brought in a hurricane lantern for when the power went out, as it always did during big storms in Wainiha. She filled the two bathtubs and all her spare jars with water, in case the water went out, too.

She would never forget the two hurricanes she'd lived through in this house: Iwa in 1982, and Iniki in 1992. Her home, built on heavy recycled telephone pole pilings sunk deep into Wainiha's valley walls, had only lost some roof and a few windows—but many trees had fallen to block the road, and she and her family had been trapped in the valley for days without power or water.

Her beloved Kimo had been with her then. This time she would be alone.

Her daughter, Lehua, had called, offering to come over, and so had her grandson, Alika; but she preferred solitude in times like these. Solitude to meditate, pray, and to feel the feelings that rode through her—and solitude to ride the winds from a spirit body.

Esther took her precious collection of Hawaiian musical instruments down from the narrow shelves, in case the wind got bad, and stacked them against the wall. She'd already secured the garden beds and the chickens, and had kenneled the dogs.

Now it was time to wait—and pray.

Esther sat down and got comfortable on her teaching pillow, a plump little round that made it easier for her to sit cross-legged. She closed her eyes and alternated murmuring the Lord's Prayer and Psalm 23, bringing herself into a calm place of listening trust.

The wind grew louder, keening around the louvers like a lost wild creature. Torrents pounded on the leaves of the sheltering kukui nut and mango trees near her house. Fingers of breeze teased in through the high louvers and swirled around her with the promise of movement.

Esther flew up from her seated position as an iwa, a great black-winged frigate bird, rose above the sturdy roof of her house to soar over the valley. From her bird's-eye view, she could see that the Wainiha River was already swollen and brown, surging against the metal bridge, making it hum with the pressure of water pushing against the struts.

She rode the winds easily with just little adjustments of her wings or tail, all the way to the estate outside of Kapaa, where Alika lived. She glimpsed him through the window just above the ground in the downstairs wine cellar he'd built for that showplace of a house. He was stripped to the waist, pumping weights to pass the time—and his once-broken body was magnificent again. She could hear music cranked up loud to drown out the sound of the storm.

After all of Alika's injuries and heartbreak, Esther was blessed to remember that he was healthy and strong now. *He is safe.*

Esther flew on, past turgid waterfalls and whipping coconut palms to the sturdy cabin in Kilauea, snug against the lee of a sheltering hill that Sean Wolcott had built for her daughter, Lehua. She swished by their windows and saw the couple playing cards on a picnic cloth in front of a wood-burning stove. *They are safe.*

She flew to check on more friends and relatives, finally turning the bird's sharp, long-sighted gaze toward Maui—but that was too far away to see.

Esther felt the dilation of that inner eye that meant a knowing was imminent. She left the body of the iwa and returned to her sanctum. She smiled at the fancy of her imagination that allowed her to soar with the birds—but sometimes it felt so real that she was sure she really could. Esther closed her eyes, waiting, and a moment later, that inner knowing eye opened.

Once more she saw Lei straining in labor—and this time, Esther knew she was seeing events in real time.

The storm was just as strong on Maui as it was as on Kaua`i. Water pummeled the land. The wind winnowed and thrashed, tossing trees whose roots struggled to grip the deeply drenched soil. A huge tree fell, trapping the little family inside the house.

"Oh, Lord, please protect them," Esther prayed. "And whatever happens, give me the name of their child. They need that name, no matter what. You've always been so faithful to tell me before."

She opened her eyes. The studio had gone dim beneath the sheets of rain and howling wind. She heard nothing but the chaotic voice of the storm.

CHAPTER TWENTY-TWO

Lei

Lei struggled to stay in her body, not to dissociate, even as she was racked with pressure and pain in a way she couldn't have prepared for. A stretch of measureless time went by, filled by increasingly long contractions and shorter rest periods. Tiare coached her through the wrenching cramps. Stevens comforted her with his solid physical presence. Thus she endured. There was no room in this terrible landscape for anything else.

And then it was time to push. Just like Tiare had said, the urge was unstoppable, the need to rid herself of the massive bulge in her belly beyond any extremity.

Voices said things to her, hands supported her, but Lei was barely aware. She bore down with all her strength, biting her lip and tasting blood, struggling forward through a red haze to some unknown promised land, pressed against Michael's chest, riding it out in his arms.

A cresting of agony was followed by a whoosh of relief.

Lei collapsed, eyes shut, unable to even lift her head as Tiare exclaimed, "You did it! It's a girl!"

She felt Michael weeping, shudders of joy and relief trembling through his arms as they held her. Then Tiare unbuttoned Lei's shirt and set the baby, warm and slippery, on her chest.

Lei struggled to focus, feeling disoriented. Was the ordeal really over?

Her arms came up to hold the baby purely by reflex, and Stevens scooted her to sit higher in his lap, cuddling them both close.

Lei finally opened her eyes and looked down.

Their daughter had a lot of wet, curly brown hair, and she'd hunched her tiny body like a turtle. Her eyes were tightly shut, but she began snuffling and rooting, clearly looking for something.

"See if she'll nurse," Tiare directed. "That helps the placenta be delivered."

Stevens helped Lei put the baby to her breast, where she clamped on with vigor, making Lei jump and both of them laugh.

"Rosie," Lei said tentatively. Lei didn't recognize her own voice, it was so raspy and tired. They'd decided on Rosie for a girl, a shortened version of her beloved aunt's name. She tried out the word again. "Rosie. You're really here."

As if she recognized her mother calling her name, Rosie opened cloudy, dark eyes. They fixed on Lei's face. Her tiny hand spread on Lei's skin. Lei felt a prickle of tears and a swelling sensation in her chest.

"My beautiful baby girl," she whispered. "Hello, darling."

The afterbirth arrived with no fuss, and Tiare gathered the linens and tidied up efficiently. "I'm trying the phones again. You both did fantastic." With kind tactfulness, Tiare left them and shut the door.

"You did it," Stevens murmured into Lei's ear, looking down at Rosie's face. "You were amazing."

"We did it." Lei turned her head. His lips met hers in a tender kiss. "And she's here now, and all that's behind us."

"Never to be repeated, if I have anything to say about it."

Stevens pushed Lei gently upright and eased out from behind her. "My nerves couldn't take doing this ever again."

"What? You don't want to get started on another one?" Lei grinned, settling the baby closer. "It was no big deal."

"No big deal. Right." Stevens held out his arms so she could see the marks on them, bruised by Lei's relentless squeezing. "And I lost a patch of hair, too." He shuddered, lying down on his belly beside Lei to watch Rosie nursing. "I was a wreck the whole time."

"You were a rock, you mean. You kept me going. And Tiare! What a saint." Lei couldn't tear her gaze away from Rosie's sweet, tiny face as the baby nursed. "I can't believe how strong she is."

Stevens reached out a long finger to touch the baby's cheek. "She seems to know what she wants. Takes after her mama."

"What would we have done without Tiare?"

"I think I heard my name." Tiare opened the door carefully, balancing a plastic basin of warm water on her hip. "Stevens, you get to bathe the baby when she's done nursing."

The wind and rain seemed to be backing off, and the premature dusk had given way to weak afternoon sunlight when Rosie finished her first meal and burped delicately. Lei watched as Stevens took his tiny daughter and bathed her carefully in the shallow plastic basin, clearly enraptured. The baby didn't even cry, just looked up at her father from eyes Lei could tell were going to be big and brown.

Tiare snuffed the candles, opened the curtains, and helped Lei sit up. "Don't want you walking around for a while, so let's just sponge you off a bit and get you into something clean. Company is coming." She helped Lei clean up with a washcloth and then handed Lei her favorite terry cloth robe. Lei eased into it, feeling exhausted, sore, but also pampered as Tiare propped her up with a couple of extra pillows.

Done with settling Lei, Tiare pulled out a measuring tape and measured Rosie as Stevens held her in the bath. "She's good size for an early baby. Stevens, get on this bathroom scale." She'd brought the device in. "Then we'll weigh you with her in your arms."

They did so. Rosie came in at close to six pounds. "She's well developed. Guess she was just ready to join us," Tiare said. Relief flooded Lei—she hadn't done anything wrong to bring on the birth, and Rosie appeared totally healthy. Lei's old hurts and fears felt washed away, purged by the storm they'd just been through.

"I hear chainsaws." Stevens turned his head toward the front of the property, still fully occupied with the baby.

"Yeah. They've been working out there for a while. I got through to Pono and Jared. They're cutting through it with a few other guys from the fire department," Tiare said.

"What's going on out there?" Lei asked. "Did something happen?"

"Big tree fell and blocked the gate. We couldn't get to the hospital. But you were too busy having a baby to care," Stevens teased.

"Whoa! I can't believe I missed all the drama!" Lei exclaimed.

"Just rest. You had a baby less than an hour ago. Stay in bed. There should still be some contractions as your uterus goes down, and this is where everyone's going to want to come, anyway, to meet Rosie. By the way, the phones are back up and I took a call on the house phone from Esther Ka`awai on Kauai. She called with the baby's Hawaiian name," Tiare said.

Lei and Stevens gave Tiare their full attention. "Esther is Rosie's godmother. What did she say?" Lei asked.

"She told me to tell you that the baby's Hawaiian name is Maluhia," Tiare said. "It means peace."

Stevens lifted his tiny, fragrant, clean daughter out of the tub and wrapped her in the soft towel Tiare handed him, smiling down at the baby. "Perfect," he said. "Just perfect."

"I love it. I can't wait to tell Esther how exactly right her name is. Now give her back to me. I need another Maluhia fix over here." Snuggling the baby close, Lei's eyes fell peacefully shut.

Stevens

Stevens put a microscopic diaper on Rosie and then a snap-up pajama while Lei rested a little later. The baby gazed intently at his face, calm as her name implied. He finally sat down with her in the rocking chair they still owned from the early days with Kiet. Rosie's tender head lay in the palm of his hand, her body on his forearm as he rested it on his bent knee.

They took each other's measure for long moments, and then she yawned, her tiny body drawing up as she stretched. She shut her eyes and went to sleep, going limp as a kitten.

No fuss. No drama. Maluhia, indeed. He cuddled the infant close on his chest and tucked his chin over her, breathing in her sweet new baby smell.

It was hard to believe so much had happened in such a short time. Rosie's birth couldn't have been more different than the extreme trauma of Kiet's. His son had been cut from his mother's dying body, flown to Oahu, put in foster care . . . Stevens shook his head to clear it of sad memories and old regrets. Kiet was a sensitive kid, but he was fine, especially now that Stevens was sober and he and Lei were getting along.

In the distance, through the fading sounds of the storm, he could still hear the chainsaws. He should probably go out and help, open the gate . . . do something. But nothing seemed more important than this moment with his baby girl.

So soft. So helpless and trusting. Thank God the dark days of the Chang family and the shroud killer were behind them . . .

He started awake to see Tiare smiling down at him. "The guys are almost through the log."

"Oh, great." Stevens tipped forward and stood up, turning to Lei—but she'd fallen asleep, too, clean in her yellow robe, her hair a fuzzy nimbus around her pale face. She looked wiped out, but even sleeping, there was a shadow of a smile on her face.

"Why don't we let Lei sleep? She certainly deserves a nap. You can take Rosie out and introduce her when the guys get through," Tiare said.

Stevens felt a grin split his face. "I gotta tell Wayne and Mom. They're going to be surprised it's over so soon."

"You got that right. Let's keep her inside. We should have everyone wash. No exposure to anyone that's sick. Keep her head warm." Tiare sounded very "professional nurse" as she handed him a tiny cotton cap. "Do you have somewhere to put her?"

"Kiet's cradle." Stevens had spotted it in the corner of the living room. Lei must have gotten it ready—the mattress pad in the bottom was clean and fresh. He set Rosie down on her back, working the cap gently onto her head, and Tiare covered the infant with a flannel blanket, tucking it in.

Rosie looked petite and cherubic in the cradle. Stevens could stare at her all day. He stretched up, arms overhead, and his spine crackled. The short nap seemed to have restored him.

"Tiare, we can't thank you enough. We couldn't have done it without you." He reached out and pulled the tall, statuesque woman in for a hug. "Not too many people I can think of trusting with something so personal. Pono's a lucky man."

Tiare's soft brown eyes gleamed with pleasure at his words. "I think you two might have surprised yourselves if you'd had to do it on your own, but it was my honor to help."

"On our own!" Stevens shuddered dramatically. "No way—that was scary enough for me, thank you very much. Take a break, woman. You deserve it! I'm going over to Wayne's to let him and Kiet know Rosie's here. Then I'll take a look at how the log demolition is coming along." Tiare nodded, and Stevens went out onto the porch.

Colors seemed too bright and the sounds of the chainsaws and occasional shouts too loud, so Stevens just stood there for a moment, feeling the mist of lightly blowing rain as the storm passed. They'd gone deep into their intimate cocoon in the house —but now he felt ready to rejoin the outside world.

Wayne had come out onto his little porch. Stevens was surprised to see that he had his arm around Ellen, who must have been over visiting Kiet when the storm hit. Stevens grinned big and gestured for them to come over. "Come meet your grandbaby! Rosie is here!"

Kiet came running out of the house, pitching himself off the steps, the dogs right behind him. He ran the short distance and flung his arms around Stevens's legs. Stevens hugged him and patted the dogs.

"You have a baby sister named Rosie, little man! But you have to be really gentle meeting her, okay?"

"Is Mama okay?" Kiet's dark green eyes squinted with worry.

"Your mama's just fine. She's taking a nap, though. Everyone has to be quiet," Stevens warned as Wayne and Ellen came across the grass, still holding hands. They must have really bonded during the storm or something. The two of them headed up the steps with Kiet to where Tiare was guarding the doorway.

"Oh, my goodness, that was fast!" Ellen hugged him. "So everything was fine?"

"Intense, but Tiare tells me it was textbook. Lei's crashed out but doing great. You all can go meet Rosie. I'm gonna check out the log demolition," Stevens said. After hugs all around, Stevens walked down to the gate, the dogs at his side. Water still spattered him, but it was mostly side-blowing moisture off the trees. He hit the button to retract the gate and it rumbled open.

The tree had been dismembered into giant disks. Some of these had been hauled out of the road, but others still remained upright, huge ringed brown pancakes.

Jared walked toward him. His brother was soaked with rain and sweat, eyes alight, and he held an ax in his hand. "Bro! We finally got the road open so you can get to the hospital, but Pono tells me everything's over with already."

"You have a niece named Rosie," Stevens said. Just saying her name brought a shit-eating grin to his face. "Mama and baby are fine."

"Tiare called me. She says you guys did awesome." Pono clapped Stevens on the shoulder in a man hug. "Gave my wife a workout, but she's as proud as if she had the baby herself."

"She should be. We'd have been lost without her." Stevens's brows lifted in surprise to see Kathy Fraser, with Ikaika and Maile, walk out from behind one of the huge sections of log. All three carried axes and appeared to have been helping clear the road. Kathy wore a too-big Maui Fire Department T-shirt under a clear poncho.

"Glad to hear everyone's okay," Kathy said. "We were really worried."

"It was freakin' intense, not gonna lie." Stevens pushed a hand through his hair. "But we made it. How'd you get roped in on this project?"

"She was with me when the storm hit." Jared pulled Kathy close possessively. She melted into him, smiling.

Stevens knew all he needed to know about what they'd been up to—and how they felt about each other. "Excellent," he pronounced. "Where are we at with this tree project?"

Wayne

Wayne stood on the porch of Lei and Stevens's new house—it would always be the "new" house to him, even though it had been completed five years ago. He felt a tremble in Ellen's fingers. Her hand was cold. He tucked it in against his side.

Tiare met the three of them at the door as Stevens left to check out the action in front of the gate. Kiet bounced with excitement and tried to dart around Tiare, and the Hawaiian woman knelt to his level.

"Honey, I know you're excited. I'm only letting you in because I know you can be a great big brother and let your little sister sleep. She is extra tiny because she got born early, and she needs her rest. Okay?"

"Okay." Kiet nodded vigorously.

"And your mama is resting, too."

"I'll be quiet."

Wayne smiled at Tiare. "Thanks. For everything. We didn't expect this."

"It was all kind of a surprise, but everything went fine." Tiare's glance flicked between them. "You two get through the storm okay?"

"We played a lot of Go Fish with Kiet," Ellen said. They stepped over the threshold into the living room.

Kiet walked straight over to the wooden cradle that had been his and knelt beside it, peering in. Wayne's heart swelled at the expression of wonder on his little face. He and Ellen came to stand above the little boy.

Rosie had sweet round cheeks. A pink bud of a mouth. Curly brown hair escaped from under her cotton cap. "She looks just like Lei did as a baby." Wayne's voice was thick. He blinked moisture out of his eyes as Ellen put both her arms around his waist and hugged him.

"Our grandbabies are so beautiful." Ellen's voice choked.

"When can she play with me?" Kiet whispered loudly.

Wayne chuckled. "Give her a few years, buddy."

Kiet lost interest then, going over to the coffee table and pulling out his bin of Legos from underneath. "I'll make you something, Grandma Ellen. Want a boat?"

"Sure." Ellen followed him and sat down on the couch beside the little boy. Wayne took one more look at Rosie's precious sleeping face and went into the kitchen. Tiare was frowning into the refrigerator.

"Those firefighters are going to be hungry," she said. "Not much in here."

"I've got some food in my big freezer at my cottage. Why don't you go join your family?"

"Yeah, why don't you?" Pono entered, coming forward on stockinged feet after toeing off his boots at the door. "I want my wife back."

Wayne grinned as Tiare turned to her husband, opening her arms. Pono pulled her close in a huge bear hug and kissed her enthusiastically. "So proud of you, honey," he said.

Ikaika and Maile tiptoed in and joined Kiet by the coffee table, peeking over at the baby.

"I better get that food." Wayne lifted a hand to Ellen, the only person who noticed as he left.

At his cottage, Wayne took a huge batch of frozen laulau out of his freezer and put it in a glass pan, microwaving the steam-cooked Hawaiian meat dish with its covering of kalo leaves. Ellen appeared at the door as he was serving the laulau up onto a large china platter.

"It's turning into a party over there," she said.

"Sure it's not too much for the baby? Or Lei?"

"Both are still sleeping, if you can believe it." Ellen took the glass pan, piled high, from his hands. "I'm so grateful we're sharing these grandbabies. That we're family."

Wayne gazed at her, trying not to be too intense. "Is that all we are?"

He'd been afraid to say anything as his affection for Ellen deepened. Putting a name to it might scare her away, but he'd lived for those little moments of holding her hand or giving her a hug.

"Is that all you want us to be?" Ellen whispered. Her blue eyes watched him steadily—eyes he saw every day in his son-in-law's face, bluer than the skies over Maui's ocean. Five years of family and sober living had restored much of the beauty she'd once been.

Wayne took the glass dish from her hands and set it on the counter. He took her soft face in his hands, worrying that his were too rough and calloused, but she turned her cheek to kiss his palm. Encouraged, he drew close, looking into eyes that gazed into his, unwavering until their lips met. The kiss was sweet, and tender, and a little reckless, too.

The years rolled away. Everything was new, and possible, and filled with deep joy.

The laulau had to be reheated by the time they carried it to the main house.

CHAPTER TWENTY-THREE

C.J.

The next day dawned clear and bright, the world washed fresh and soggy. C.J., riding beside Abe Torufu in his truck, arrived at the site of the log's demise around noon. Pono had called her the previous day to tell her that the baby had been born and that all was well in spite of the storm.

Clearly, the tree had paid for falling in the way of the Texeira-Stevens home. Huge discs of sliced-up trunk had been pushed and pulled to the side of the road. A giant pile of cut branches reached to the top of the fence. Abe navigated past protruding debris and stopped at the keypad facing the gate. He turned to C.J. "You sure you're ready to do this?"

"Yes." She smiled. "I'm ready to go public."

"Glad you finally got over yourself."

C.J. punched his rock-hard shoulder, and Abe winced comically, grinning. He leaned out the window and pressed the intercom button on the gate control.

Stevens's voice came through tinny and hollow. "Hello?"

"This is Abe Torufu. And Captain Omura. Here to pay our respects to the new arrival."

"Captain's with you?" Surprise in Stevens's voice. "Great. We need to catch up on the case. We've got a bunch of company, but the more the merrier at this point."

The gate retracted with a rumble. Abe braked at the sight of a cluster of vehicles jamming the parking area. "Looks like a party in here."

"And we're fashionably late." C.J. had taken the morning off. She wore a pair of slim black jeans and a tee paired with a jean jacket, since the weather was cool with the earth still soaked from the storm. She touched up her lipstick, fussing a little nervously with her hair, as Abe found a parking spot under a macadamia nut tree's spreading branches.

"You look amazing. As usual." Abe gave that gap-toothed grin that she might be coming to love. "And I'm going to mess that lipstick up anyway." He hooked a big hand around her neck and hauled her over for a kiss. C.J. flapped her hands against his chest eventually, and he let go.

"Someone could see," she scolded.

"We're a couple now, remember? No more sneaking around?"

"Oh, yeah." C.J. opened her door and stepped out of the truck onto the squishy lawn. "Oh, no. My shoes!" She gazed down as her favorite Jimmy Choo slides disappeared into the muddy grass. "Dang it."

"Let me help." Abe came around the front of the truck and scooped her up. C.J. squeaked, but there was nothing to be done but hook her arms around his thick neck and let herself be carried up to the house.

Stevens's mouth hung open in shock as Abe set C.J. on the bottom step and took her hand. "Her shoes were getting wet," he said, by way of explanation.

"Ah . . . sorry about that. We had a bit of rain, as you can see. Come on in. Got a lot of company, but I know Lei will be happy to see you both. So you're . . . ah . . ." Stevens seemed to be groping for words. "A thing?"

"Indeed we are," C.J. said. "More than a thing. We're a couple, aren't we, Abe?" It actually felt good to say it, and she hadn't stopped smiling since he'd picked her up on the lawn.

"I'd like us to get married, but she's playing hard to get," Abe told Stevens. The lieutenant's eyes bulged.

"One step at a time, babe." C.J.'s heart stuttered a little—he was always pushing, the brat. "Why don't you go in for a minute and say hi to everyone, so I can update Stevens on his case."

"Sure, Cherry." Abe kissed her and went inside.

"Cherry?" Stevens had begun to grin, and it took up half of his face.

C.J. fluffed her hair self-consciously. "It's my first name—Cherry Joy—which I don't go by for obvious reasons. But Abe likes it." C.J. could feel a blush heating her chest, so she hurried on to safer topics. "We had a lot of action on the case after you left yesterday. Mahoe is solid. Got more under the hood than I initially gave him credit for."

"How'd that interview with André Métier go?" Stevens still had a smile lurking at the corner of his mouth.

"We cracked that kid. Turns out he had a recording of the murder he'd taken off of Bukowski's body. He'd been at the site of the murder, all right, but at Bukowski's invitation. He arrived too late to help his cousin, who'd called him and told him he'd witnessed the murder of François Métier. Bukowski was going to blackmail Kitty Summers and wanted Métier there for backup. Métier was delayed, and the woman went nuts on Bukowski, as you saw—really let her rage out of the cage. When Métier got there, he searched the body for the phone—Bukowski had told him the murder was recorded on a voice memo. He listened to the recording and staged the scene to point to Summers—he'd brought the bracelet along from her locker, in case they needed to implicate her." C.J. slid out of her damp shoes and set them alongside the impressive assortment of footwear on the welcome mat. "Métier got blood on his clothes and burned them. Didn't want to come forward because he thought it would look bad for him—on a number of levels."

"And it did. So you believed him? Kitty Summers was the doer?" Stevens's blue eyes narrowed.

"Oh yes. She did both victims." C.J. told Stevens about the dramatic interview at the jail. "We were able to trap Summers into admitting to killing François Métier by playing Bukowski's recording. Mahoe and Kevin from the crime lab are at her apartment, going over it for trace. So far they've found blood around the shower drain and her clothes in the washer—we picked her up before she had a chance to wash them a second time, so some pretty nice blood spatter showed up. We got her."

"You sound like you're having fun." Stevens grinned. "Enjoying being out in the field, are you?"

"A little bit, yeah." C.J. pointed to the door. "Enough shop talk. Where's that baby?"

"Right this way." Stevens held the door ajar for her.

The modest living room hummed with conversation. People she knew and some she didn't ebbed and flowed around the room. Directly ahead of her, an older Japanese man who must be Lei's grandfather was building a Lego construction on the coffee table with Kiet.

Lei was seated like a queen in the corner of the couch, a flannel blanket over her shoulder as she nursed the baby.

C.J. approached. "That looks good on you, Texeira."

"Captain!" A smile bloomed across Lei's face. "What looks good? My crazy hair, the spit-up on my shirt?"

"Motherhood," C.J. said. "Motherhood looks good on you." She sat down next to Lei. "Let me see."

Kiet scrambled up helpfully, moving the blanket aside so C.J. could see the baby's face. "My baby sister," he said proudly. The baby nursed on, eyes closed, mouth working.

"Looks like a baby." C.J. never knew what to say about the larva-like appearance of infants—they all looked the same, but parents never seemed to think so. Some compliment was called for. "She's a cutie. Does that hurt?" She gestured to the machine-like movement of the baby's jaws.

"Kinda. I'm sure we'll get used to it." Lei slanted C.J. a glance. "I saw that you came with someone."

"Me," Abe boomed from behind the couch. "She's with me now." He handed C.J. a paper plate of food. "We're a couple."

Lei blinked. "Nice score, Abe."

C.J. cleared her throat. "I expect it will raise a few eyebrows, but life is short, right?"

"Amen to that," Stevens said. C.J. might have envied the loving smile he gave his wife and children if Abe's hand hadn't been resting on her shoulder, firm and solid.

Lei

Lei looked around the room, feeling a bubble of happiness tighten her chest. Everyone who was near and dear to her had gathered to meet Rosie, and even if it was a little hectic on top of a night of broken sleep, she wouldn't have traded it for anything.

All she had to do right now was sit and hold her daughter and feel the love that filled the room.

Directly in front of her, Grandfather Soga deliberately hunted for just the right Lego piece for his meticulous construction as Kiet held up different ones for his inspection. "What about this one, Grandfather?"

Behind Lei, in the kitchen, Captain Omura and her surprise boyfriend, Abe Torufu, made conversation with Ellen and Wayne, who seemed to have a glow about them, too. And she could hardly glance at Jared and Kathy without being burned by the chemistry they were throwing off over there on the love seat.

Out on the deck, her best friend Marcella juggled baby Jonas on her hip and a sippy cup in her hand as she talked to Captain Bruce Ohale and Dr. Wilson, over for a few days to meet the baby.

Her techie friend Sophie Ang, moving with feline grace, sat down in the spot on the couch that Captain Omura had vacated.

"So glad you came," Lei said. "I'm sorry we haven't had much time to catch up. What's new with you?"

"Nonstop action and constant change. Nothing new under the sun but this little one. She's so beautiful." Sophie's husky voice was tender as she gazed at Rosie's sleeping face, tucked in the corner of Lei's arm. "I love her name. Rosie Maluhia. How wonderful to remember your Aunty Rosario that way."

"Yes." The dear people who surrounded Lei also reminded her of the ones who were gone. Easy tears prickled her eyes and she sniffed. "Sorry. I keep thinking how happy Aunty would be to see the baby."

"She's watching right now from heaven," Stevens said from behind her as he put his big warm hand on the back of her neck. His palm slid up, caressing and massaging away tightness, sensual and supportive at the same time.

Rosie's eyes opened and she looked up at her parents, one tiny hand flailing. Lei reached out and the baby grasped her finger reflexively. Her daughter's digits were so delicate that they were almost transparent, but her grip was surprisingly strong.

"Rosie Maluhia Texeira-Stevens, welcome to the world," Stevens said. The baby's mouth twitched, and though it was way too early, Lei was sure it was a smile.

Turn the page for a sneak peek of Razor Rocks, book 13 in Paradise Crime Mysteries.

SNEAK PEEK

RAZOR ROCKS, PARADISE CRIME MYSTERY #13, WITH LEI TEXEIRA!

DETECTIVE SERGEANT LEILANI TEXEIRA clutched the dashboard of her partner Pono's jacked-up purple truck, affectionately nicknamed Stanley. "Can you slow down?"

Pono grabbed the chrome skull shifter, and changed gears. Stanley roared forward even faster. "No." He whipped around a line of rental cars, the cop light on his dash strobing, as they zoomed down Highway 380 toward Ma`alaea Harbor.

Lei shut her eyes. "Bruddah. Getting killed on the way to the harbor won't find your cousin any faster, and besides, if we get in a wreck, Tiare will kill us both." Pono's beautiful and formidably competent wife, Tiare, was not to be messed with.

Pono's big brown hand tightened on Stanley's shifter, but he eased up on the gas pedal.

Lei sat back in her seat. "I know this is hard—but whatever's happened has already happened. You gotta stay objective about the case, or Captain Omura will pull you off of it."

Pono scowled like an angry tiki god, his pidgin thickening. "It's my cuz. Not jus' any kine cuz—dis my uncle's oldest boy Chaz Kaihale. We been close since small kid time."

"I know. Chaz is good people." Lei touched Pono's tense bicep, her fingers lightly brushing the slash of a scar where a tribal tattoo of interlocking triangles had been torn by a meth dealer's bullet. She still remembered how terrified she'd been when the man who was her brother in everything but name had been shot… "Tell me again what you know. Let's get a plan before we meet with the Coast Guard."

Pono blew out a breath and put both hands back on the wheel. The truck slowed to a reasonable rate at last. "Chaz called me from sea. You know how he's a captain; goes out with a couple of guys to crew luxury yachts for that company, Deluxe Dream Vacations. Anyway, I wen' get one call from him just yesterday; he stay yelling. "Pono! You gotta help us! Get pirates coming!" and then damn if the phone didn't cut off." Pono flexed his fingers on the wheel. "Ho, I was laughing. I thought Chaz was pranking me cuz was April first! But when I tried to call back, it nevah go through. So I'm thinking, eh, he pranked me but even with the sat phone, half the time his calls get cut off." Pono glanced over at Lei. Even with his favorite Oakleys hiding his eyes, she felt his pain. "Turns out, the call was legit."

"You couldn't have known! I mean, it was April Fool's Day!" Lei shook her head. Drifts of curls, whipping in the breeze from the partly-open window, hid her view of her partner, so she grabbed handfuls of her wayward hair and bundled it back with a rubber band from her pocket.

"I should have tried harder to check. Chaz, he one prankster, but I should have called the ship-to-shore radio at least…anyway, I did nothing. Then just now, I get a call from that Coast Guard guy we worked that Molokini case with—Aina Thomas? Remember him? He called my cell, telling me they found the yacht my cuz was captaining washing up on the reef off Lana`i. No one on board, but get bloodstains." Pono speeded up again.

"No, Pono, no…" Lei's stomach lurched under the sensible

black polo shirt she wore with jeans and athletic shoes, and she rubbed it reflexively. "You didn't tell me anything but 'go get in the car, we got a case involving my cuz.' This is big, if it's pirates. If it's murder."

"I know."

"Are you sure Thomas was calling you as an investigator? Maybe he was calling you as a witness, because you and Chaz are close. He found your name listed somewhere in Chaz's phone or something."

Pono's mouth just tightened, and Lei had her answer—*Pono wasn't thinking, right now.*

Lei needed to take charge. "I'll call Omura and brief her with what we know. And let me take the lead when we talk to Thomas." She dug a Maui Police Department ball cap out of the backpack, loaded with investigation paraphernalia, that she carried in lieu of a purse and duty belt. She tugged the cap down low and tight on her head, threading her thick ponytail through the back. "We got dis, partner."

LEI HADN'T SEEN Petty Officer Aina Thomas in several years, not since they'd shared a gut-wrenching case involving the murder of a beautiful young marine biologist in the waters off of Molokini atoll. A lot had happened since she'd been briefly attracted to the handsome Coast Guardsman, including the birth of a daughter and the rescue of her husband, Michael Stevens, from foreign kidnappers.

Wind characteristic of the area whipped the palm trees as they pulled into the marina parking lot of Ma`alaea Harbor. Lei hopped down off the chrome step of the lifted truck, patting her weapon in its shoulder holster and straightening her jacket over it, checking that her badge was clipped onto her belt.

"We go!" Pono boomed, his usual mellow attitude gone as he slammed his door. Lei jogged to keep up as they moved along the waterfront, the ocean glimmering in the distance and the clang of wind-whipped rigging and squeak of boats at their moorings, a strange kind of music. Lei spotted the Coast Guard inflatable, and hurried to get in front of her partner.

Pono felt like a thundercloud at her back, pushing her forward, and a quiver of purely personal nervous tension sharpened Lei's voice as she hurried toward the nattily-uniformed young man standing on the dock in front of the powerful, rigid-hulled Coast Guard Defender zodiac. "Petty Officer Thomas. What have we got?"

"Sergeant Lei Texeira and Detective Pono Kaihale." Thomas's voice was brusque; he put his hands on his hips. His crisp Coast Guard uniform still looked really good on his trim, athletic frame. "Long time. I see you came with your partner, but I only called Pono. As a witness, to be interviewed."

"That may be what got this going, but Captain Omura has authorized us to investigate these missing persons and signs of foul play on behalf of the Maui Police Department. So, going forward, this is going to be a joint investigation." Pono's body heat shimmered just behind her; her partner was barely containing his anxiety, but even without seeing him, Lei knew he'd be looking as intimidating as hell with his arms crossed over his bulky chest and those inscrutable Oakleys hiding his worried eyes. "Why don't we go to your conference room in the Coast Guard building where we can speak privately?"

Aina Thomas had a face much like her own: tawny, light brown skin, a few freckles across the nose, the tilted eyes of mixed Asian/Hawaiian and Portuguese descent, well-marked features, curling dark hair buzzed military-short. Other than his hair, looking at him was like looking at a male twin.

Thomas shook his head in negation. "We need to get back out

to the wreck. We can brief on the way. Follow me." He spun with precision and headed for the ladder leading up onto the deck of the craft.

Lei glanced around as she ascended the ladder onto the rigid-hulled inflatable twenty-five-foot Coast Guard Defender. Two huge Honda outboards idled harshly; as soon as she and Pono were on board, a crewman handed them life vests and Thomas ushered them into the cramped quarters of the small navigation cabin. "We can talk in here. It's about thirty minutes to the site."

"Wow, this thing really rips," Lei said. "it's usually an hour from Ma`alaea to Lana`i on the ferry."

Thomas's quick, triangular grin reminded her why she'd found him so attractive. "You have no idea. Grab onto something."

Lei caught hold of a support stanchion on the inside wall just as the boat surged forward, spinning away from the dock and violating the usual inside-harbor speed limits. Pono jostled against her until they both found seats on a padded storage bench against one wall.

"Why don't you tell us what you wanted to talk to Pono about?" Lei shouted over the noise of the engines. "It must be pretty urgent if we didn't have time to talk about it somewhere quieter—and more private." She indicated the Guardsman driving the boat with her head.

In answer, Thomas handed the man a set of earmuffs. "It's ear protection and a comm unit," Thomas told them. The Guardsman put them on, his eyes front and full attention on driving the speedy craft.

Thomas removed a touchscreen tablet from a drawer and sat in one of the two bolted-down captain's chairs, swiveling to face them. "I called you because we suspect foul play. I called Pono because of his relationship with Chaz Kaihale, the captain. We think Kaihale may be involved with whatever went on."

"Why you say that about my cousin?" Pono rumbled, fierce

with defensiveness for his family member. "He's a good man. Never been in any trouble."

"Because Kaihale's nowhere to be found, nor are the passengers…and the boat was robbed of valuables. Usually these kinds of hits are an inside job," Thomas said. "Otherwise, we're talking pirates, and that seldom happens in Hawaii for a number of reasons I won't get into right now. Good thing the ship hung up on the rocks, or we'd have nothing to investigate at all; I saw a hole in the hull other than what the rocks made, and I think the perp tried to sink it."

Pono folded his thick arms and opened his mouth to defend his cousin some more, but Lei held up a hand. "Guys. Let's agree at this point that this shipwreck seems like a crime scene and move forward without further assumptions. So, Aina. Did you notify the police on Lana`i yet?"

"I did. Sergeant Gary Miller was on duty and said he'd be going down to the beach to meet us."

"I'll get ahold of him." Lei took out her phone and routed her call to the on-island officer through Captain Omura. Maui County consisted of five islands of varying sizes: Maui, Kahoolawe and Molokini atolls, Molokai, and Lana`i. The two atolls were uninhabited, and officers rotated out to Lana`i for shifts, while larger Molokai had its own force.

Lei knew Miller from other cases, and it would be good to have backup from on-island with the energetic young black man, though the Lana`i police station was tiny with little investigation resource equipment. They'd have to process all evidence on the main island of Maui.

Once Lei had established contact with Miller, who'd be picked up on the beach, she put away her phone.

The Guardsman driving the Defender turned his head. "Ship ahoy. We're here."

Lei's pulse picked up with the familiar hit of adrenaline that made being a cop so addictive.

Click to find out more about Razor Rocks, Paradise Crime Mysteries #13!
tobyneal.net/RRwb

ACKNOWLEDGMENTS

I feel as exhausted getting to the end of this book as Lei did after having a baby! *Nine points of view?* What was I thinking!

Turns out, I was thinking that it was going to be impossible to top the nonstop blistering action of *Red Rain*, so I needed to go in a completely different direction. I realized afresh what a colorful, multicultural cast of characters populate the series, and I wanted a new writing challenge—to show this story through the points of view of lesser, but still fascinating, characters.

I've tried hard to keep every book fresh and surprising, not an easy task fourteen books in (including my companion books *Stolen in Paradise* and *Unsound*). I hope I achieved that in this story as well. It was certainly more difficult doing it this way, trying to keep each character's "voice" distinctive, avoiding retelling the same facts of the plot but driving the story forward, and worrying about crossing timelines…

I loved writing the scene with all of Lei's favorite people in the room...very emotionally satisfying. I hope you thought so, too. I took a break after this book to write TEN books with Lei's friend Sophie! Please check out the Paradise Crime Thrillers, listed in the bibliography that follows. They start with Wired In, and I promise you won't be sorry! Sophie's got a whole different set of problems to solve, but they are no less interesting than Lei's.

That said. I got to missing Lei, Stevens and their growing family, so read on for an excerpt from *Razor Rock*s, Paradise Crime Mysteries #13!

Thanks so much to Ret. Capt. David Spicer, for keeping Lei and Stevens's police work honest. Thanks to Holly Robinson, ever and always, and to Penina Lopez for copyediting. Special thanks also to Shirley, Angela, Don, and Bonnie, who've been faithful typo hunters for the journey.

Another *mahalo* goes out to chef/farmer James Simpliciano of Simpli-Fresh Farms in Lahaina. You were the inspiration for Teo Benitez and his organic farm! Thanks for all you do for the farm-to-table movement on Maui.

Sugar agriculture is ending on Maui, and I'm worried about the massive, valuable acreage throughout our island that is covered in beautiful, waving sugarcane. I fear that it will, as happened on my home island of Kaua`i, end up getting parceled out into yet more real estate for rich off-islanders.

This book is dedicated to the hope that, instead, small farmers will be allowed and encouraged to work the soil of Maui to grow enough crops right here so that we can feed and provide for ourselves and aren't so dependent on imported food.

The Hawaiians lived in abundance on this island. Why can't we? Change begins with having a dream.

If you enjoyed the story and/or the series, please leave a review. They're the best thanks an author can get.

Much aloha,

Toby Neal

FREE BOOKS

Join my mystery and romance lists and receive free, full-length, award-winning novels *Torch Ginger & Somewhere on St. Thomas.*

tobyneal.net/TNNews

TOBY'S BOOKSHELF

PARADISE CRIME SERIES

Paradise Crime Mysteries

Blood Orchids
Torch Ginger
Black Jasmine
Broken Ferns
Twisted Vine
Shattered Palms
Dark Lava
Fire Beach
Rip Tides
Bone Hook
Red Rain
Bitter Feast
Razor Rocks

Paradise Crime Mystery
Special Agent Marcella Scott
Stolen in Paradise

Paradies Crime Suspense Mysteries

Unsound

Paradise Crime Thrillers

Wired In

Wired Rogue

Wired Hard

Wired Dark

Wired Dawn

Wired Justice

Wired Secret

Wired Fear

Wired Courage

Wired Truth

ROMANCES

The Somewhere Series

Somewhere on St. Thomas

Somewhere in the City

Somewhere in California

Standalone

Somewhere on Maui

Co-Authored Romance Thrillers

The Scorch Series

Scorch Road

Cinder Road

Smoke Road

Burnt Road

Flame Road

Smolder Road

YOUNG ADULT

Standalone

Island Fire

NONFICTION

Memoir

Freckled

ABOUT THE AUTHOR

Kirkus Reviews calls Neal's writing, *"persistently riveting. Masterly."*

Award-winning, USA Today bestselling social worker turned author Toby Neal grew up on the island of Kaua`i in Hawaii. Neal is a mental health therapist, a career that has informed the depth and complexity of the characters in her stories. Neal's mysteries and thrillers explore the crimes and issues of Hawaii from the bottom of the ocean to the top of volcanoes. Fans call her stories, *"Immersive, addicting, and the next best thing to being there."*

Neal also pens romance, romantic thrillers, and writes memoir/nonfiction under TW Neal.

Visit tobyneal.net for more ways to stay in touch!
or
Join my Facebook readers group, *Friends Who Like Toby Neal Books,* for special giveaways and perks.

www.ingramcontent.com/pod-product-compliance
Lightning Source LLC
LaVergne TN
LVHW091125080826
845145LV00008B/2051

* 9 7 8 1 7 3 3 7 5 1 7 7 3 *